Also by Ray Hobbs and Published by Wingspan Press

An Act of Kindness	2014
Following On	2016
A Year From Now	2017
A Rural Diversion	2019
A Chance Sighting	2020
Roses and Red Herrings	2020
Happy Even After	2020
The Right Direction	2020
An Ideal World	2020
Mischief and Masquerade	2021
Big Ideas	2021
First Appearances	2021
New Directions	2021
A Deserving Case	2021
Unknown Warrior	2021
Daffs in December	2022
A Worthy Scoundrel	2022
Fatal Shock	2022
Last Wicket Pair	2022
Knights Errant	2022
A Baker's Round	2023
Confusion to Zeus	2023
Ways of Gentleness	2023
An Eye to the Future	2023
Stage Direction	2023
Dogs in Daft Outfits	2024
Taking the Stick	2024
People are Like Bottles	2024

Published Elsewhere

Second Wind (Spiderwize)	2011
Lovingly Restored (New Generation Publishing)	2018

I0611578

A FAMILY EFFORT

RAY HOBBS

Wingspan Press

Published in the United States and the United Kingdom
by WingSpan Press, Livermore, CA

The WingSpan name, logo and colophon are the trademarks
of WingSpan Publishing.

ISBN 978-1-63683-068-1 (pbk.)
ISBN 978-1-63683-944-8 (ebook)

Printed in the United States of America

www.wingspanpress.com

This book is dedicated to those who held the fort at the most critical time.

As ever, I wish to acknowledge the assistance given to me by my brother Chris, who acted as a sounding board for ideas, occasionally lending his own and helping to fuel my enthusiasm throughout the writing of this story.

RH

Author's Note

For my characters to have communicated without slipping occasionally into navalese would have rendered the story and its dialogue unrealistic. I must therefore act, once again, as translator.

A **writer** is a clerk. The Navy's use of the word possibly originated at a time when literacy was comparatively rare, so that a rating with that ability was regarded as something special. Members of today's Logistics Branch no doubt still agree with that assessment.

A **flag officer**, i.e. a commodore or above, is so called because a pennant appropriate to his rank is flown by the ship in which he sails. It helps the captains under his command keep track of his movements as well as being particularly careful about their own.

The **wardroom** is the naval equivalent of an officers' mess, although it functioned as a depository for the spoils of war until civilisation regulated the Navy's buccaneering traditions.

Pompey is the sailors' familiar name for Portsmouth. The most likely explanation is that it is a contraction of the landmark 'Portsmouth Point'. After all this time, however, no one really cares.

The **first lieutenant** is usually the executive officer. His name says it all, even when the captain and his fellow officers call him 'Number One', and the lower deck refer to him as the 'Jimmy' or 'Jimmy the One'.

The **hook** referred to in this story is the wooden anchor or 'killick' depicted on a leading hand's insignia. The rating himself is sometimes referred to as a killick, at least when his subordinates are being polite about him.

Gash is basically refuse, although a **gash hand** is one who is currently surplus to requirements, e.g. a rating awaiting his draft (*qv*).

A **draft** is to a rating what a posting is to an officer. Differentials must be maintained.

A sailor's **oppo** is his friend. A relic of the days of 'green' and 'red' watches, the term stems from 'opposite number', or the rating who performs the same function in the opposite watch. Nowadays he can have as many oppos as he likes.

A **capital ship** is one that is important enough to be escorted by an anti-submarine screen. They are easily identified as there are so few of them left in service.

Good conduct badges in the form of stripes worn on the left arm, are awarded each for four years' good conduct or, in lower-deck parlance, 'undetected crime'. A **three-badge** rating is therefore deemed to have kept his nose clean for twelve years. Junior ratings with that distinction are usually regarded as unambitious.

Unlike the massive, bronze artillery pieces of Nelson's time, the **cannon** referred to in this story were small-calibre automatic weapons that fired explosive shells.

The order, **'Splice the Mainbrace'** had nothing to do with the joining of ropes but was simply the authority to issue a double tot of rum, after which most sailors would have difficulty in splicing anything. It was used in celebration, e.g. the monarch's birthday, or as a reward for a particular achievement. A famous instance occurred in 1949, when HMS *Amethyst* escaped the clutches of the Chinese Communists, prompting King George VI to issue the popular order.

A **deflection** is the distance allowed in aiming ahead of a moving target, taking into account its speed, so as to hit it, rather than have the shot fall astern of it.

No one knows why the sea is called the **oggin**. One suggestion is that it stemmed from a mispronunciation of 'ocean' – no doubt after the mainbrace had been spliced.

Goffers are non-alcoholic drinks. The word was most likely plucked out of nowhere, and yet it found a place in the naval lexicon.

A **pot-mess** was a stew cooked in a saucepan, but the term has also been used for decades as a metaphor for a shambles or disaster.

A **pongo** is a soldier. Again, the origin is obscure, but the irreverent sailor divides the armed forces into matelots, pongos and crab-fats, the last being a reference to the colour of the RAF uniform.

A **hand-out** is not, as many readers might suspect, a gift, but assistance of the practical kind; thus, a hand-out to fold bedding was simply an extra pair of hands to perform the task.

Before the Navy adopted more modern and practical facilities, bedding in a shore establishment was arranged for inspection in a **biscuit**. The mattress cover, sheets, blanket, pillow and pillowcase were folded neatly and wrapped in the counterpane so that the embroidered anchor central to its design pointed to the foot of the bed.

'**Chatty**' was the familiar name for Chatham Naval Base, as well as a reminder that no one can be witty all the time.

The order to **secure** is basically permission to go off-watch. The origin, presumably a connection with rigging of some kind, is now forgotten, presumably in the euphoria of going off-watch.

A **sprog** is a baby or youngster. As in this story, it can also be used to describe a new recruit, derisively or otherwise.

Lastly, '**Tiddley**' means 'posh' or 'fancy', and it can be applied to anything. Not surprisingly, the battleship HMS *Royal Sovereign* was known as the 'Tiddley Quid'.

I hope you enjoy the story.

RH

APRIL 1940

A COASTAL TOWN IN KENT

1

TO EACH A TASK

A visitor to the town might have given *Chloe* and her occupants a second look, although more out of curiosity than for any other reason. Half a dozen boys, possibly in their mid-teens, and an elderly man would have seemed an unusual complement, and the boat herself was something of a hybrid. Originally a 27-foot whaler, she had been converted to sail, although it was a four-stroke engine that was now bringing her and her crew into Sandbrook's ancient boatyard. The fresh breeze they had enjoyed two hours earler had stiffened, gusting angrily and giving the sea the appearance of beaten pewter. With a young and inexperienced crew, Arthur had elected to bring *Chloe* in under power.

A boy in the bow caught a mooring post with his boathook and steadied the boat.

'Well done, Andrews,' said Arthur. 'Make fast, now, with a figure of eight and a locking hitch on the cleat, and secure her to the post with a bowline, as I showed you.'

'Aye, aye, sir.'

'You too, Mortimer,' he called to the boy furthest aft.

'Aye, aye, sir.' Mortimer went cheerfully about his task; in fact, all but one of the boys were in good spirits. The exception, an unfortunate youth called Phillips, was recovering slowly from the misery of seasickness.

'Don't be downhearted, Phillips,' Arthur told him. 'It's happened to most of us, you know, and you'll find your sea legs soon enough.'

'Sir,' said Andrews, the boy in the bow, 'do you mind if I ask you a question?'

'You can always ask, Andrews.'

'It's a bit personal, sir.'

Arthur laughed. 'As I said, you can always ask, but whether or not I'll give you an answer is another matter.'

'Of course, sir. I just wanted to ask, if you don't mind, how old you were, sir, when you joined the Navy.'

'I was fourteen, a little bit younger than you are now, I imagine.'

'Yes, sir, I'm sixteen.' With undisguised impatience, the boy said, 'I won't be eighteen for another fifteen months.'

'What's the hurry?' Arthur suspected he already knew the answer. The previous war had taught him about boys impatient to enter a man's world.

'My dad won't let me join up, sir. He says I'm too young, but I'll be able to join without his consent when I'm eighteen.'

Arthur stood up to step ashore, and said, 'Don't be in too much of a hurry, Andrews. Now we're at war, I can see your father's point of view.' Turning to the rest of them, he said, 'Well done, lads. You can secure, now.'

There was a chorus of, 'Aye, aye, sir,' followed by their individual thanks for the afternoon's sailing, before they all clambered on to the jetty and made their way home, trawling the wretched Phillips in the rear.

Training sea cadets was a new experience for Arthur, but he'd taken to it with a level of enthusiasm that had surprised even him. He'd felt driven to do some kind of war work and had been told that the only option open to a man of his advanced years was Air Raid Precautions. He decided then that he would be more usefully occupied in training the next generation of seamen than in enforcing the blackout. He had to bear in mind, of course, that the cadets needed gentle handling. They were, after all, neither boys from HMS *Ganges* nor midshipmen hotfoot from Dartmouth, but youthful civilians. He had also to make allowances for their instructors. He still smiled when he remembered his first visit to the training centre. He'd been warned that the unit was struggling for lack of officers and senior ratings, but he was surprised when the only adult he could find was a sedentary-looking petty officer, who asked him how he might be of assistance.

'I've come to offer my services,' Arthur told him.

'Oh, yes?' The PO looked at him squarely, possibly seeing an old man, tall, solidly built and seemingly fit, but with too much time on his hands. At the same time, there was more than a hint of authority in his tone. Arthur spoke and sounded like a man who expected obedience. 'What experience have you had?' asked the PO.

'Currently, I own Ellis's Boatyard.' He paused, knowing that what he had to say must surely take the petty officer by surprise. 'Otherwise, forty-six years in the Royal Navy. I entered HMS *Britannia*, Dartmouth, in 1884 and was commissioned in 1889.' He was conscious of the look of sudden alarm on the PO's features but continued mischievously. 'I assumed my first command, HMS *Chloe*, a *"Daphnis"* Class Destroyer, in 1912, and went on to serve at Gallipoli....' By this time, the PO was red-faced with embarrassment. Taking pity on him, Arthur left the rest of his credentials unlisted.

Clearly forcing himself to look into the newcomer's pale-blue, gently smiling eyes, the PO said, 'I'm sorry, sir. I had no idea.'

'You had no reason to know, PO. Think no more about it.'

Still visibly embarrassed, the petty officer reached for a notepad and said, 'I'd better take down some particulars, sir.'

'Very well. My name is Arthur Edward Clement.' Pointing to the notepad, he said, 'If you like, you can add "Rear Admiral, retired". My date of birth, a matter of some recent embarrassment, I have to say, is the eighth of July, eighteen-seventy, but that doesn't mean I'm too old to give your cadets a few tips about seamanship.'

'I wouldn't doubt it for a minute, sir, but I have to point out that the authorities could take the line that you're... that you're maybe a little too....'

'Too old? A minor detail, PO, and I've never been impressed with higher authority.' His oft-resented independence of thought was the reason he'd retired as a rear admiral, leaving the dizzy heights to those who still enjoyed Their Lordships' approval. Smiling again at the unfortunate senior rating's dilemma, he said, 'If they won't let me join, I'll simply turn up at frequent and regular intervals and give the boys the benefit of my experience. It won't cost anyone a penny, so why should they care one way or the other?'

'I really believe you will, sir.' The PO looked again at the details and said, 'I just need your address and, if possible, a telephone number, sir.'

Arthur supplied the information, after which he asked, 'Tell me, PO, which branch did you serve in?' The medal ribbons on his tunic suggested he was not without service time, but his right sleeve bore no badge of branch or category.

'The Paymaster Branch, sir,' he said modestly. 'I came out after twelve years as a leading writer.'

'And I imagine you were quite useful as such, but who else is there at this place? I mean, you can't be the only senior rating, and there must be an officer or two secreted about the building.'

'I'm the only senior rating, sir,' he said apologetically, even though the deficiency was clearly none of his making, 'and I'm afraid there are no officers currently attached to this unit.'

'Well, bugger me,' said Arthur, laughing. 'This establishment really does need some new blood.'

That conversation had taken place the previous November. It was now April, and the authorities had still failed to communicate their decision, supposing they'd made one, so Arthur kept his word and became a familiar figure at the centre, a respected instructor and, as always, a law very much unto himself.

He locked up the boatyard, started the Morris Commercial and made his way through the leafy streets to the Victorian detached house that was now his home. On retirement, he'd moved reluctantly from the larger, six-bedroom residence he and his late wife Elizabeth had shared.

He found his cook/housekeeper in the kitchen, peeling potatoes, and he greeted her. 'Good afternoon, Mrs Hogben.'

'Good afternoon, sir. Did you have a pleasant afternoon's sailing?' She was a short, tidy woman, capable and serene. The last quality he admired almost as much as he valued her cooking and household management.

'Very pleasant indeed, thank you, Mrs Hogben. We had only one casualty.'

She looked at him in alarm. 'A casualty, sir?'

'A sad case of seasickness. He'll recover, I've no doubt.'

'I hope so, sir. Still, it's ever so good of you to take the boys sailing the way you do. Everybody says so.'

'It's kind of everyone to say that, but those lads are tomorrow's sailors, and anything I can teach them will stand them and the country in good stead. The days of sail have long since passed, but seamanship skills are as vital as they ever were.' He looked around the kitchen and sniffed inquiringly, but had to ask, 'What are we eating this evening, Mrs Hogben?'

'One of your favourites, sir, fish pie.'

'Oh, good.'

'I knew you'd be pleased, sir.' Remembering something else, she said, 'A letter came for you in the second post, sir. It looks like Miss Penelope's handwriting, although I'm not prying, sir.'

'Of course not, and thank you for telling me about it.' He'd have found the letter soon enough, but Mrs Hogben knew he'd want to know about it as soon as he got in.

He had two granddaughters, as different as pitch and powder. Joan, the elder, had always been regarded by her parents as the more responsible and reliable of the two, so Arthur had tried to redress the balance, with the result that Penelope, or 'Penny', as she now insisted on being called, had come to occupy a special place in his affections. He loved them both and tried very hard to live with Joan's controlling ways, but he couldn't help the way his feelings leant. He picked up the envelope from the hall stand and opened it.

Dearest Grandpop,

I hope all is well with you. How is your private navy? I'm so proud of you for doing that.

Well, I've arrived here at HMS Pembroke III. *Apparently, the original HMS* Pembroke *is Chatham Barracks, but you'll know more about that than I do.*

We start training properly tomorrow, although I don't know when we'll be kitted out with our uniforms and everything. We're going to receive a lecture about naval life, apparently, although I must be at a distinct advantage, having grown up with a flag officer as my grandfather! Anyway, I can't wait to get started.

Keep well, and don't make those boys work too hard!

Yours with lots of love, as always,

Penny XXX

He didn't think he would ever become used to being called 'Grandpop' – it was one of the silly but harmless ways Penelope had picked up at school – but he was looking forward to seeing her at the end of basic training. Her joining the WRNS had been a surprise, but he'd quickly adjusted to the news and decided that it would compensate in some small way for his not having a son or grandson to follow him into the service.

* * *

Penny's journey into London had been a succession of new experiences. For one thing, London seemed to be protected almost entirely by sandbags that lined doorways, gateways, and every public building, including the new air raid shelters. Also very much in public view were the huge, clumsy barrage balloons tethered by steel cables, which they tugged this way and that in the gusting wind. Most particularly, she noticed the ubiquitous servicemen and women, and the sight of them excited her, because she was about to become one of them.

In boarding the underground at Charing Cross for the short journey to Finchley Road Tube Station, she found other girls in the compartment, all bound for the same destination and each as excited as the next. Being a gregarious soul, Penny soon found herself in conversation with one of them, a girl called Sybil, who said, 'It's all going to be very strange. I chose the Wrens because of the uniform, but I don't know the first thing about the Navy. Do you?'

Physically, the two girls were very similar, with light-brown hair and bright blue eyes, of which Penny's betrayed a sense of irrepressible fun. It was the look of someone who took few things seriously.

'Quite a lot,' she said modestly, realising that it would be awful if she sounded too self-assured on her first day. 'My grandfather's a retired rear admiral.'

'Gosh. I don't suppose it'll be long before you join the commissioned ranks.'

'I really don't know,' said Penny. 'I've certainly not given it any thought.'

'Well,' said Sybil, 'it's the first avenue I'll explore. I mean, to heck with doing all the hard work and having to wash and iron my own clothes. I'd far rather leave those jobs to someone else.' On brief reflection, she went on to say, 'I'm surprised you haven't considered it, Penny. With an admiral as your grandfather, you'd be a racing certainty for a commission.'

Penny shifted her gaze from the ever-fascinating advertisements that lined the walls of the compartment, and said, 'It makes sense, surely, to learn how to do the job before putting yourself in charge of it. At least, that's what I think.'

That was where the conversation ended, at least for the time being, because the train pulled into the station, and they made their way on to the platform.

With no obvious official presence outside the tube station, three of them shared a taxi, which brought them via a surprisingly short route to a sandbag-framed portico guarded by sailors with rifles and fixed bayonets.

'Abandon hope,' said Penny, who nevertheless experienced a surge of excitement at arriving at the next stage of her life.

* * *

At the far end of the Mediterranean, the aircraft carrier HMS *Glorious* had left Dekheila Harbour and had begun the voyage back to home waters.

Lieutenants Clive Newing and William 'Bill' Stevenson had just occupied two of the armchairs that lined the large and capacious wardroom, when the Tannoy crackled.

'D'ye hear there! D'ye hear there! This is the captain speaking. With so many buzzes doing the rounds, I think it only right and sensible to tell you what really is happening. The fact is, we're heading for home waters and Scapa Flow, where we shall join the rest of the Home Fleet. As you already know, the enemy have invaded Norway, and a counter-invasion by British and allied troops has been deemed necessary. Our task will naturally be to carry out air strikes and provide air cover. We shall also be required to ferry aircraft from Great Britain to Norway for the benefit of the Royal Air Force. I shall tell you more when I am in possession of the details. In the meantime, I urge everyone to remain as vigilant as ever. That is all.'

'I think that calls for a drink,' said Clive, attracting the attention of the wardroom steward.

Dutifully, Bill said, 'I can't disagree with that.' The two were physically very much alike, slim, tall and dark-haired. They only differed in personality, Bill being forthright, often speaking without thinking too much about what he was about to say, whereas Clive was more likely to size-up a given situation before passing judgement.

'Two pink gins, please, Daniels.'

'Aye, aye, sir.' The steward wrote the order on a mess chit and returned to the bar.

'By the sound of it,' said Clive, 'there'll be no time for leave.' He hadn't seen his home in South Kent for almost a year and, whilst that wasn't at all unusual in service life, he would have welcomed a seventy-two-hour pass, at least.

'Instead of that,' said Bill, 'we're going to be dodging penguins.'

'There are no bloody penguins in the Northern Hemisphere, you blockhead,' said Clive, signing the mess chit for the drinks. 'Thank you, Daniels.'

'You're most welcome, sir.'

'Well, what are those seabirds that dive on unsuspecting picnickers to pilfer their hard-boiled eggs and pork pies?'

'Skuas, cormorants, gannets…. That sort of thing.' In truth, Clive had only the vaguest knowledge of seabirds, but he did know that penguins confined their activities to the Southern Hemisphere.

'Thanks, Clive.' Bill took the pink gin from his friend and pilot. 'Norway, here we come.'

* * *

At about the same time, Acting Leading Seaman Wilfred Gregory was summoned to the First Lieutenant's cabin aboard the destroyer HMS *Wrathful*. He stopped at the curtain and knocked on the bulkhead next to it.

'Yes?'

Wilf pulled the curtain aside and said, 'JX one eight two seven five nine Acting Leading Seaman Gregory, W. T., sir. I was told to report to you, sir.'

'That's right, Gregory,' said Lieutenant Soames. 'Come in.'

Wilf stepped forward and came to attention.

'Stand easy, Gregory. I'm happy to tell you that your promotion has been confirmed and that you are now Leading Seaman Gregory. Congratulations.' He offered his hand.

'Thank you, sir,' said Wilf, shaking the officer's hand. The promotion meant a modest increase in pay, but an important step forward for an ambitious rating.

'A leading hand is an important member of a ship's hierarchy. Do you know what I mean by that?'

'I think so, sir.' It was the first time he'd heard the word 'hierarchy', but he thought he could guess its meaning.

'As a leading hand, you will be the first link in the chain of authority. You will be in direct contact with the most junior ratings, the men who do the job and, as such, you will be invaluable to the senior ratings and officers above you. I want you to bear that in mind as you go about your duties.'

'I understand, sir. Thank you for explaining that, sir.'

'You're very welcome. I believe you're going on draft when we reach Portsmouth.'

'That's right, sir. Pompey Barracks and then on draft.'

'In that case, I wish you well. Carry on, Gregory.'

'Aye, aye, sir. Thank you, sir.' Wilf came to attention again before turning about and leaving the First Lieutenant's cabin.

On his way to the messdeck, he passed the Chiefs' and PO's Mess. Petty Officer Little saw him and called out, 'Gregory?'

Wilf stopped. 'Yes, PO?'

'Congratulations on your "hook".'

'Thanks, PO.'

'What did the "Jimmy" have to say to you?'

'He just said, "Well done" and told me how important killicks are.'

'Yes, he's the only officer I've ever known who does that, but it's good that he makes you feel appreciated.'

'He does that all right, PO.' Those few words from the First Lieutenant meant a great deal to Wilf. He would be leaving the ship, very soon, but he was unlikely to forget them. He wondered idly, as he was a 'gash hand' for the time being, if there were any imminent likelihood of leave. His home was in Kent, where his father worked in a boatyard owned by, of all people, a retired rear admiral. He would have to mind his manners if he ever encountered him.

2

SCRUBBING BRUSHES AND SHOP WINDOWS

Instead of the smart uniform they'd seen in the recruiting posters, the recruits at Mill Hill were issued with bluettes and thick, lisle stockings. The bluette was an overall-type dress in an unrecognisable, washed-out material that clung to its wearer in an unflattering way, so that it resembled prison garb. It would remain the recruits' only uniform until they passed out. In it, they would scrub the lecture hall, dining room and messdeck floors, being careful to call them 'decks', wash and dry the crockery and cutlery used by the entire company, and scrub out the lavatories and ablutions, now known as the 'heads'. In between those duties, they learned about naval life and terminology, about badges of rank and rate, and when and how to salute. They also learned squad drill and the initially incomprehensible orders associated with it. At first, it seemed impossible, but before long, they learned that 'How!', ''Tan' at heise!' and 'Haybout turn!' meant, respectively, 'Attention!', 'Stand at ease!' and 'About turn!' Performing those tasks, however, was another matter and, as with most skills, some learned more readily than others. For Penny and a few others, it came under the heading of harmless fun. After all, what did it matter if the instructor shouted at you and ridiculed you? The joke was surely on him or her, and the important thing was not to give way to laughter at such times. They'd heard various unsubstantiated stories of Wrens suffering corporal punishment by caning, but they decided that such a terrible sanction must be inflicted for only the most serious offences, so they disregarded all such rumours. Some girls, however, found it harder than others to subscribe to their philosophy, and Penny entered the messdeck one day to find one of them, a quiet and reserved girl called Gloria, face-down on her bunk with her shoulders heaving, sobbing hopelessly into her pillow.

'Shift up, Gloria,' said Penny, slipping easily into the messdeck argot as she perched on the edge of the bunk. 'What's the matter?'

Gloria's reply was garbled, to say the least, partly because her speech was impeded by the pillow, but mainly because of her uncontrollable sobbing. Penny managed to make out, 'I want... to... go... home.'

Sybil sat on the adjacent bed and asked, 'What is it?'

'She wants to go home,' Penny told her.

'It's one option,' said Sybil with a shrug, 'but not one I'd take. Not with my horrible brother on leave, anyway.'

Presently, Gloria's sobs grew fewer and less violent, and she turned on to her side to face them both with reddened, swollen eyes.

'You could go home,' said Penny thoughtfully. 'It's still an option, as Sybil said, and we've been here less than a fortnight.' Two weeks was the probationary period, during which a recruit could be discharged as unsuitable, or leave the service voluntarily. 'What's the trouble, exactly?'

'Being... shouted at... just because I... can't do... things.'

'Oh, that.' The intake had just spent much of the afternoon on the parade ground, engaged in squad drill, and Penny couldn't fail to notice that Gloria, being a seemingly natural victim, had been the instructor's prime target. 'You mustn't let old "Rubber Lips" upset you. She really isn't worth it.' PO Wren Holmes was instantly recognisable by her thick, protuberant lips, and because she was unpleasant as well, Penny found it impossible not to christen her appropriately.

'Is... that what you... call her?'

'Yes, it came to me just now. You know, when her mother took her to the shops, to keep her away from mischief, I bet she told her to lick her lips, and then stuck her to the shop window, like a rubber sucker.'

'It sounds feasible,' said Sybil. 'Lips like hers aren't much use for anything else.'

'Yes,' said Penny, 'you can bet no man's ever been near them, and no one will even consider it.'

The thought appealed to all three of them, and soon, even Gloria was laughing.

Eventually, Penny said, 'Squad drill's all right if you go about it with the right attitude. I think up silly rhymes about the instructors while I'm doing it, and I march in time to them.' She shrugged. 'It passes the time.'

'I recite dirty limericks to myself,' said Sybil.

'You would.' Penny was acquainted, by that time, with Sybil's ribald sense of humour.

'Rubber Lips is like a prefect we had at school,' said Sybil. 'She was called Daisy Brigstock, and she was utterly foul. Anyway, when we'd had as much of her as we were prepared to take, one night, just before sixth-form bedtime, one of the girls put a lizard in Daisy's bed. We heard the screams two dormitories away. After that, whenever she was horrible to us, we thought about the lizard, and it made us feel better.'

'As for going home,' said Penny, remembering how the conversation had begun, 'if you did that, you could live the rest of your life regretting the fact that you'd run away from your opportunity to do something useful in this war. On the other hand, basic training will soon be a part of your past. Get through this, and the rest will be easy.' She didn't really know that, but she suspected she was right, and it was always good to sound positive.

'In any case,' said Sybil, 'why on earth would you want to go home when you've got oppos like Penny and me to brace you up?'

Gloria couldn't find an answer to that.

Later, when they were about to go to the dining hall for supper, PO Wren Holmes came to the messdeck to speak to Gloria. 'Probationary Wren Turner,' she said, 'don't think you're going to get away with this afternoon's feeble effort. You're going to perform the about-turn on the march tomorrow until you get it right. I'll see that you do, supposing it kills me. Right?'

'With that inducement, she can't fail to get it right, PO,' Sybil assured her.

'Yes,' said Penny in a dreadful impression of Al Jolson, 'Stick around, PO. You ain't seen nothin' yet.'

The whole intake gave way to raucous laughter, although PO Wren Holmes remained baffled. Thereafter, whenever possible in PO Holmes's company, someone would insert 'stick', 'stuck' or 'sticking' into the conversation, with a similar result. More practically, however, after supper, Penny and Sybil set about showing Gloria how to do an about-turn on the march.

'The word "turn" comes when you're on the left foot,' Penny explained with an impression of PO Wren Holmes. 'Squad will turn about. Squad, haybout *turn!*' Demonstrating, she went on. 'Then you turn to the right on your right foot, right again with your left, and your right foot brings you back the way you came.'

After several attempts, Gloria was still struggling, and Sybil, who had been watching her, said, 'I think it helps to think of it as making letters with your feet.'

'Spill the beans,' said Penny. 'You've lost me and possibly Gloria as well.'

Gloria confirmed that such was the case.

'It's easy. Look.' Sybil took centre stage to demonstrate. 'Your left foot goes down on "turn", you bring your right heel to your left to make a letter "L", your left comes across to form the horizontal stroke of a "T" and, finally, your right forms a "V" with your left, and off you go. Try it.'

They did, with the whole class exuberantly shouting 'L, T, V', which rather symbolised, at least to Penny's way of thinking, the comradeship that had developed in less than two weeks. Politicians had spoken in the past of equality, and the French had thrown in liberty and fraternity for good measure, but there, at HMS *Pembroke*, was true equality as well as sorority. They'd come from a multitude of social backgrounds, but they were now a class of equals, and happy to remain so. Happiest of all, though, was Gloria, who could now face her *bête noire* on the parade ground without fear.

'I learned more from you two in ten minutes,' she said, 'than I have from her in all the time we've been here.'

'It's a fact,' said Penny, 'that there are some instructors who should recognise their limitations and stick to shop windows instead.'

* * *

Walter Gregory, the boatyard's foreman, had just stepped on to the concrete slipway to light his pipe, smoking being prohibited elsewhere in the boatyard, when Arthur joined him to do the same.

14

'Good morning, Chief. What's the buzz?' Walter had retired from the Navy in 1931 as a chief shipwright artificer, and Arthur still addressed him by his former rate.

'Good morning, sir. I just had a letter from my lad.'

'Oh, good. How's he faring?' Arthur remembered Walter s son coming regularly to the boatyard before joining the Navy as a boy seaman.

'He's just waiting for his hook to be confirmed, sir.'

'Good for him. Where's he serving?'

'All I know is he's with the Home Fleet, sir, HMS *Wrathful*, one of the old *"V and W"* Class destroyers.'

'I remember them.' They were excellent ships, he recalled, built towards the end of the Great War.

They lapsed into silence, and it was obvious to each of them that the other was thinking similar thoughts. They'd both been frustrated in their attempts to interest the authorities in their services, and Walter was even considering joining the Auxiliary Fire Service, although he was still a sailor at heart. Eventually, he said, 'I'd better get back to work, sir.'

Arthur nodded absently.

'I fancy you'll be out with the sea cadets again this weekend, sir.'

'All being well, Chief.'

'I'd like to do something like that, but I don't know what an ex-shipwright "tiffy" could tell 'em.'

All at once, Arthur was jerked out of his thoughts. 'They need induction, Chief,' he said. 'Most of all, they need someone with a wealth of experience to tell them about the ways of the service. You could do that.'

'I suppose I could, sir,' said Walter, knocking out his pipe against the heel of his boot. 'I hadn't thought about that.'

'Think about it and come down to the centre if you've a mind. We need all the help we can find.' He added wistfully, 'Unlike this place.' Trade was slow, and the war had brought the leisure business almost to a standstill. 'I wrote to the Admiralty a month ago. Now that they're using coastal craft again, they're going to need yards like ours.'

'Do you mean coastal motor boats and motor launches, sir?'

'Yes, although the CMBs have been superseded, apparently, by motor torpedo boats. The MLs have never gone out of date.' Now warming to the subject, he said, 'You know, I think I'll write to the Air Ministry as well. Their boats will need someone to attend to their bumps and scratches, too.'

* * *

HMS *Glorious* was approaching Orkney, about to enter the fleet anchorage in Scapa Flow, and the first of her aircraft, the Skua and Sea Gladiator fighters, had been flown off ahead of the northerly gale that was forecast. Now, her Swordfish were ranged on the flight deck. They were biplanes of the torpedo/spotter/reconnaissance type, and they were known for their ability to operate in weather conditions that kept other aircraft in their hangar. Clive Newing sat in his open cockpit, wiping his goggles. A squall of rain had just hit his windscreen, showering him as well. They had sailed from Dekheila, where rain was rationed, and cold weather was an exotic mystery, and they had come home to a taste of early spring in the North Sea.

The Fairey Swordfish was a remarkable aircraft, despite its obsolete design. With a steel frame clad in canvas, it was reminiscent of aircraft of the previous war, and its top speed was certainly less than impressive when compared with the performance of more modern aircraft, but it was able to carry a torpedo, a mine, three depth charges or a substantial bombload. In fact, such was its versatility, one of its test pilots had christened it the 'Stringbag', because it carried almost anything. Also, it was powered by the extremely dependable Bristol Pegasus engine, itself a blessing at sea.

Eventually, the signal was given to take off, and Clive's squadron commander rolled forward, gathering speed, and finally taking off. Each of the squadron followed suit, and soon it was Clive's turn. He opened the throttle, and the Swordfish gathered momentum, finally taking off and joining the climbing spiral until the squadron was formed astern of its commander. No sooner were they in formation than they made the short journey across Orkney and began their descent on Hatston, where they must remain until *Glorious* was ready for them to re-embark.

They landed to hear stirring news. Less than a fortnight previously, a force of Skua dive-bombers had taken off from Hatston and, flying to the limit of their endurance, attacked and sunk the light cruiser *Königsberg* in Bergen harbour, making her the first-ever capital ship to be sunk by aircraft.

* * *

Having successfully escorted her convoy to Liverpool, HMS *Wrathful* left the rest of the escort and changed course for Portsmouth.

Wilf's feelings were mixed. He knew that, as a leading seaman, he would be given a new draft, and the knowledge carried with it an element of excitement, but *Wrathful* was a happy ship, and he'd enjoyed his time as a member of her company. He would be sad to leave her, and those were his thoughts when he heard the pipe, 'D'ye hear, there! D'ye hear, there! All drafts and leave are cancelled until further notice.' After a moment spent in absorbing the message, Wilf adjusted to the news that he wasn't about to leave the ship yet. He found a cosy kind of security in that knowledge, although, like the rest of the ship's company, he wondered about the reason for the cancellation.

3

A Warm Welcome and a Stern One

For the RAF pilots being ferried to Norway, the voyage presented a lesson in communication.

One of them, an eager, fair-haired pilot officer called Farrand, referred to it when Clive guided him to the Wardroom. 'It seems to me, sir,' he said importantly, 'that, ever since we handed the Fleet Air Arm over to the Navy, you've been working on a new and incomprehensible lingo.'

'Since you returned it to its rightful owner,' Clive corrected him. 'I was here when it happened,' he said with a feeling of residual pleasure, 'and what a wardroom party that was. By the way, the language has been in place for four hundred years. This is the Senior Service, remember. Anyway,' he said, remembering his duty as a host, 'what would you like to drink?'

'Beer, if they have one, sir.'

'It's a well-stocked bar,' Clive assured him. 'Whose beer do you favour?'

'Do you mean you have more than one?'

'I should hope so,' said Clive airily. 'You can have Guiness, Bass, Worthington, Watney's or Mann's, at least, although I should warn you that aircrew are not actively encouraged to drink beer. It all adds to the weight on take-off, you know, rolling off a comparatively short deck as we do.'

'Surely not.' He was nevertheless half convinced.

'Only joking. It's the need to ease springs when you're in the air that's the real problem.'

Clearly suspecting another leg-pull, Farrand asked, 'What do you mean by "ease springs". sir?'

'Relieve oneself.'

'Ah.' It made sense. 'As we're not about to take off yet, do you think I might have a bottle of Worthington's, sir?'

'I think that might be arranged.' Clive caught the steward's eye and said, 'A pink gin and a bottle of Worthington's, please, Daniels.'

'Aye, aye, sir.'

'It's a language all of its own,' said Farrand, reverting to the original topic.

'I only joined the service eight years ago,' Clive told him, 'but they tell me the practice has continued unabated in the Fleet Air Arm, despite Trenchard's draconian decree in nineteen-eighteen, forbidding further use of naval terminology. Thank you, Daniels.' He signed for the drinks and handed Farrand his beer.

'Thank you, sir. In fairness, I think all Lord Trenchard was trying to do was create a completely new service. The thing is, we rather revere him and think of him as our founding father.'

'Rather than as a blinkered, jaundiced half-wit. Well, we all have our attitudes and preferences, Farrand. Where would we be if everyone drank Worthington's ale?'

Farrand's thoughts were already elsewhere, despite Clive's harsh words about Lord Trenchard. 'I've been wondering about flying off, sir,' he said. 'The Gladiator needs a run of a hundred-and-fifty feet. Do you think that will be possible?'

'You people do demand a lot, Farrand. I suppose we can juggle things to give you a little more flight deck. The main thing is that you remember to wear woollen underwear, double thickness, if you can cope with it.'

'Because of the Norwegian climate, sir?'

'No, it'll keep you warm when you're swimming in the North Sea.'

'Oh, I see, sir. Very funny.'

* * *

Now re-fuelled and re-ammunitioned, HMS *Wrathful* had left Portsmouth and the English Channel, and was making her way northward, on the final leg of her voyage. In a broadcast, the captain told the crew all they needed to know for the present.

'We are proceeding to a position off Namsos on the coast of Norway, where we shall be providing an anti-submarine screen for the fleet. Enemy aircraft are known to be active in the area in which we'll be operating, so much will depend on our close-range weapons and their crews. I know you will all make the greatest effort, and I wish every one of you the very best of luck. That is all.'

The news was especially important to Wilf, whose action station was on the port two-pounder twin cannon, known familiarly as the 'pom-pom' because of its characteristic sound. The ship had two such mountings as well as two twin Lewis machine guns, relics of the previous war and little enough to defend a ship against the bombers of the modern Luftwaffe.

'Hard luck on you, "Hooky",' said Albert Fisher, the three-badge doyen of the messdeck. 'If it hadn't been for this Norway carry-on, you might have landed a soft draft somewhere.'

'The way things are,' said Wilf, 'how many soft drafts can there be?'

'There'll be a few, you can bet.'

Wilf decided not to argue. There was no point and, for all he knew, Fisher could be right. Instead, he pulled on his foul-weather jacket preparatory to going on watch. Whatever happened off the Norwegian coast, he could only do his best. After all, the captain had said he expected that of everyone in the ship's company.

* * *

Watching the squadron of Gladiators take to the air had been quite exciting. Three of them had narrowly escaped a ducking but, in the end, they had all got away safely. Taking off at sea was a particularly serious task for the inexperienced, because to fall into the sea over the ship's bows would be fatal. By the time one of the escorting destroyers could reach the incident, the pilot would, in all probability, be drowned, and no one wanted that to happen.

Next to leave the ship was Clive's squadron, bound for Trondheim. Each aircraft carried a bombload of 1,500 lbs, although they took off easily enough, climbing in a wide spiral and finally forming up on their squadron commander. With their extra weight, they were making 85 knots, and Clive had just made a mental note of the fact, when a shout via the Gosport tube claimed his attention.

'ETA Trondheim oh six four five,' said Bill Stevenson.

'Thanks, Bill.'

Entering service in 1936, the Fairey Swordfish had no means of air-to-air signalling other than flashing light or prearranged hand signals. As for communication within the aircraft, Clive and his observer were only connected by the primitive Gosport tube, invented during the previous war. Any communication with Leading Airman Bright, the telegraphist/air-gunner, had to be made via the observer.

The squadron flew on until, at oh six three five, the coast first became discernible through the gusting rain. With any luck, the foul weather would keep enemy fighters grounded, so that the only hazard would be anti-aircraft gunfire, although German gunnery was reputed to be extremely accurate.

The squadron was almost over Trondheim harbour when the enemy batteries opened fire, creating startling, crimson bursts on either side of the formation, the explosions rocking the aircraft with the shock waves they created.

The squadron commander gave the hand signal to attack and banked over to port, going into a seventy-degree dive on the ships in the harbour. One by one, the others followed him, releasing their bombs at a little over a thousand feet. Anti-aircraft fire was now so intense that there was no time to gauge the damage, and Clive had already seen one Swordfish go down in flames.

When they were a safe distance from their target, he looked around him and counted the aircraft. There was just one missing. At that stage, he had no way of knowing whose aircraft it was. It was sufficient to know that three members of the squadron were lost.

* * *

Louisa Dowland peered through the smoke created by the arriving train. Doors opened, and passengers alighted, their dim shapes vaguely discernible, although, when they came closer, none of them turned out to be Penelope. Louisa was about to deduce that her daughter had missed the train in London when she heard a familiar voice behind her.

'Hello, Mum.'

Louisa turned, irritated for the moment by the casual form of address. Joan still called her 'Mother', but Penelope's standards had plummeted to new depths lately. She was about to remark on it when she realised that her wayward daughter must have emerged from a third-class compartment, the rearmost of the train. 'Penelope,' she said, accepting a kiss, 'what on earth were you thinking of, travelling third class?'

'All the first-class compartments were full, and a lovely man in third class gave up his seat for me.'

'I'm sure any of the men in first-class would have done the same.'

'Don't you believe it, Mum. The ruling class ain't what it used to be.'

Louisa resisted the temptation to argue. Instead, looking at Penny's canvas bag, she asked, 'Can you manage with that thing?'

'Oh yes, I don't need a porter.'

'Very well.' She led the way past the colourful planting boxes and hanging baskets tended faithfully by the stationmaster, through the ticket barrier and out to the station yard, and said in a surprised way, 'I rather expected you to be in uniform.'

'We don't have to wear uniform when we go ashore.'

'Ashore?' Louisa unlocked the car and reached over to open the passenger door. 'You're sounding like your grandfather already.'

'Why not? As examples go, his is good enough for me. I'm going to call on him tomorrow.'

'I thought you might. I've no doubt he'll spoil you to death, as usual.'

'It's not just that, Mum. It'll be lovely to see Grandpop, but I need to see Mrs Hogben, as well.'

Louisa turned into Folkestone Road and sighed heavily. 'Must you refer to your grandfather in that silly way?'

'He doesn't mind.'

'Of course he doesn't. He lets you get away with murder. Anyway, why do you need to see Mrs Hogben?'

'My uniform skirts need altering. I don't know just what the remedy is, but she'll be able to tell me what to do.'

Why on earth her daughter wanted to consult a cook/housekeeper about something of that kind seemed to defy reasonable explanation, but then a possible reason suggested itself to her, and she asked. 'How long have you got?'

'Leave? I have to report to HMS *Nelson* in Portsmouth by oh-eight-hundred, next Thursday.'

Louisa changed down, causing the gears to grind. She repeated her sigh, although it had nothing to do with her clumsy gear-change. 'What on earth is "oh eight hundred"?'

'Eight o' clock in the morning.'

'What a silly language. Still, it would be short notice for Mrs Binns, and past experience tells me you wouldn't want to ask her to make the alterations, anyway.'

'True.' Mrs Binns, the dressmaker, was authoritative and judgemental, two failings that alienated Penny most of all. 'Mrs Hogben will know what to do,' she told her mother confidently.

'Well, don't be a nuisance. Remember that she's your grandfather's housekeeper, and she has her own work to do.'

'She won't be too busy to say, "Congratulations on completing your basic training, Miss Penelope. What are you going to do next?"'

If Louisa were aware of any criticism, she gave no sign of it, but said, 'I don't suppose she will be. She's as ready as your grandfather to pander to your whims and desires.'

Had the word 'Welcome' been woven into the doormat, it seemed to Penny it would be the only kind she was likely to enjoy at home. However, she could look forward to seeing her grandfather the next day, and that made up for a great deal. For the present, she was content to enjoy the tree-lined, winding road that led to her home. Spring had already taken hold in Kent, and the trees were coming rapidly into leaf.

* * *

No one had seen any of the crew of Swordfish 4F bale out, but the last two to make their attack had seen the unfortunate aircraft hit the ground. The resulting explosion had been all the greater because 4F's bombload was still intact and because her final act was to hit an enemy fuel dump, although that in no way compensated for the loss of three lives. Fresh sorties, however, were planned for the next two days, and it was necessary to look ahead to them.

'One thing puzzles me,' said Bill Stevenson, later, in the wardroom.

'Only one thing, Bill? My life is an on-going mystery.'

'Seriously, Clive, I've been thinking about all these aircraft we're ferrying for the RAF. I mean, it's one thing flying them off, but how are they going to get them back home when they've done their job? They can't land-on, crating would be a huge task, and they obviously lack the range to fly home.'

Clive had been thinking about that, too. 'Have you wondered why the RAF are sending their second eleven to Norway and keeping the Spitfires and most of the Hurricanes at home or in France? I have. I think those aircraft are going to be sacrificed.'

'If that's the case, what's the point of this operation?'

'It strikes me it's no more than a bluff, an attempt to make the Boche think again about collaring Norway's assets.'

Bill humphed at the thought. 'It certainly has the makings of a half-arsed show.'

'I don't know who dreamt up this whole debacle,' said Clive, 'but what kind of mastermind sent ships to Norway without air cover in the first place? Damn it, they had to bring us all the way from Egypt to provide what we can.'

'This kind of mental gymnastics calls for refreshment, Clive. What do you say?'

'I agree.'

Bill hailed the steward and ordered two pink gins so that the debate might continue in a civilised manner. Meanwhile, a hundred miles or so up the coast, HMS *Wrathful* was preparing to reinforce the fleet at Namsos.

4

SUCCESS AND RETURN

HMS *Wrathful*'s immediate task was to protect the anti-aircraft cruiser HMS *Curlew* against U-boat attack. The main threat, however, came from the air in the shape of the Heinkel 111 medium bomber and the Junkers 87 dive-bomber, known as the Stuka. The latter had a particularly daunting reputation, even among those who had not yet seen it first-hand, but whose impression was gained solely from newsreel footage from Spain and, more recently, Poland. Its appearance alone had a malevolent quality, with its inverted gull wings, its claw-like fixed undercarriage and 'Jericho Trumpet' sirens, which emitted a deafening scream when the aircraft was diving, creating a sensation as unnerving as their designer had intended.

As French troops were landing at Namsos, a wave of aircraft was reported to be approaching from the south, and the information was communicated immediately to the destroyer screen.

At his action station on the port pom-pom, Wilf kept a careful watch and waited. The breath-taking beauty of the fjord and the turn of events that had brought him unexpectedly to Norway were now temporarily forgotten in the immediate concern. Inside his duffel coat, steel helmet, anti-flash hood and gloves, he perspired copiously despite the freezing weather. By contrast, his mouth was completely dry, and his tongue felt like a cinder. The knowledge that others must be similarly affected meant nothing to him as he coped with his own apprehension.

All his training as a boy at HMS *Ganges*, then as an ordinary seaman at HMS *Raleigh*, and finally, at HMS *Excellent*, the Royal Navy's gunnery school, had led him to this moment, and he went through his drill, meticulously training and elevating the twin cannon, ensuring that everything was running smoothly and in perfect order.

He hadn't long to wait before a lookout reported aircraft approaching from the north. Tiny specks to begin with, they soon became identifiable as Stukas.

As they came within the range of the small-calibre guns, the voice of *Wrathful*'s First Lieutenant, came through the loudspeakers. 'Barrage, commence, commence, commence!'

Wilf and his crew took careful aim and, as the first of the Stukas was about to cross their sights, Wilf squeezed the firing lever, sending a stream of shells to join the kaleidoscope of fire put up by the flotilla's guns. There was a sudden and massive explosion as one Stuka received a hit from *Curlew*'s secondary armament. Wilf knew better than to waste time watching debris fall into the sea, however, and he trained his guns again on the remaining attackers.

Incredibly, the enemy seemed to ignore the French troopship at the jetty and concentrated instead on the shore installations and the disembarked French troops, who were now scattered in all directions. The last three Stukas, however, now turned their attentions to *Curlew* and the destroyers, and their hideous screaming reached a new level.

Wilf fired again, only to see his efforts fall wide of their target when the captain took evasive action by turning the ship hard a-starboard. He saw two bombs hit the water, and realised, despite his frustration, that the manoeuvre had probably saved the ship. As the Stuka that had dropped those bombs came out of its dive and began its laborious ascent, Wilf squeezed the firing levers again and saw his shells rip into its fuselage and explode. It faltered, and then stalled, finally plunging into the harbour. He had scored his first victory.

Taking evasive action again, the captain turned the ship to starboard, and the bombs of the remaining Stukas fell harmlessly into the waters of the fjord.

As the last of the aircraft disappeared, the First Lieutenant gave the order, 'All guns, cease firing. Check, check, check,' and Wilf and the others were able to breathe naturally, relieved and elated by their early success.

The familiar crackling of the Tannoy system claimed their attention again. 'D'ye hear, there! D'ye hear, there! This is the captain speaking. Well done, everyone, and particularly the port pom-pom crew, who have just shot down our first aircraft. This is a milestone for the ship, and we shall celebrate it in the usual way at our first opportunity. That is all.' There was a loud cheer from the ship's company at the promise of a double tot of rum, and Wilf and his crew exchanged a celebratory handshake.

* * *

Mrs Hogben picked up one of the navy-blue serge skirts and examined it, asking, 'What's the problem, Miss Penelope?'

'It's here, on the right,' said Penny, showing her the place. 'The folded-over cloth where the buttons go and the other one with the buttonholes are both far too thick. It makes us look hideous.'

'Oh dear.' Mrs Hogben saw the problem immediately.

'Well, maybe it's not quite hideous, but it looks untidy,' said Penny.

'The plackets for the buttons and buttonholes are very thick, as you say.' said Mrs Hogben, looking closely at the opening. 'My late husband told me when he was in the Army, that he had two of everything – one to wear and one to keep for kit inspections.'

'That's right. If you'll tell me what to do, I'll alter the skirt I'm going to wear, and keep the bulky one for inspections. It's the same with the knickers – "blackouts", we call them – the elastic top-and-bottoms will pass muster at inspections, but we've already hemmed some of them up without elastic, so that they're more like French knickers.' On brief reflection, she said, 'No one's going to see what we're wearing beneath our skirts, anyway.'

'I should hope not, Miss Penelope.' Examining the skirt once more, she said, 'I think your best plan is to leave the alteration to me. I have a navy-blue zip fastener that I think is about the right size.'

'Oh, Mrs Hogben, I don't want you to be out of pocket. Tell me what I owe you, and I'll make it right with you.'

'Bless you, Miss Penelope. It must have been in the bottom of my sewing box many a year. It certainly doesn't owe me a penny, so you're welcome to it. Leave the skirt with me and I'll have it ready for you to take home.'

'You're too kind, Mrs Hogben. Thank you.' Penny was reminded of the times when she was little, and when she was home from school, when things had been too awful at home. On those occasions, she'd come to her grandfather's house, often when he was away, and found instant comfort in Mrs Hogben's company. She had no children of her own, having lost her husband in the previous war, so she had love and motherliness to spare, and Penny was glad of it.

The kitchen door opened, and her grandfather said, 'I detect a lull in the women's talk. Is it safe for me to come in, yet?'

Laughing, as she often did, at her employer's silliness, Mrs Hogben said, 'I think the coast is just about clear, sir. I've some sewing to do, so I'll brew some coffee for you and then I'll leave you and Miss Penelope to catch up with each other's news.'

When they were alone, the admiral forsook the old jacket he'd been wearing in the garden for an equally old and comfortable cardigan and sat down to hear a disorganised but excited account of Penny's spell of basic training, including some wildly irreverent remarks about some of her instructors.

'It sounds as if you got a hundred percent out of it, Penny. Good for you, but what are you going to do next?'

'I have to report to HMS *Nelson* by oh-eight-hundred, next Thursday.'

Her grandfather looked at her quizzically. 'Pompey barracks? What are you going to do there?'

'I'm joining the Signals Branch, Grandpop,' she told him proudly, pouring coffee for them both and handing her grandfather's cup and saucer to him.

'Thank you, Penny. Shore establishments must have come and gone since I was in the service, but *Nelson* barracks will always be there. At all events, what are you going to do in the Signals Branch?'

'Wireless telegraphy.' She uttered the words proudly, although she had very little knowledge of the subject.

'Good heavens. Well, it's very important, and you'll be doing what it says on the posters.'

'That's true, but I don't think many Wrens look like the girl on the poster.'

'You will,' he told her confidently.

'Even to the "pudding basin" hat.'

'Is that what you call it?'

'Yes, and it's very descriptive.' As something else occurred to her, she said, 'The girls going into visual signalling will be given a pair of bell-bottomed trousers because they do everything out of doors.'

'My word. Girls in bell-bottoms, indeed. I never thought I'd see the day.'

'Apparently, it can be quite cold and windy in some of the places they'll be drafted to.'

'Well yes, quite.'

Smiling confidentially, she said, '"Pop" says trousers are not ladylike. In fact, they're almost as unspeakable as his younger daughter calling her parents "Mum" and "Pop".'

He smiled, trying hard not to laugh. 'Maybe he believes that respectable wars are waged only by ladies and gentlemen of exquisite taste and bearing.' Penny's father had served on Field Marshall Haig's staff in the previous war, and now occupied a post in the Treasury, to which he commuted daily.

'You don't believe in that tosh, do you, Grandpop?'

'Certainly not. Tell me one thing, though,' he said, suppressing his laughter again. 'When did you begin calling your unfortunate parents "Mum" and "Pop".'

'When I was at *Pembroke*. I met every kind of girl there, Grandpop. There were girls who'd been to my kind of school; girls who'd never been to school at all, but had a tutor at home. There were girls from very ordinary schools and ordinary homes, and girls who thought that the food they prepared in the galley was wonderful and that the greatest luxury was to have their own bed. We all mucked in together, regardless of background, and it was wonderful.'

The old man smiled happily. 'I'm delighted to hear you say that, Penny, and I'm extremely proud of you, too.'

'Gosh, Grandpop, it was worth coming home, just to hear you say that.' Self-consciously changing the subject, she asked, 'How do you think the war's going?'

'It's difficult to say at this stage, and there's certainly a great deal of complacency about. In my view, the American politician or journalist, whoever he was, who called it a "phoney" war, should have been around when HMS *Courageous* was sunk, or when the *Graf Spee* was shooting holes in *Exeter*. What concerns me now, though, is this thing in Norway, which seems to be going less well for the Army than any of us would prefer.'

* * *

The target was an enemy troop convoy moving northward towards Trondheim. The weather had improved, so the Swordfish were escorted by Sea-Gladiator fighters. Clive looked up at them, envying them their acrylic canopies and wondering why the Swordfish had been designed with an open cockpit. His train of thought was disturbed, however, when the squadron commander alerted everyone with a hand signal that meant he'd spotted the target. Clive looked ahead and downward to see the line of lorries and self-propelled guns, and was distracted again by the activity overhead. The enemy had seen them, and the antiquated Sea-Gladiator biplanes were now fully engaged with the Messerschmidt BF109s, forcing the Swordfish to lose altitude. Meanwhile, the squadron commander was giving the signal to attack.

One by one, the Swordfish peeled off, diving on the convoy and releasing their bombs at a lower altitude than usual, and feeling something of the blast from their own ordnance. As Clive made his attack, he saw an ME 109 go down in flames, followed by a Sea-Gladiator. He released his bombs and was pulling out of the dive, when he felt a jarring and realised with some alarm that his aircraft had been hit. Turning to the Gosport tube, he shouted, 'Are you all right back there?'

'We're okay,' said Bill. 'Whatever it was must have hit the aircraft further forrard.' Almost as he spoke, the engine note changed, but it was naturally impossible for Clive to see any damage. Fuel contents and oil pressure seemed to be holding up, but the aircraft had lost power. With its bombs gone, it should have been capable of over 100 knots, but the air-speed indicator showed that it was labouring at between 70 and 80, and the Swordfish would stall at 50 knots. Clive hoped desperately that it wouldn't lose even more power.

Evidently alerted to the fact that one of his squadron was failing to keep up with the formation, Sandy Bishop, the squadron commander, made a U-turn to fly alongside Clive's machine, presumably to ascertain the problem. As he drew level, Clive pointed agitatedly to the engine and waved his hand from side to side to indicate that there was a problem with it. Sandy signalled that he understood and gave the 'good luck' sign.

From the observer's seat, Bill shouted, 'What's happening?'

'Losing power. At least they'll know where to look for us.' He hoped they would. In a lively sea and poor visibility, three men in a dinghy would be difficult to spot.

Bill shouted, 'Continue on two-seven-five degrees.'

'I will,' said Clive, adding grimly, 'for as long as I can.'

The Swordfish ground on, maintaining something still below 80 knots, but now the needle of the fuel contents gauge was falling. The loss was gradual, but Clive had serious doubts about their chances of returning to *Glorious*. The prospect was bleak. If they had to ditch, they would need to board the dinghy dry, because, even in late April, the North Sea was less than hospitable, and cold, wet, ditched aircrew seldom survived for long.

Still, the Pegasus engine roared on, clearly in some kind of mechanical distress, but with the obstinate will for which it was celebrated. Maybe, just maybe, they might reach *Glorious*.

* * *

With the number of fighters in Norway hopelessly inadequate, the role of the surface ships in providing anti-aircraft defence remained as vital as ever. However, within a very short time, enemy bombing had rendered Namsos Harbour unusable, and the flotilla was ordered to Andalsnes to cover a withdrawal.

The experience at Namsos had been most useful. In particular, it had revealed the Stuka's principal weaknesses. One was that having committed to a dive it was incapable of altering course, and this meant that, where there was room to manoeuvre, a ship could take evasive action. The second was that whilst the Stuka was very difficult to hit whilst diving, once it had pulled out it was slow and vulnerable. The knowledge was used to some effect during a subsequent raid on Andalsnes.

In turning to port and starboard in order to evade the falling bombs, the ship presented two of its gun crews with convenient targets. One

Stuka fell to the Lewis machine guns of a reservist from the forrard messdeck, and the other became Wilf's second victim.

The captain's promised celebration, the splicing of the mainbrace, would have to wait until the ship was in friendly territory, but that didn't prevent the seamen's popular practice of 'sippers'. It was strictly forbidden but, with no officer or senior rating on the messdeck at 'Up Spirits', the others gladly plied Wilf and the other gunner, a Yorkshireman called Jack Farthing, with sips all round of their rum issue. The rum ration, two-and-a-half fluid ounces of over-proof spirit per man, was strong to begin with, but the result was two very happy ratings, who insisted that, if the need arose, they would still be able to shoot the core out of an apple.

* * *

The fuel contents needle of Swordfish 6F was flickering only a little above zero when, peering through the half-light, Clive sighted *Glorious* on the horizon. Bill must have seen her at about the same time, because he yelled into the Gosport tube, '*Glorious* green one-oh!'

'I see her! Get on the lamp!'

He never heard the telegraphist operate the signal lamp; that would have been impossible, but he saw *Glorious* turn into the wind and, crossing everything, he made his approach.

The deck landing control officer beckoned him to land, he felt the tug of the arrestor wire as his hook caught it, and the wheels touched the flight deck. There might have been only a teaspoonful of fuel in the tank, but it had been sufficient to bring them home.

Only later, when he and Bill were in the Wardroom, did he hear the report from the hangar. Three of the nine cylinders had been shot away. The engine had brought them home despite losing a third of its power and a great deal of fuel. For the time being, however, they were a crew without an aircraft, which meant they would be 'grounded' and therefore free to celebrate their return without the usual constraint.

5

A Chance Meeting

On Saturday, the 27th of April, HMS *Glorious* returned to Scapa Flow to embark a crated squadron of RAF Hurricane fighters. To make available extra space, she flew off several of her own aircraft. She also left behind Clive, Bill and their air-gunner, L/A Bright, who were all granted a welcome seven days' leave. It was fortunate that they were given the full seven days, because to travel to most places from Orkney was a time-consuming business. Eventually, however, Clive took his leave of the others and caught the train from Edinburgh to London and then to Sandling Junction in Kent. It was a wearisome journey lightened only by the knowledge that he would soon be with his family, having been away for the greater part of a year, and he was heartily glad to climb down and join his mother on the platform.

After they'd exchanged greetings, she asked, 'Have you had an awful journey?'

'I've had worse,' he assured her, and it's been worth coming all these miles to be home again. He put his arm around her waist, resisting the urge to lift her off her feet in sheer exuberance. 'How's Audrey?'

'She seems happy enough in London, but she couldn't be with us, I'm afraid.' Audrey was his younger sister, now a staff-nurse at King's College Hospital. 'Where have you been, Clive? You telephoned from Edinburgh, as I remember.'

'I've just come down from Scapa Flow.' He thought it best not to mention Norway.

'Where's that?'

'Orkney.'

'Good grief, that's halfway across the sea.'

'No, you're thinking of Shetland. Orkney's closer.'

'It's distant enough.' She stopped at the barrier and Clive gave up his ticket to the stationmaster, who performed a curious kind of salute. 'Welcome home, sir.'

'Thank you.' Clive returned his salute.

His mother unlocked the car, and they got in. 'I don't know how much longer we'll be able to do this kind of thing,' she said. 'Petrol's going to be scarce, even with your father's allowance for the orphanage and the other place.'

Clive smiled. His father was a dentist, who made regular visits to the local orphanage and the home for the elderly and bewildered, that his mother always referred to as 'the other place'. 'I'm surprised they haven't evacuated the children from the orphanage,' he said.

'Yes, they seem to have concentrated on London and a few other places. They're obviously not expecting any bombing here.' Reaching the end of the approach to the station, she made a left turn into Folkestone Road, and Clive lowered his window to enjoy the freshness of the air. They were only a couple of miles or so from the sea, but he fancied he could scent the salt air already. 'Oh, it's good to be home,' he said, unashamedly stating the obvious.

They passed the house on the right, where a dinghy sat perpetually, it seemed, on its trailer. No one knew the people who lived there; they kept largely to themselves and were therefore of no particular interest to their neighbours.

Clive's mother turned into the sloping drive and parked the car at the top. 'Yes, she said, almost absent-mindedly picking up the threads of their previous conversation, 'the war seems to be happening elsewhere, and I can't imagine why the Germans would want to bomb a place such as this.'

Clive made no comment. He'd seen from his vantage point over Norway how the Nazis had bombed civilian and military targets alike, but there was no need to tell his mother that.

As soon as the door was closed behind them, he hugged her, lifting her off her feet for the sheer joy of seeing her again.

'Be careful,' she said, laughing, 'you'll hurt yourself.'

'Nonsense, you're as light as a feather.'

'Well,' she said, disentangling herself from him and looking pleasantly flustered, 'I'm going to make us some tea. I'm sure your father will be in shortly.'

Clive's father had a surgery in what had been the dining room of the original 1920s house, with its own entrance and facilities. Clive called it his 'torture chamber', so it was fortunate that his father had a sense of humour. The new dining room was built on to the back of the house, next to the kitchen, but surrounded by flower beds. Everywhere, however, the light was limited by the obligatory gummed tape that was arranged in a criss-cross pattern on each window. The blackout curtains were also prominent, ready to be closed at the appointed hour.

'Clive, my boy!'

He hadn't heard the door open when his father came in. 'Hello, Dad.' They were performing the customary double handshake when Clive's mother came in with the tea things. 'Clive's got a whole week,' she told his father.

'Less travelling,' Clive told her.

'A week's little enough after all this time,' said his father.

They chatted, bringing Clive up to date with local matters, avoiding anything relating to the war as far as possible, but finding it impossible to ignore completely.

'You'll never guess what the admiral's doing now,' said his mother, clearly itching to tell him.

'Go on, Mum.' Rear Admiral Clement was a well-known figure as Clive remembered him, busy and dynamic. He imagined serving under him must have been a nerve-racking experience.

'He's taken over the training of the local sea cadets. According to Mrs Hogben, his housekeeper, he calls them "the sailors of tomorrow". He takes it very seriously.'

'Good for him. He must be sixty-five, if he's a day.'

'More than that,' said his father, 'but I'll leave it at that, because he's a patient.'

'Poor devil.'

'Clive, you're awful,' his mother chided him gently, the banter between her husband and her son being a familiar feature of family life when they were together.

His father asked, 'Where are you going next, Clive, or shouldn't I ask?'

'It's a secret, Dad, even from me. I should receive a telephone call this week, but I can wait happily until it happens.'

Something had been puzzling his mother, and she asked, 'How did you get from Egypt to Orkney?'

'We rowed and rowed, Mum. I'll show you the lashes on my back if you like.'

'You know what I mean,' she protested.

He did, as it happened. Being as one with his parents was one of the joys of coming home. It was just a shame Audrey couldn't be there as well.

* * *

A couple of hours later, in the same village, another family sat down together after dinner. Penny and her parents had been joined by Penny's sister Joan and her husband Charles, an accountancy officer in the RAF, who was currently on leave. He and Penny's father Harold were engaged in an earnest discussion about the recently-proposed Purchase Tax and the increase in tobacco duty. At the far end of the room, Joan and her mother were talking about rationing and shortages. Penny was bored and waiting for the Nine O' Clock News. The minute hand of the large wall clock seemed to have fallen asleep, no doubt as bored as Penny. It was twelve minutes to nine, and it seemed likely to remain so for a very long time.

Those three weeks at HMS *Pembroke* had been vital and stimulating, spent in the company of girls of around Penny's age, and that made all the difference. Joan was only two years older than her, but she might have been forty, talking about everyday matters with her mother, and when there was so much going on around them. Penny returned her attention to her knitting. The log settled in the grate, sending a shower of sparks up the chimney, that seemed to cling desperately to the sooty fireback for as long as they could before the draught tore them away and sent them on their upward journey. The log was half-burnt, but no one did anything about it. It didn't really matter, because the room felt warm, anyway. It was almost May, so things should be warming up soon. Penny looked again at the clock, which was now at seven minutes to nine. She counted the rows of her knitting and realised she had only a few more before she attempted the clever stuff. It wasn't one of her favourite pursuits; she was only doing it to pass the time, and because it was considered patriotic to knit for the services.

When she looked at the clock again, she saw that it was five minutes to nine. There was a lull in the deathly conversation beside her, so she asked, 'Should we give the set time to warm up?'

Her mother looked up at the clock and said, 'Yes, dear, I think that would be a good idea.'

Penny went over to the wireless set and turned the Bakelite knob. The valves inside began to glow and, gradually, the sound of a violin and a piano came to her ear. The piece, whatever it was, seemed to have reached its exciting coda, which was as well, because it had to end in time for the news.

Eventually, Big Ben boomed out the hour and a well-known voice said, 'This is the BBC Home Service. Here is the Nine O'Clock News, and this is Alvar Lidell reading it.' He went on, in his beautifully-modulated voice, to report on developments in Norway. Even to Penny's untutored way of thinking, things sounded far from encouraging. 'Falling back on prepared positions' sounded suspiciously like retreating, and 'Enemy forces have launched a series of attacks on British and French positions, which are being effectively resisted' sounded less than positive. It was difficult to know what to make of it.

At the end of the bulletin, Penny's mother said brightly, 'The news was read in Norwegian this morning.'

'How versatile and obliging of them,' said Charles. 'Whatever next, eh?' Then, catching Penny's eye, he asked, 'And where are you off to, now you've joined the colours, Penelope?'

'HMS *Nelson*.'

'Oh, and when does she set sail?' He was joined in laughter by Joan and her father.

'On the evening tide, I believe.' Penny had read that in a book, and considered it a suitably polite answer to an inane question.

'Penelope,' said her mother, 'must you be so prickly?'

'I was entering into the spirit of the conversation. For what it's worth, Charles, HMS *Nelson* is the Royal Naval barracks in Portsmouth.'

'That was all Charles wanted to know, dear,' said her mother.

Penny refrained from comment. Some things were better left unsaid.

*　*　*

The next morning, Clive was in the garage, taking the dustsheet off his Norton CJ350. He'd given it a thorough service and cleaning the last time he was home, and he'd also had the forethought to fill the petrol tank, even though war was more a threat than a reality at the time. Even so, he was pleasantly surprised when it started at the third kick. Strapping his uniform cap to the pillion saddle, he set off, stopping briefly at the end of the drive. Because of petrol rationing, there was very little traffic about, but he checked carefully before turning left into Sandbrook Road. As he rode beneath trees that, he was told, had existed since before the turn of the century, it seemed impossible that his part of Kent might be threatened yet again. Something so ancient and permanent couldn't be laid waste like parts of Norway that he'd seen. Common sense told him, however, that the same thought must have been in many a Norwegian's mind before their country was trampled and desecrated by the invaders.

Sandbrook High Street was another landmark he associated with home, and he loved everything about it, the higgledy-piggledy skyline, the shops and awnings in their various colours, and the general sense of pride and involvement in a bustling community that deserved to go about its business unmolested.

Reaching the end of the High Street, he turned down Corunna Street, reminder of the great evacuation of the Peninsular War, and wondered a little about Sir John Moore and the ignominy of being remembered largely for an evacuation. Maybe it wasn't so bad after all, he reflected; evacuated troops could fight again, unlike those left behind, and Moore had also been responsible for some much-needed reforms.

He continued towards the fish market, where keen housewives had formed a queue. Fish wasn't yet rationed, so there was an even greater demand for it than before the war.

He rode on past one of the odd-looking, cylindrical Martello Towers, built originally as a defence against Bonaparte. It now supported an anti-aircraft gun in defiance of another tyrant, as history was inevitably repeated.

Eventually, he came to the boatyard, which had fascinated him from childhood. Its founder, Jacob Ellis, had died in 1932. Clive was sure of the date, because it was the year he'd entered Dartmouth, and he'd heard subsequently that Rear Admiral Clement had bought the yard. He remembered avoiding it on his infrequent leaves; as a midshipman of sixteen, he'd regarded any officer of flag rank as little less than an ogre and, now he thought about it, the prospect was much the same for a lieutenant of two years' seniority. Even so, the lure of the boats under repair drew him inevitably to the place. Some were quite elderly, and he liked to think of them fishing in quieter times. Others were pleasure craft, which really were a feature of peacetime Britain. He'd often thought he'd like to own a boat. He'd done quite a lot of sailing at Dartmouth and enjoyed it, but that was a luxury for another time.

He switched off his engine and swung the bike on to its centre stand. In taking his cap from the pillion, he became suddenly conscious that he had company.

'Hello,' he said, finding that his company was a rather pretty girl. She had fair hair and a flawless complexion, but the feature he noticed immediately was her engaging blue eyes.

'Good morning, sir.' She smiled confidently, thus making herself even more attractive.

Her form of address caused him to smile, too. He asked, 'Why did you call me "sir"?'

'Because I'm a Wren, sir. I've only just completed my basic training, so I haven't been in the service all that long, but the commitment is there. I'm off to Portsmouth next week, to train as a telegraphist.'

Smiling at her keenness, he said, 'In that case, I wish you well.'

'Thank you, sir.' She looked over his shoulder and said, 'My grandfather's about to join us. We'd better introduce ourselves before he tells me off for talking to strange men.'

'That's a good idea. I'm Clive Newing. I'm sure I've seen you before.' He offered her his hand.

'We both live in Sandbrook Road,' she said, shaking his hand. 'I'm Penny Dowland.'

'I'm glad to meet you. Does your grandfather work here?'

'You could say that, sir. It's his boatyard.'

'Oh, good lord.' Clive hurriedly straightened his cap.

'Relax, he's a sweetie, really.'

A deep voice said, 'Who's a sweetie?'

'You are, Grandpop,' she told him.

The admiral was wearing a peaked cap with no recognisable badge, but Clive saluted him all the same.

The old man returned his salute, but addressed his granddaughter. 'Are you going to introduce your friend, Penny?'

'Of course, Grandpop. This is Lieutenant Clive Newing.' She added helpfully, 'He's a pilot.'

'I can see that.'

'Lieutenant Newing, this is Rear Admiral Clement.'

'Retired, of course.' He shook Clive's hand and asked, 'What brings you to the boatyard, Lieutenant?' His pale-blue eyes were alert but friendly, not at all what Clive had expected.

'Curiosity, sir, and a passion for boats.'

'Oh yes?' He perched on the low wall. 'Done much sailing?'

'I did rather a lot at Dartmouth, sir. Unfortunately, events have rather intervened since then.'

'Quite. Hitler has a lot to answer for.'

'Well, I suppose it's why we're here, but it's a shame for people at home.'

'So it is. There's talk, you know, of them closing Sandbrook to all but essential businesses. I heard that from the manager of the Salamanca Hotel, and he's been worried enough by the downturn in business.'

'That's awful,' said Penny, adding wistfully, 'there's a dance at the Salamanca tonight, to raise funds so that they can organise a party for evacuated children.'

'It does seem a shame,' agreed Clive.

'Well,' said the admiral, rising again to his feet, 'I must be away. Feel free to call in any time you're on leave, Lieutenant. We could maybe take *Chloe* out for a sail, sometime. They haven't mined the coast yet.' He indicated the boat tied up at the top of the slipway.

'Thank you, sir. I'd enjoy that. I'm actually waiting to hear about my next appointment.'

'Well, good luck.'

'Thank you, sir.' He saluted again.

'Oh, never mind that,' said the admiral offering his hand. ''ll see you about the place, I imagine.' He continued on his way.

'I told you he was a sweetie,' said Penny.

'You did.' His thoughts were momentarily elsewhere. 'Look, Miss Dowland….'

'Penny,' she prompted.

'Penny, I know it's rather short notice, but would you care to come with me to the dance at the Salamanca? That's always supposing I can get tickets, of course.'

'I'd love to, sir.' Her eyes twinkled as she spoke.

'Clive,' he told her. 'Where can I telephone you to tell you whether or not I've been able to get tickets?'

'Have you something to write on?'

He took out his diary and a pencil. 'Here,' he said, opening the diary at the back.'

'Okay, I'll give you the number for the boatyard – I'll be here most of the day – and my home number,' she said, writing them on the first blank page of his diary.

6

Pumpkins Have a Short Life

Clive arrived at the Salamanca in time to secure two of the remaining tickets, a piece of good fortune he communicated to Penny as soon as he could, having been informed helpfully by his mother that girls needed notice of such things.

As the distance to and from the Salamanca was less than half-a-dozen miles, his father had lent him the Wolseley, reasoning that a motorcycle was unsuitable transport for a lady in a frock.

When he arrived at Penny's home, she was ready to leave, so he had only the briefest of meetings with her parents, but they told him politely that they expected their daughter home by midnight.

'I don't know why,' she said, getting into the car. 'I'm sure they'd rather have a pumpkin than me.' Looking around her, she said, 'This is rather grand.'

'But very suitable for a girl as glamorous as you.' Her dress was a very pale blue with a low back, and it complemented her neat figure.

'Thank you, Clive.'

'Also, my dad insisted I took the car rather than have you ride on the Norton. I think he had visions of frills and petticoats flying in our wake.'

'That would have been fun. I've never been on a motorbike, but this is a lovely car.' Changing the subject, she said, 'We hardly know each other, not that it matters, but I know you have a dad and a mum. What else have you got?'

A little taken aback by her unashamed curiosity, he said, 'Just a sister. She's twenty-one and a nurse at King's College Hospital. How about you?'

'I have a sister, two years older than me, although you wouldn't know it if you met her. She's twenty-two going on forty, and she's married to a boring clot of an accountancy officer in the RAF. She's very respectable and sensible, whereas I'm the *enfant terrible*.' She hesitated and asked, 'Should that be *enfante terrible*, or do you suppose all French children are masculine?'

'I really couldn't say, but I'm sorry you're out of favour.'

'I don't care. I spend most of my time with my grandfather. He's a lot more fun.'

'I imagine he is.' Clive pulled up outside the Salamanca Hotel and opened the passenger door, offering Penny his hand.

'Thank you, Clive. If you don't mind my asking, where have you been until now?' Seeing his look of surprise, she explained, 'I didn't mean that in the sense, "Where have you been all my life?" I just meant, where have you spent the war so far?'

'Ah, I see. The Mediterranean and Norway.'

'Oh, gosh. Was that awful? Norway, I mean.'

'It's very cold,' he told her, leading her into the hotel and handing the tickets to the doorman to be torn in half. Proceeding into the lavishly-decorated ballroom, with its ornate plaster mouldings, chandeliers and marble pillars, he asked her, 'What would you like to drink?'

'I don't drink very much. What are you having? Don't tell me—pink gin?'

'You're an admiral's granddaughter all right. Yes, pink gin '

'May I have the same, please?'

'Of course. Let's find a table.' He steered her towards a small table that wasn't too close to the band, and went to the bar, returning with two pink gins.

'This is wonderful,' she said. 'I wonder when they're going to start things off.'

'I think they're waiting for someone to make a speech about the evacuees,' he said, covertly admiring her smooth neck and shoulders against the delicate shade of her dress.

'What sort of aeroplane do you fly?' Belatedly putting a hand to her mouth, she said, 'Maybe I shouldn't ask you about that kind of thing.'

'It's absolutely forbidden,' he said seriously, 'but, unless they have other plans for me, I usually fly a Swordfish.'

Clearly, that meant little to her, because she asked, 'What does that look like?'

'It's a biplane. That means it has two wings, one beneath the fuselage and one above it and, until this evening, being completely devoted to it, I thought it was the most exquisite thing I'd ever seen.'

She blinked uncomprehendingly. 'When did you change your mind?'

'When you opened the door of your house and I saw you in that frock for the first time.'

'Oh, you!' Suddenly, she was distracted. 'Someone's going to make a speech,' she said.

'Let's hope she makes it a short one.'

An elderly woman in a long gown stood in front of the band and called for everyone's attention, and then Clive's wish was fulfilled when she spoke briefly about the plight of the evacuees and thanked everyone for supporting the cause. There was loud applause, possibly for the brevity of her speech, rather than her style or its content, and the bandleader announced the first foxtrot, 'Somewhere Over the Rainbow.'

Clive asked, 'May I have the pleasure?'

'Of course.'

As he led her on to the floor, she said, 'I haven't danced with a lot of men.'

'It really doesn't show.'

'Good.' Reassured, she moved closer. 'I went to a very strict school, where we weren't allowed even to talk about boys, let alone mix with them. When they taught us dancing, we had to dance with girls.'

'It was the same for us at Dartmouth.'

Her eyes grew wide as she asked, 'Did you have to dance with boys?'

'Yes, but I prefer it this way. Boys tend to pick their noses and sweat.'

'Don't be disgusting.'

He nuzzled her cheek, inhaling discreetly as he did so. 'What perfume are you wearing?'

'Oh, it's Floris something. Do you like it?'

'It's quite magical.'

'If you really mean that, I'm glad.' Then, in a way that was becoming familiar, she suddenly changed the subject, asking, 'What will happen to your aeroplane while you're on leave?'

'I hope it'll be mended.'

'Is it broken?'

'Yes, that's why I'm on leave.'

'I don't believe you.'

He told her sagely, 'You're quite right not to believe everything you're told.'

'You talk as if you're donkeys' years older than me. How old are you?'

'Twenty-four.' There was no point in hedging.

She nodded, as if her suspicions were confirmed. 'You are quite old,' she said.

'I'm no spring chicken,' he agreed. 'As a matter of fact, I've been wondering, lately, how I'm going to spend my retirement. Do you think, if I were to ask him nicely, your grandfather might offer a suggestion?'

'He's noted for it,' she said, 'especially when someone asks him a silly question.'

At that point, the number reached its end, so they applauded the band, and Clive led Penny back to their table.

'You dance very well, for a naval officer,' she said.

'Thank you. Do you find us generally lacking as a species?'

'I've only danced with my grandfather and an old friend of his. My grandfather tends to plod, and his friend has two left feet.'

It was possibly the most unusual conversation he'd had on a first rendezvous, but he was enjoying it. He asked, 'Is your father a naval officer?'

'Good heavens, no. He works at the Treasury, and during the last war, he was in the Army, on Field Marshall Haig's staff. My grandfather teases him about it, and it makes him indignant, so I have to feel sorry for him. Life can't be easy when you have no sense of humour.' She asked, a little belatedly, 'Do you think I'm terribly disloyal?'

'No, no one can blame you for seeing your family the way you do.'

Like someone who has unearthed a secret, she said, 'Your father's a dentist. I know that because he gave me a filling after I'd left school, and I once saw you leaving the house on your motorbike.'

'Your life is an endless catalogue of excitement, isn't it?'

'Beast.' She gestured towards the band and asked, 'Are you going to ask me to dance again?'

'Of course.' He got up and offered her his hand. The band was playing 'Change Partners' from the film *Carefree*. The male vocalist was fairly ordinary, but that didn't matter for dancing.

'Was your dad a dentist in the last war?'

'Yes, in the Army.' Grimacing, he said, 'And they say the British don't use torture.'

'Don't be awful. He never hurt me at all.'

'He wouldn't. He's a chump for a pretty face.'

'You are awful about him.'

'Actually, he and I get on very well together. We tease each other, but we each give as good as we take.'

They danced for a while in silence, and then Penny said, 'I've seen your mother around the village. She seems very pleasant and she's rather lovely.'

'She is.'

'What about your sister? What's she like?'

'This is like that card game that children play.'

'Happy Families?'

'Yes, that one.' He gave a mock sigh and then answered her question. 'Audrey's bossy with me, even though she's younger than me, but it's all in fun. I haven't seen her for more than a year, though. I hope I'll recognise her when I see her again.'

'You do talk the most awful nonsense, Clive.'

'You're not impressed, obviously.'

'I wouldn't say that.' After a while, she asked, 'Did you see this film?'

'*Carefree*? Yes, I used to make a point of seeing anything with Ginger Rogers in it.'

'I bet she's nothing like the parts she plays. I bet she's a horror in real life.'

'Oh, don't say that,' he pleaded.

'You have to face up to these things, Clive. It's like learning that Santa Claus doesn't exist.'

'Oh, no.'

'All right, I'm only teasing. She's probably just as fluffy in real life.'

'No, it's not that,' he said, making his lower lip tremble. 'It's what you said about Santa Claus.'

'Oh, come on.' They applauded the band and returned to their table.

'Are you ready for another drink?'

'Mm, just one, please. I don't want to get blotto.'

'No, I don't relish the idea of carrying you into your house and facing the flak within.' He went to the bar and ordered two pink gins, one of them well diluted with Indian tonic water.

When he returned, Penny asked, 'What is flak?'

'When it's not a tirade from angry parents, it's a name for anti-aircraft fire.'

'Have you ever been shot at?'

'By angry parents or the Nazis?'

'By the Germans, silly.'

'Occasionally, but they don't mean anything by it. It's all in fun.'

She glared at him in mock-impatience and said, 'Let's dance. I love this one.' The band was playing 'Love Walked In'.

Even without that disclosure, Clive would have been in no doubt about her feelings for the song. She danced with closed eyes, and her features took on a dreamy look. As he'd begun to suspect, talking with her at the boatyard, she was a girl of truly independent spirit, and he wondered fleetingly how she would fare in the disciplined environment of the WRNS. He quickly dismissed the thought, however, and gave himself up to the pleasure of holding her in his arms and dancing to the enchanting music of George Gershwin.

The whole evening continued to be just as enjoyable, although, with regrettable promptness, at least from their point of view, the bandleader brought the proceedings to an end by thanking everyone for supporting the event, and announcing the last dance, which was 'The Perfect Waltz' by Wayne King. Clive and Penny took to the floor and danced very closely to the dreamy music, perfect, as its name professed, for the end of a romantic evening, which, even allowing for Penny's unusual style of conversation, it had been.

When they were outside, Penny asked, 'What time is it? I can't see my watch in the blackout.'

He consulted the luminous dial of his wristwatch and said, 'Twenty-three twenty-five.'

'Oh, gosh. I imagine I'll be talking like that before very long.'

'I'm sorry, it's a habit. It's five-and-twenty minutes past eleven.'

'I haven't to be back until midnight, but I don't suppose we should cut it too fine.' Impatiently, she said, 'It's too awful, being treated as a child.'

'You're no child,' he assured her, offering her his arm.

'Can you see where you're going in the blackout?' It was very difficult, with an overcast sky that hid the moon completely.

'Yes, I've got cats' eyes.'

'I believe you.' She allowed him to lead her to the car and waited while he opened her door. When she was gathered in, he got into the driving seat and said, 'You've been marvellous company, Penny.'

'Have I really? I'm not terribly used to this, you know. I haven't known all that many men.'

'In that case, you've taken to it in the manner born, and I mean that in the nicest possible way.' He started the engine.

'You think I'm just an innocent young girl, really, don't you?'

'I'm sure you're innocent, not that there's anything wrong with that, and there's no denying that you're young. From what you've said, I gather you're twenty.'

'That's right.'

'When's your birthday?'

'It's on the twenty-seventh of May.'

'Excellent. In less than a month, you'll have reached your majority and there'll be no argument about it.' He let in the clutch and moved off. 'Pumpkins have a short life, but you can look forward to a much longer one.' On reflection, he added, 'I'd like to be at home for your coming-of-age, but I shan't be.'

'When do you have to go back?'

'I don't know. They gave me a week's leave and told me to await further orders. I imagine a great deal will depend on what's happening in Norway.' He drove the short distance up Sandbrook Road and turned into Penny's drive.

'Thank you for a lovely evening, Clive,' she said, reaching for the door handle with discernible regret.

'Look,' he said, anxious not to let her out of his sight so soon, 'I've been thinking. I hope you don't think I'm being too demanding, but

I wonder if you'd like to do something else while we're still both on leave.'

Her face brightening immediately, she said, 'It makes sense. What have you in mind?'

'We could maybe see a film. They're showing *Blind Folly* at the Picture Palace. I know nothing about it, of course, except that it's not about the war.'

'That's a recommendation in itself. Yes, let's do that.'

'Can you be ready for eighteen— I'm sorry, six-thirty?'

'Eighteen-thirty?' She laughed. 'Aye, aye, sir.'

'I'll let you out.' He climbed out and walked to the other side of the car to open her door. 'Thank you for coming,' he said. 'You made everything far better than you can imagine.' He kissed her cheek. 'Good night. I'll see you tomorrow.'

'Yes. Good night.'

He waited until she'd opened the door of the house, and then drove home.

7

'THEY CAN'T BLACK-OUT THE MOON'

Penny viewed the Norton apprehensively as it ticked over on her drive.

He asked her, 'Have you ever ridden pillion?'

'No, what do I do?'

'Don't worry. Tuck your skirt between your legs – both fore and aft, that is – and climb on to the saddle, put your feet on the footrests and hang on to me.' As an afterthought, he said reassuringly, 'It's a friendly way to travel.' He mounted the bike and looked discreetly away while she arranged her skirt and climbed on to the pillion.

'Are you okay?'

'I think so.'

He lifted his arms and looked behind him to each side to check that her feet were in place, before moving off. As he ran down the drive, he felt her arms tighten around his waist, and he turned, when he reached the road, to reassure her. 'You'll be fine,' he said. 'Just hang on to me.' Her response was to hold him even more tightly.

They rode the short distance down to the Picture Palace, where Clive chained and padlocked the Norton.

'That was lovely,' said Penny. 'It's a shame, really, that it's such a short journey.'

'I could tell you were enjoying it.' Retrieving his cap from one of the panniers, he said, 'I have a longer journey tomorrow, but it'll have to be by train. I got a telephone call shortly before I left the house. I have to report to HMS *Kestrel*.'

'Oh, no. Is that a ship or an air station?'

'It's the naval air station at Worthy Down in Hampshire. It looks as if you and I are going to be near neighbours.'

'Good, but why are they sending you there?'

'Search me. I've no doubt I'll find out soon enough.' They entered the cinema, and Clive bought two tickets for the balcony.

As they climbed the stairs, Penny unbuttoned her coat, and Clive saw the royal blue dress she was wearing. 'I like that,' he said. 'Blue's your colour, isn't it?'

'Yes, that's why I joined the Wrens.'

'Hush,' said the usherette at the top of the stairs, pointing with her torch to two adjacent seats.

Clive apologised and thanked her politely.

They watched an American comedy starring someone Clive had never heard of. The humour was heavy, and the film really wasn't very good, but British Movietone News was next, which meant that they hadn't missed anything important.

There was a clip about the King and Queen visiting an Army barracks and a factory in the Midlands, and then the newsreel moved on to an item about Norway, showing a group of British and French soldiers who'd obviously been asked to pose for the camera, the British giving the clichéd 'thumbs up' gesture, and the French demonstrating comradeship in a more Gallic fashion. The commentator was relating a hearty account of the way the British Army and its allies rested together after giving the enemy what-for. He succeeded in making Clive chuckle, if nothing else.

'Hush,' said Penny, 'you're not supposed to laugh.'

'I'm sorry. I thought this was meant to be a comedy.'

After more fatuous footage, the newsreel reached a welcome end, and the lights came up.

'Those newsreel people can get excited watching icicles thaw,' he said.

'I suppose they have to sound interested.'

He asked, 'Can I buy you an ice cream or something?'

'No, thanks, I've just eaten.' Pointing towards the screen, she said, 'They used to have an organist here.'

'I bet he was a rotten substitute for ice cream.'

'Don't be silly.'

Continuing sensibly, he said,   'I expect he's been called-up. I wonder if he's in Norway. Judging by the numbers on that newsreel, everyone else seems to be.'

Frowning, she said, 'It looked as cold as you said.'

'It gets even colder than that. Norwegian babies are born in woolly jumpers and on skis.'

'Don't be silly.'

Eventually, the lights went down, and the main feature began. Clive reached for Penny's hand and was rewarded with a welcoming smile.

After a short while, he lost the thread of the story. It wasn't at all difficult to follow, being a lightweight comedy, but his mind was elsewhere, thinking of possible reasons for his peculiar posting. After a while, he settled for watching the film in a passive, superficial way, except when Lilli Palmer was on screen, and he would have defied any functioning male not to give her his full attention.

Eventually, the film reached its end, but Clive didn't feel he'd missed anything. Even though he and Penny had only just met, he was surprised to find that he was growing increasingly drawn to her, and his intention had been simply to spend more time in her company before his leave was up. Now it had been cut short, he was glad he had. He gave her hand a final squeeze before standing up, being a uniformed officer, for the National Anthem.

When they were outside, Penny looked at her watch and said, 'We've lots of time. It's not ten o'clock yet. What shall we do?'

'We could call at the Salamanca again and have a drink.'

'Yes, let's.'

They walked the short distance to the hotel, the journey made easier this time by a clear, moonlit sky, and went into the Channel Bar, which was quite busy. Clive asked, 'What would you like to drink?'

She wrinkled her nose in thought. 'I think I'll stick to "goffers" tonight,' she said. 'Lemonade, please.'

'Did you learn that word from your grandfather?'

'Who else?'

'I've always thought of it as lower deck slang.'

'You'd be surprised at some of the things he says.'

'He strikes me as particularly human for a flag officer.'

She considered that briefly and said, 'He's intolerant of slipshod workmanship and what he calls "flannel", and he's not keen on being contradicted. Otherwise, he's very human,' she concluded.

Two people got up to leave, and Clive claimed their table before anyone else could. 'Guard this,' he said, 'while I get the drinks.'

He returned shortly with a glass of lemonade and a pink gin.

'Thank you.' She asked, 'What did you think of the film?'

'It was rather above my head, I'm afraid.'

'Surely not.' She laughed and then hesitated, unsure for the moment. 'Do you mean that?'

'No, I was distracted.'

'By what?'

'By the truly lovely girl beside me.'

She looked at him uncertainly. Eventually, she said, 'I never know when you're joking.'

'It's the worst kind of form to play around with a person's feelings, and I'm not a cruel person. Believe me, I says it as means it.'

'In that case,' she said, weighing up what he'd just said, 'thank you for the compliment.'

'I've got lots more,' he assured her, 'all equally sincere, genuine and unrehearsed.' He studied her briefly. 'Are you shocked?'

'Not shocked, but a little bit surprised. If I'm honest, though, it's good to hear you say those things, because I like you an awful lot, too.' She placed her hand on his, as if to underline her words, but then she said uncertainly, 'You must know lots of girls.'

'I spend most of my time at sea, and the one luxury we don't enjoy in a warship is girls. There are pictures of them, of course; sailors line the inside of their locker doors with glamorous photos, and some even receive letters from their wives and sweethearts, but the real thing is as rare as snowflakes in September. The Admiralty simply don't allow it.'

'That makes sense,' she conceded, still looking thoughtful.

'What's on your mind, Penny?'

She hesitated. 'Just.... I was thinking about those people who receive letters from their wives and sweethearts. If I were to write to you....'

'Yes?'

'Do you like me enough to write back?'

'More than that,' he affirmed. 'If that's all you want, consider those letters written and in the post.'

'Right,' she said, taking out her diary. 'How should I address my letters to you?'

'Lieutenant C. R. Newing, RN,' he dictated, 'HMS *Kestrel*, Worthy Down, Hants.'

'I've got that.'

'Fair exchange,' he said, taking out his diary. 'What's yours?'

'Ordinary Wren P. E. Dowland eight four three one nine two, HMS *Nelson*, Portsmouth. Did you catch my official number, or shall I give it to you again?'

'No, I think I have it. I'll read it back to you. "eight four three one nine two". Is that correct?'

'Spot on. What's your middle name?'

'Roger,' he said, adding, 'the lodger, the dirty old codger.'

She gave him an odd look.

'It's a limerick,' he explained, 'not really for your unsullied ears. Fair dos again, though. What's yours?'

'Elizabeth. It was my grandmother's name, although I never knew her, because she died giving birth to my mother in eighteen ninety-nine.'

'Did your grandfather never marry again?'

'No.' Smiling, she said, 'He says I sometimes remind him of her.'

'That's nice. It answers another question, as well. I've been wondering if he'd named his boat *Chloe* after her, but evidently not.'

'No, HMS *Chloe* was his first command, a destroyer. He took command of her in nineteen-twelve.'

'You know his history, don't you?'

She shrugged. 'I should. He's been one of the most important people in my life for as long as I can remember, he and Mrs Hogben, his housekeeper.'

Taking her hand, he said, 'You haven't had the happiest of childhoods, have you?'

'It might have been worse. Thanks to those two and my school, it hasn't been too awful.'

'Did you enjoy school?'

She nodded. 'Tremendously.'

'Apart from having to dance with girls?'

'I didn't say it was perfect.' Her eyes took on the kind of pensive look that was becoming endearingly familiar.

'What is it, Penny?'

'Oh, I was only wondering if we might walk along the shore while it's still allowed. I'm thinking of what my grandfather said yesterday, about them closing the seafront.'

'I think we should.'

As they left the bar, he offered her his arm and, together, they took the steps down to the promenade. In contrast to the previous evening, the sky was cloudless, and the almost-full moon created a glittering path across the sea that seemed to draw them to the horizon, where, if they looked to southward, they could just make out the dim outline of the French coast. It obviously made an impression on Penny, because she said, 'Boulogne's just eighteen-and-a-half miles from Hythe. I don't know what the distance is from here, but it can't be much more than that. When you think of it, there's very little to separate us from France.'

'Let's hope so,' he said, mindful of the British, French and Polish troops currently facing the enemy in Norway.

'You're thinking about the war, aren't you?'

'It's difficult not to.'

'I know.' She shivered involuntarily.

'Do you feel cold?'

'A little.'

'Come into my Burberry.' Unbuttoning his gabardine coat, he opened it and drew her into its folds.

'Mm,' she murmured, 'you're warm and cosy.'

'You're welcome in here anytime. It's something the war can't prevent us from doing. Not permanently, anyway.'

Penny looked over her shoulder at the moonlit English Channel and said, 'They can't black-out the moon, either.'

'That's a good song, and it's true. Are you feeling any warmer?'

'Yes, but I like it inside your Burberry.'

'Oh, but it can be a dangerous place.'

'Why?' Her tone conveyed more than a hint of anticipation.

'You never know what dangers may befall you. Just as an example, I might even kiss you.'

'Do you really think so?'

'There's always that risk,' he said, kissing her softly on her lips.

'That wasn't so awful,' she assured him.

Encouraged, he bent again to kiss her, coaxing her through the hesitancy of her inexperience, and teasing her lips until they parted and responded naturally.

After a while, they drew apart, he to look at his watch, and she to say breathlessly, 'I told you I was innocent.'

'I'd never have known it, and innocence is guilty of nothing, as I told you earlier.'

Suddenly anxious, she asked, 'What's the time?'

'Twenty to twelve.'

'Will you kiss me again? Then we must go.'

He did, deeply and at length. Finally, he gave her his arm and they walked back to the Norton.

It might have been his fancy, but it seemed to him that she clutched his waist more tightly than ever on the way home. It was the shortest of journeys, and they pulled up in Penny's drive well inside her parents' curfew.

'You won't turn into a pumpkin, after all,' said Clive, checking the time.

The news was lost on Penny, who drew him to the side of the house. There, secure in the blackout, they kissed again.

She asked, 'You will write to me, won't you?'

'I said I would, and I shall.'

'And I'll write to you. Be careful, and don't do anything silly.'

'Who, me?'

'Who else? Kiss me, and then I have to go indoors.'

Eventually, they disentangled, and Penny moved reluctantly towards the door. 'Goodnight, Clive.'

'Goodnight, Penny.' He waited until she'd closed the door behind her, and rode the short distance home. Goodness knew what lay in wait for him in his new posting, but he gave the matter little thought. Instead, his mind was full of the evening he'd just spent and the girl with whom he'd spent it.

8

RUM, MAIL AND SURVIVAL

Convinced of the hopelessness of their position at Andalsnes, the Allies had decided to withdraw from the port, and HMS *Wrathful* was one of the ships covering the evacuation.

Wilf Gregory had two Stukas to his credit, and he was hoping for a third, at least. He wasn't at all bloodthirsty, but there was something hateful about the Nazi dive-bombers. Their 'Jericho Trumpets' were designed to demoralise an enemy, and Wilf was sure they'd done that over Spain in the Civil War and Poland in 1939, but all they did to him was make him angry. It was a cold anger, too; fierce reaction was of no use to an anti-aircraft gunner, who had to lay his guns coolly, estimating his deflection shots and choosing the moment. That was the only way to hit a moving target, and it was the essence of anti-aircraft gunnery.

Those were his thoughts when the next wave of Stukas was sighted. He'd already checked that his loader had inserted a fresh belt of ammunition, and he waited for the order to open fire.

When it came, he'd already selected his target, which was now into its dive. The hideous screaming began, he saw the bomb carrier descend so that the bomb wouldn't foul the propellor, and then it was released, aimed at another ship, which was making a turn to port to avoid it. The bomb fell into the sea maybe a hundred feet away from its target, creating a deluge, but without causing any damage. Wilf estimated his deflection and squeezed the firing levers, only to lose his target when *Wrathful* made a turn to starboard in order to avoid a bomb from another Stuka. It was a regular occurrence, as he complained to his messmates that evening.

'As soon as I get one lined up, the ship changes direction, and the bugger gets clean away,' he said.

'You're just greedy, Greg, said one of them. You've got two, and now you want the whole Luftthingummybob.'

'I've always said you can carry ambition too far, said Albert Fisher.

'You've never done that, "Stripey",' said Wilf looking at Albert's good conduct badges, 'we can tell.'

'Well, you can make yourself unhappy if you try to do too much. I mean, you've got your hook, you've got two Stukas, and you want even more. You don't know what contentment is.'

'I do,' said Ernie Taylor, hearing the Tannoy crackle. There was the whistle of a bosun's pipe and the order 'Up Spirits!'

'And stand by, the Holy Ghost,' said Albert. It was the oldest joke in naval history, but its appeal had never faded.

'Come on, Ernie,' said Wilf, 'give us a hand.' The two climbed the ladder and reported to the Master-at-Arms, who issued a measured quantity of rum and water, and the requisite tot glasses and pewter measure. They were accompanied back to the messdeck by a stony-faced petty officer, whose task was to ensure that no man would consume more than his tot, and that any left-over rum would be discarded.

Under his strict scrutiny, Wilf poured the regulation mixture of two-and-a-half fluid ounces of over-proof rum and five of water into each glass, handing them to his messmates. The dilution of the rum ration with water had begun in the eighteenth century as a safeguard against sailors bottling their tots and saving them for binge drinking, and the regulation was as unpopular as the law that said, 'No man shall give another man all or part of his tot.' In particular, the latter ensured that the celebration of birthdays and other events, by sippers, was only possible when no officer or senior rating was present. It would have surprised no one that the ship's company of HMS *Wrathful* were eagerly awaiting the double tot their captain had promised them.

* * *

Clive arrived at HMS *Kestrel* after a long train journey, to be reunited with Bill Stevenson. It appeared that their purpose at Worthy Down was to patrol the Channel, searching for blockade runners and U-boats. The experience of Norway had taught the Admiralty that the surface ships of the Kriegsmarine were only likely to venture into open waters when there was little likelihood of their being engaged by equal or superior forces.

Clive asked, 'Have you seen anything of Bright?' Bill had arrived earlier, as his home was in Hampshire.

'No,' said Bill, 'we have a new air-gunner, a leading airman called Carson.'

'Not old "Kit"?' It was another old joke, as any Carson in the service was inevitably nicknamed 'Kit', but it seemed no one could resist it.

'We also have two celebrities in the Wardroom,' said Bill. 'You'll meet them later. One is the actor Ralph Richardson, who's been here for some time, and his old theatrical oppo Laurence Olivier arrived last month. He'd recently finished a film called *Rebecca*.'

'What's that?'

'I believe it's based on some romantic novel or other.'

'What are these chaps?'

'Both pilots. Olivier is yet to get his wings, and the word is that, if Richardson's not careful, he may grow a pair of his own and acquire a harp into the bargain. He's already earned the name "Pranger". I imagine we'll find out about Olivier soon enough. Apparently, he has a private licence, but he hasn't yet satisfied the service that he's fit to fly.'

Clive met both of them that evening and decided that, whatever ability they showed or lacked in flying, they provided entertaining company in the Wardroom.

* * *

In the morning, Clive and Bill were told off, as the Navy called the process of briefing; they met Leading Airman Carson, who seemed very capable, and spent the forenoon over the Channel, but without sighting anything of interest.

One thing that was of interest, however, was the letter that Clive found on his return. It was postmarked 'Hythe, Kent' and, as he'd guessed, it was from Penny. He took it to his cabin to read it.

Dear Clive,

I hope your journey wasn't too unpleasant. After Thursday, we'll be able to compare notes.

Believe it or not, my mother telephoned my grandfather on Monday afternoon, after I'd told her we were going to the dance, to ask him if he thought you were a suitable escort. She actually owned up to the offence without an ounce of shame. Huh! Of course, he'd only just met you, and then only briefly, but he told her you seemed 'a steady sort of chap'! I told him he was spot on with that assessment, but he wasn't surprised. He has total faith in his own judgement.

Monday and Tuesday evenings were wonderful. Please tell me they were for you, too. Tuesday, particularly, was one of those occasions when everything was just perfect, and I'll never forget it. Maybe we can get together, sometime, in Portsmouth. That would be marvellous.

Please write soon.

Love and best wishes,

Penny X

Clive folded the letter and put it safely away. He would reply to it later.

* * *

Yet again, Wilf was denied his third Stuka. The last onslaught was particularly fierce, and the captain was obliged to give frequent helm orders to avoid the almost incessant bombing, a manoeuvre that had so far proved successful. One ship that was less fortunate, however, was one of *Wrathful*'s sister ships, HMS *Wenlock*. Wilf saw her under attack, he saw the explosion, and fully expected her to sink, but her damage control party somehow managed to contain, and finally extinguish, the fire. Thick, black smoke poured from somewhere abaft the after funnel, and an Aldis lamp was winking on her bridge. In due course, *Wrathful*'s company learned something of the content of its signal. *Wenlock* had suffered heavy casualties, including her captain and first lieutenant, and she needed an experienced officer and a number of seamen and stokers to man her again and take her home. A list was read out, and Wilf's name was among them. Hurriedly, he packed his kitbag and went to the upper deck to report to the First Lieutenant.

'I'm glad to see you, Gregory,' he said. 'We need leading hands.

We're taking both whalers. As soon as everyone's mustered, we'll get under way.'

With everyone on board, the deck crew lowered the two 27-foot whalers into an uncompromising sea, and Lieutenant Soames gave the order to give way together. It seemed that he was going to take command of *Wenlock*. First of all, though, he and the emergency crew had to reach the stricken destroyer before the Luftwaffe returned to finish the job.

* * *

Arthur heard the office door open and turned to see Penny. 'Your mother's going to accuse me of monopolising you,' he said, smiling in spite of his words.

'I think she knows the truth by now, Grandpop.'

'I think she does.' He beckoned to her to take a seat. 'Tell me about this young man she was so keen to hear about.'

'Clive?'

'I didn't know his name. Even his surname escaped my memory, but it was a very brief meeting, as you know.'

Taking the chair that was offered, she said, 'He's called Clive Newing, and he's lovely. He knows I've only recently joined the Wrens, but he's not at all patronising or disparaging about it.'

Arthur nodded appreciatively. 'Is he from a naval family?'

'No, his father's the dentist in Foxhill, just up the road from us. They tease each other, but he says they get on well together.'

'Of course. I know Mr Newing. He's an excellent man, and it's always as well to be on good terms with a dentist.'

'He was lovely to me when he filled one of my teeth.'

Smiling at her artless observation, he asked, 'And what has Lieutenant Newing been doing so far?'

'He was in the Mediterranean in HMS *Glorious*, and then he was in Norway.' She reflected on that and said, 'Well, not *in* Norway, exactly, but off the coast.'

'I bet he's glad he's no longer there.'

'Why?'

'As far as I can make out, it's a shambles, Penny. We can only hope that whoever's in command in France has the job weighed off somewhat better.'

'Clive's at HMS *Kestrel*, now, the air station at Worthy Down, near Portsmouth.'

More seriously, he said, 'You're obviously quite taken with him.'

'Yes, I am.' As ever, she was open about her feelings.

He sat back with his fingertips together and said, 'Things were very different when I was young. For one thing, girls were chaperoned in those days, and young men were carefully vetted. When I met your grandmother, I was allowed to take her gloved hand very genteelly, and the whole business of courting took place over a long period of time, during which, more often than not, I was at sea.'

'How wonderful.' She was fascinated by the picture that formed in her imagination.

'I could tell you lots of things, Penny. I could tell you that you're very young, which you already know, and that you mustn't let your heart rule your head, which is too obvious for words. I could also remind you that we're at war, and that being a pilot in the Fleet Air Arm isn't the safest occupation, but whatever I say will make not a scrap of difference to the way you feel, so I shan't warn you about anything. Instead, I just want you to remember that, whatever happens, I'll be here whenever you need me.'

'Oh, Grandpop,' she said, leaving her chair to hug him, 'and my parents wonder why I spend as much time with you as I do.'

* * *

At length, the relief crew were on board and the whalers were on their way back to *Wrathful*. Lieutenant Soames assessed the situation and detailed men to their tasks. 'Both pom-pom mountings are wrecked,' he told Wilf, 'so I'm putting you on the port Lewis guns. You'll have to manage without a loader, as we haven't a man to spare.'

'I'll manage, sir.'

'Excellent. Carry on, Gregory.'

'Aye, aye, sir.'

Wilf made his way to the port Lewis mounting, steeling himself when he saw the blood-soaked deck. Elsewhere, the stench of wet, charred timbers was almost overpowering. He closed his mind to it and concentrated on searching the sky for enemy aircraft. As he did so, he heard someone reporting to Lieutenant Soames via the voice pipe, and then Soames's order, 'Start engines.' The ship was under way, the engines were pumping out the flooded compartments, and the time was 2050. In another hour, they would have darkness as their ally. The only hazard, then, would come from the U-boats, although the sheer number of destroyers on the coast might well deter them. They would soon know.

Within the hour, Lieutenant Soames broadcast to the ship's company, telling them he estimated that, with the current sea state and the need to steam at a reduced speed to conserve fuel, their journey to Scapa Flow would take 36 hours. 'Tomorrow forenoon,' he told them, 'we will bury the dead. Good luck to you all. That is all.'

* * *

Clive, Bill and 'Kit' Carson landed at Worthy Down, having again encountered no identifiable enemy shipping. It seemed very strange to Clive and Bill after the carnage of Norway, but all they could do was follow orders.

After a drink in the Wardroom, Clive returned to his cabin to write to his parents, his sister and Penny. It was quite difficult, as there was very little he could write about, but it was expected of him, so he made a determined effort.

By the time he was able to begin his letter to Penny, he was finding it easier to write about trivia, but there were other things he wanted to tell her, as well.

Dear Penny,

Thank you for your extremely prompt letter! It arrived the day after I did, and very welcome it was, too.

Yes, Tuesday evening was very special for me, too, and perhaps we shall be able to get together in Pompey. The powers that govern your outfit may well be less than generous with leave at first, as you're new and under training, but I think we should get together again before long. Let me know when you can get away, because it will be easier for me.

It was kind of your grandfather to put a word in for me with your mother. As you said, it was the briefest of meetings, but I get the impression that very little escapes his notice.

Now, for obvious reasons in wartime, I can't name names, but I find I'm in daily communication with two well-known theatrical and film actors. Are you interested in that kind of thing? If you are, I should be able to get their autographs for you quite easily. Just say the word, and it shall be done.

Naturally, I can't tell you what I'm doing, although it would only bore you mindless if I did, but I can say that it's both quieter and warmer than the place I left behind.

I wish you the very best of luck on the course, and I'll give you one invaluable piece of advice. The Navy is a small world and a big family, so don't upset anyone in authority, because you're bound to meet them again later, and you may need their help, influence, understanding or mercy.

Speaking of mercy, you're the only girl to have known the inside of my Burberry, and that makes you very special indeed. Stay fit and healthy, and we'll meet again. Vera Lynn says so, therefore it must be true.

Love and fondest wishes,
Clive XX

* * *

'We therefore commit his body to the deep, to be turned into corruption, looking for the resurrection of the body, when the sea shall give up her dead, and the life of the world to come…. according to the mighty working, whereby he is able to subdue all things to himself….' Lieutenant Soames reached the end of the Prayer of Committal, and the burial party lifted the table, retaining the ensign as the last of the dead slid over the side and into the sea. Those present raised their heads, the service reached its conclusion, and the burial party was dismissed, each man as grim as the next, not simply because of the ceremony they'd just attended, but also because most of them had been on watch the whole night. Barely seaworthy and steaming at less than half speed, HMS *Wenlock* was being nursed along each mile she covered on her voyage to Scapa Flow in Orkney.

Wilf was as tired as anyone, having been relieved at his post on the bridge to join the party of seamen steering the ship by hand because the linkage between the wheelhouse and the rudders was now a mess of broken, trailing wires.

As he toiled, Wilf thought about his parents and his home in Kent, because they were eight hundred miles away and, at least for the time being, thought was all he had.

9

DOTS, DASHES AND DANCING

Penny and the others of the intake went through the same joining
routine as they had at Mill Hill, and were given a bewildering
amount of information, little of which they remembered as they
were marched from their quarters in Victoria Barracks to the Signals
Training Centre. In her naivete, Penny had expected a modern,
purpose-designed establishment, and was shocked to find that signals
training was to take place in four large, but elderly, wooden buildings.
The recruits were separated into their four specialisms, which
were Coding, Message Handling, Wireless Telegraphy and Visual
Signalling. The instructor in WT, a tall, good-looking, dark-haired
man of around thirty, introduced himself as Petty Officer Telegraphist
Stanhope. He walked with the aid of a cane and was recovering from
injuries sustained in the River Plate action. He also wore the ribbon
of the Distinguished Service Medal, which added to his prestige and
the high regard in which his trainees already held him. He took them
into the classroom and gave them an idea of what would be required
of them during their course.

'If an officer comes in while you are seated in the classroom,' he
explained, 'as they are wont, I will call you to attention, but you will
not stand. Instead, you will sit to attention with your arms folded, thus.'
Somewhat unnecessarily, he demonstrated the arms-folded posture. As
the course wore on, the girls learned that 'wont' and 'thus' were only
two of the old-fashioned words that characterised his delivery, but his
drollness of speech was soon forgotten in the demanding schedule.

That afternoon, they began learning the Morse code, which PO Tel
Stanhope told them confidently would shortly become their second
language.

'You will live, breath and even dream in Morse,' he told them, 'and then, very soon, it will become second nature.' We will begin with the vowels.' He listed them, writing them on the blackboard against their Morse symbols.

In what seemed no time at all, they were able to read high speed combinations of the five symbols. *Di-dah, dit, di-dit, dah-dah-dah* and *di-di-dah* became as familiar as their own names, and just for fun, or so he told them, PO Stanhope threw in the semi-vowel 'y', or *dah-di-dah-dah*. The girls saw the wisdom of his method when he extended their repertoire by adding the consonants 'b', 'c' and 'd'. With those nine letters, they knew a third of the alphabet and could read various combinations of them at the optimum operating speed. It was much easier than trying to learn the whole alphabet at once. They also had to learn the Radiotelephony Spelling Alphabet, which they found easy enough.

Within a few days, personalities began to emerge. On the desk to Penny's right was a cheerful, friendly girl called Betty. Her parents owned a fish and chip shop in Burnley, Lancashire, and they quickly became friends. Not all the girls were as pleasant, however, and Penny's fond memories of everyone mucking in together as a classless society at HMS *Pembroke* had to remain memories only. Two girls, in particular, Daphne and Annabelle, already had ambitions to rise above the rest, but not necessarily through hard work. In their ignorance, they addressed PO Stanhope as 'Chiefy' and treated him as a favourite uncle. Either of them was likely to interrupt a Morse reception exercise with requests for special treatment, a favourite being, 'Do slow down, Chiefy darling. I haven't got the first word yet!' Before long, the two were sent to a separate hut to be instructed by Leading Telegraphist Bowers, a dour, three-badge rating who proved incorruptible. He was nobody's 'darling', and he would brook no silliness. Penny was less than surprised to learn subsequently that both girls had failed the course and were required to re-muster as drivers. She could only guess at the kind of conversation they would attempt to strike up with the senior officers unfortunate enough to be seated behind them.

After one week, the intake were allowed shore leave, and Penny wrote to Clive immediately to give him the news. He replied by return, telling her he would collect her that Saturday evening from Victoria Barracks at 1800.

* * *

On their arrival in Orkney, the crew of HMS *Wenlock* were given five day's leave and ordered to report thereafter to HMS *Nelson*. For Wilf, as well as many others, that five-day pass was the most welcome news, and he arrived eventually in Sandbrook, having slept most of the way from Edinburgh, much of it while seated on his kitbag in the train corridor.

On the next day, Walter Gregory reported to his employer, saying, 'I've taken the liberty of bringing my lad Wilfred, sir. He's just got back from Norway.'

'It's good to see you,' said Arthur. 'Congratulations on your leading rate, Wilfred.'

'Thank you, sir.' Wilf took the outstretched hand shyly, more than a little surprised to be addressed in that way by a flag officer, albeit a retired one.

'That's not all, sir,' said Walter. 'While he's been in Norwegian waters, he's been twice mentioned in despatches.'

'Has he, now? In that case, as soon as the sun rises above the yardarm, you must both come to the office, and we'll celebrate the fact.'

It was actually a little before eleven when Arthur called them both to his office.

'Now, I have gin, whisky and rum. What will you have?' Looking at Wilf, he said, 'We may as well start with you, Wilfred, as it's your achievements we're celebrating.'

'If it's all the same to you, sir, I'd prefer rum,' said Wilf, still barely able to believe this was happening.

'Then rum it shall be. What about you, Chief?'

'I'll join my lad with rum, if I may, sir. This is most kind of you, sir.'

'You're very welcome,' said Arthur, pouring two generous tots, and then a measure of gin for himself. Holding up his glass, he proposed the toast, 'Wilfred's hook and two mentions in despatches.'

They drank the toast, and then Arthur sat them down. 'Now I'd like to hear all about it,' he said.

With some prompting, Wilf gave a dry and artless account of *Wrathful*'s activities off Namsos and Andalsnes, making light of his two Stukas and going on to describe *Wenlock*'s plight and her rescue by Lieutenant Soames and the party from *Wrathful*. Of the latter achievement, he ended by saying, 'I was just one of a lot of hands who did what had to be done, sir, no more than that.'

'So you were, Wilfred, but you should still take pride in the part you played.'

'It's kind of you to say so, sir, but it was Mr Soames, the First Lieutenant, who took command, sir. He should get the credit.'

'I'm sure Lieutenant Soames is a very gallant and capable officer, and we shall no doubt hear more about him in due course, but I'm reminded of an observation made by the greatest naval officer of them all. Lord Nelson, himself, went on record as saying that the true hero of any naval engagement was the ordinary British seaman. Remember that, and cherish those words, Wilfred, because they still hold good, today.'

* * *

Penny stood at the main gate of HMS *Victoria* with no idea what to expect, but she was still surprised when Clive drew up in a Wolseley Hornet. He got out and held the door open for her.

She said, 'It's wonderful to see you. How long have you had this?'

He waited until he was in the driving seat to explain. 'I've only borrowed it for the evening. That part was easy. It was the petrol that took some finding, but I managed it.'

'Where are we going?'

'To a little restaurant that's been recommended to me. It's not far from here. How's the course going?'

'Famously. I can read half the alphabet in Morse at twenty-two words a minute.'

'Good for you.' He performed a mock double-take and asked, 'What about the other half?'

'We'll do that next week.'

'I see. So, Wrens do things by halves, do they?'

She laughed. 'We have a wonderful instructor who has his own ways of doing things, and he says we'll all be fluent in Morse long before the end of the course.'

'Does he know how to shorten the war? I imagine Churchill would be very interested to hear his ideas.'

'Oh, yes,' she said, suddenly reminded of the week's events, 'what do you think about Mr Churchill being Prime Minister?' His appointment had been announced only the previous day. 'Grandpop calls him "Young Churchill", because he's four years older than him.'

'Good for Grandpop. It's difficult to know what to think,' he said, turning into a narrow street and parking beside a restaurant that, like every other building, was blacked-out. 'He's made a pot-mess of every job he's been given so far, and he was as guilty as anyone of creating the chaos in Norway, but I can't think of anyone else who's capable of leading the country just now.' He switched off the engine and opened his door. 'Let's go inside and forget the war for the time being.' He took a large envelope from the back seat before locking the car, and they made their way through a curtained light trap and into the restaurant, where an elderly waiter found Clive's reservation and took their coats and hats.

'My word,' said Clive when he saw Penny's dress, 'every time I see you, you hit me for six. What colour do you call this?'

'It's cornflower blue, and you're exaggerating, but thank you, anyway.'

They followed the waiter to a table not far from the dance floor, and he handed them each a menu. 'I'm afraid the steak dishes are no longer available,' he said in a humble tone that almost suggested that the fault were his.

'Don't worry,' Clive told him. 'I'm sure we'll find something equally inviting. What's not on the menu?'

The waiter leaned forward confidingly and said, 'Hare, sir, in a sauce that is as creamy as circumstances allow.'

'We'll bear that in mind. Thank you.'

'I'll leave you to choose an *entrée*, sir.' The waiter withdrew.

'Poor old man,' said Penny, watching him recede. 'He looks worn out, and the evening's just begun.'

'I think he enjoys every minute of it. With all the young men called up, he'll be cock of the midden for the duration of hostilities.'

They chose their *entrées*, both opting for the hare as a main course, and Clive asked for the wine list.

'I hope you're not going to push the boat out,' said Penny.

'Why not? Eat, drink and be merry, for tomorrow I fly. At least, I shall in three days' time.'

She smiled inquisitively. 'I thought you usually did.'

'On Tuesday, I fly to RAF Manston, my next posting.'

'What on earth for?'

'I've no idea, but I'll tell the junior service as soon as I land that in consideration of the shameful way they treated the Fleet Air Arm between the wars they needn't think they're going to get their hands on it again. That really is off the menu.'

The wine waiter arrived with the wine list, which Clive opened and perused.

'I'll leave the wine to you,' said Penny.

'Very well.' Clive beckoned the wine waiter and asked for a bottle of the 1938 Chateau Mouton Rothschild.

'They're going to play our song,' said Penny. The bandleader had just announced 'They Can't Black-Out the Moon'.

'May I?'

'Of course.' She allowed him to lead her on to the floor. As he took her in hold, she said, 'It does seem odd, their posting you again after only a few days.'

'Hush,' he warned.

'Sorry. Walls have ears. I know.'

'So do bulkheads, and I'll hear no more of that landlubberly language, now you're in the Senior Service, my dear.'

'Of course.' They danced the rest of the number without speaking, and Penny thought again about Sandbrook seafront and the moon reflected on the waves. She doubted she would ever forget it, and she hoped Clive wouldn't, either.

They'd only just returned to their table, when the waiter brought the wine for Clive's approval. He looked at the label and nodded before tasting it.

'That's excellent,' he said. 'Thank you.'

'I'm glad you don't make a performance of it,' said Penny.

'I couldn't do that without laughing,' he said, 'and trust me, you don't want to see me with wine coming down my nose.'

'I'd rather not,' she agreed.

Their first course arrived, and Penny said, 'So much is happening just now, it's difficult to know what to toast.'

'That,' agreed Clive, 'and I haven't christened my new aircraft yet.'

71

'What was your last one called?'

'Greta.'

'After Greta Garbo?'

'No, Greta was a dog we had years ago.' He leaned forward confidentially to ask, 'Would you mind if I called the new Swordfish "Penny"?'

'I've absolutely no objection, but I don't own exclusive rights to the name.'

'But you wouldn't feel I were trivialising your name?'

'It would never occur to me, and it's the first time I've had an aeroplane named after me, so I'm quite flattered.'

'Good.' Raising his glass, he said, 'Here's to the two Pennys in my life.'

Raising hers, she said, 'You've got enough for a telephone call, now.'

'Please,' he cautioned her. 'This is a serious matter.'

'It's an awful shame I can't be at her christening ceremony.'

'And that I can't be around for your coming-of-age,' he agreed.

Changing the subject abruptly, as was her way, she said, 'The contents of that envelope must be very important for you not to allow it out of your sight.'

'You want to know what's in it, don't you?'

'Of course I do.'

As he handed her the envelope, she noticed that it was the stiffened kind, used for photographs and certificates. Still curious, she lifted the flap, which wasn't gummed down, and took out three photographs.

'You'll find two of them more entertaining than the third,' he warned her.

'Oh, my goodness, Clive. Thank you.' She was looking at signed photographs of Ralph Richardson and Laurence Olivier. The third was of Clive, and it was signed simply, 'With love, Clive.'

'I know I'm in celebrated company, but I thought you might like to have it, anyway.'

'I love it, Clive. Thank you.'

The bandleader announced 'Deep Purple', causing Clive to ask, 'Shall we?'

'Yes, let's.'

They made their way on to the dance floor. This time, they danced to the end of the number without speaking. It was that kind of song.

When they returned to their table, Clive said, 'Churchill is due to make his maiden speech on Monday as Prime Minister. At least he'll be doing something he does well, although it's going to take more than rhetoric to stop the Boche.'

'The Boche?'

'It's what my father calls them.' As the thought occurred to him, he said, 'You know, they should have had him interrogating prisoners in the last war. Thirty seconds in the dentist's chair, and they'd have told him everything, from the current battle plan to the Kaiser's inside leg measurement.'

'You're awful about him, Clive, but I'm sure you don't mean it.'

'Don't be so sure. Shall we dance again?'

'You know me well enough by now.'

They got up to dance to the ever-popular and highly-appropriate 'Cheek to Cheek', the floor being quite crowded by that time.

* * *

Clive pulled into the side of the road and switched off the engine.

Penny asked, 'Why have we stopped here?'

'To say goodnight, of course. That's something we don't do under the gaze of the main gate sentries.'

'Of course.' She leaned forward so that he could put his arm around her, and joined him in a lengthy and luxurious kiss. After some time, she said, 'Ten minutes from now, I shall turn into a pumpkin.'

'I've never kissed a pumpkin.'

'It's not recommended. Much as I'd rather stay here with you, I must be back on board by twenty-three fifty-nine.'

'You're learning quickly,' he said. '"Back on board by twenty-three fifty-nine" would have impressed Lord Nelson.' He kissed her once more and started the engine. 'You know my address, don't you? RAF Manston, Ramsgate.'

'Yes, I'll write to you.'

10

PREPARATION

In the Wardroom at HMS *Kestrel*, Bill Stevenson was reading the account in *The Times* of Churchill's maiden speech.

'It says here that he was cheered all the way to the despatch box,' he said, 'and that the applause was led by Attlee, as it was again at the end of his speech.'

'And that goes to show just how desperate the situation is,' said Clive. 'I can't see why we don't make it illegal for anyone to stand for parliament. They only make a pot-mess of it when they get there.'

'It's stirring stuff,' said Bill, ignoring him, 'but I can't help thinking that he needs a little help with his presentation. I mean, to begin with, he has no idea of cadence. He seems to rely entirely on his choice of words.'

'Believe me,' said Ralph Richardson, joining the conversation, 'he needs no help with his rhetoric, and I speak as one who knows a little about communicating with an audience.'

'He does only know a little,' said Olivier, 'but I have to admit, he uses it well.'

'I spent some time in the Strangers' Gallery of the House of Commons, studying speech patterns,' said Richardson, ignoring his irreverent friend, 'and I learned very quickly that Churchill is no ordinary speaker. For one thing, the unusual use of cadence that you mentioned, Stevenson, is one of his most powerful devices. His words alone are telling, but his delivery is both magnetic and compelling.'

For once, Bill was bested in an argument. 'I can't argue with your expert opinion,' he said.

'I shouldn't, sir,' advised Olivier. 'He'll only wear you down, as he does everyone else.'

Clive had been studying Bill's newspaper. 'There was more news last evening,' he said. 'While we were carousing in this wardroom, the Secretary of State for War made a broadcast asking for volunteers to form a sort of militia. "Local Defence Volunteers", he called them.'

'It'll make them feel useful, I suppose,' said Bill.

Still reading, Clive said, 'We may need them yet, as the powers-that-be seem so far unacquainted with the essential difference between arse and elbow. Just a minute, though, there's something else. There was an announcement after the Nine o' clock News, affecting owners of boats with an overall length of thirty feet or more. Apparently, they have to register their details with the Admiralty via their local police station.' Putting the newspaper down, he said, 'To say, "the plot thickens", does the machinations of this government no justice whatsoever. I wonder what's behind the boat thing.'

* * *

Sandbrook's tiny police station had been a part of the town since Victorian times, but Arthur had only been there once, and that had been to hand in a wallet that a careless customer had left behind. This time, he entered the oak-panelled station to find Sergeant Philpott besieged by an eager and noisy gathering.

'I have to ask you to form two queues,' said the sergeant with his usual air of patience and authority. 'Local Defence people to the left and boat owners to the right.'

'I'm here for both,' shouted one of the fishermen.

'So are we,' said the others.

'Well, we haven't the space for a special queue for "both", said Sergeant Philpott. You'll have to register for one thing at a time. Now, is there anybody here who wants to register for the Local Defence. ...' He referred to his instructions for the title, which was new enough to have escaped his memory. '...Volunteers, but who hasn't got a boat? If so, we'll deal with you first.'

A number of men formed a queue, and Arthur watched the procession of very young, middle-aged and somewhat-older volunteers go forward to give their names. Some were little more than schoolboys, no doubt awaiting conscription; some would be in reserved occupations, others were possibly veterans of the previous war, and a few were obviously in blatant but heroic denial of the upper age limit. On the far side of the room, a spider was busily spinning its web, seemingly oblivious to the excited crowd that had gathered below. Arthur was no entomologist; in fact, he knew only four things about spiders. He knew that they had eight legs, that they ate flies, that the discovery of just one of their webs in a warship or naval establishment led to at least seven days' Number Nine Punishment, and that they had no interest in joining the Local Defence Volunteers. It was meaningless, he knew, but it was a mental exercise that helped pass the time.

Recognising Arthur from the office within, a constable asked, 'Would you like a chair, Admiral Clement?'

'No, thank you. I think there are others whose need is rather greater than mine.' Some of the older end volunteering for possibly active service seemed to be unused to standing for long periods and were looking jaded. He continued to watch the queue, considerably heartened by the response to the LDV appeal. The need to register boats was a mystery to everyone, and Arthur could only guess at its purpose. He hoped earnestly that he was wrong.

Eventually, Sergeant Philpott called, 'Boat-owners wishing to register as Local Defence Volunteers.'

Arthur continued to wait as the younger fishermen stepped up to the desk. The process was simple. All that was needed was their names, addresses and dates of birth. Sergeant Philpott did the writing, so there was no risk of embarrassment, and the authorities, yet to be named, would be in touch, or an announcement would be made.

Distracted again, Arthur wondered how many drunks and petty thieves had been brought into that police station, major crime being largely unknown in a small coastal town such as Sandbrook. He was pondering the question when the sergeant spoke up again.

'Finally, anybody who just wants to register a boat.' He was sounding tired, and Arthur wasn't surprised. World wars didn't come around all that often, thankfully, but when they did, they brought upheaval and a great deal of hard work in their wake. He stepped forward, and Philpott said, 'I'll take you first, Admiral Clement. You've waited long enough, sir.'

'Thank you, Sergeant.'

'Now, sir, your full name, please?'

'Arthur Edward Clement.'

The sergeant wrote that on his makeshift form. 'And your address and telephone number, sir.'

'My home address is "Oakland", Folkestone Road, Sandbrook, Kent.' He waited until the sergeant had finished writing, and said, 'My home telephone number is Sandbrook one four one.'

'Thank you, sir. Now, the name of your boat?'

'*Chloe*, as you know.'

'This is an official matter, sir. Her overall length?'

Arthur hesitated. 'For the purpose of this exercise, Sergeant Philpott, let's say she's thirty feet overall.'

The sergeant paused to ask, 'Is she really thirty feet long, sir?'

'It's a minor detail, Sergeant. Just put her down at thirty feet.'

'If you say so, sir.' He dipped his pen in the inkwell and plied it again.

'Address where the boat is kept, sir.'

'Ellis's Boatyard, Sandbrook Seafront. You've seen it there often enough.'

'Often enough to question her overall length, sir,' agreed the sergeant. 'She has all the appearance of a twenty-seven-foot whaler.' Philpott had served as a seaman in the previous war.

'As I said, it's a minor detail that need hardly concern either us or the Admiralty.'

After such a hectic session, the sergeant was disinclined to argue, and anyone who knew Arthur could testify to his stubbornness. 'The telephone number of the boatyard, sir?'

'Sandbrook one five nine.'

'Thank you, sir. That's all that's required.'

'Have you any idea what this is about, Sergeant?'

'None whatsoever, sir. We're only carrying out orders from above.'

'And doing it remarkably well. Thank you, Sergeant.'

'Thank you, sir. Next, please.'

* * *

In the short time Penny had been at the Signal Training Centre, she and her class had learned about the propagation of radio waves, the way the Admiralty organised its communications, the tuning and loading of receivers and transmitters, and now they were embarking on WT Practical Procedure, the codified way in which stations communicated with one another.

PO Tel. Stanhope gave them each an individual callsign and assigned a collective callsign to the class. Before long, Penny heard her callsign GW4T being transmitted. The PO Tel. was asking for her readability. Naturally enough she was reading him loud and clear, so she answered, 'GB8F de GW4T QRK 5 INT QRK K.'

He answered, 'de GB8F (SVC) QRK 5 BZ AR.'

She studied his signal. 'QRK 5' meant 'loud and clear', and 'AR' meant 'End of Transmission', but 'BZ' defeated her. She asked, 'What does "BZ" stand for, PO?'

Instead of replying, he pointed mutely to the telegraph key, and Penny remembered to her embarrassment that, for the next hour, all communications were to be made via WT. Hastily, she sent him a service message, the only kind, other than the procedure message, that ratings were allowed to send on their own behalf. 'GB8F de GW4T (SVC) Request meaning of BZ K.'

He smiled and sent, 'de GB8F (SVC) BZ means Well Done AR.' Two tiny words of praise meant a great deal to her, even though she'd had to ask about them.

Gradually, the class learned about the International 'Q' Code, a vocabulary of three-letter signals that covered a wide range of uses. They also learned about the 'Z' Code, which was strictly military, but just as useful. The prosigns completed the telegraphist's repertoire. They included 'K' for 'Over', 'AR' for 'Out', 'INT' for '?', 'de' for 'this is', and 'AS' for 'Wait'. There was a great deal to learn, but learning it gave them huge satisfaction.

A moment's disquiet came when Penny was summoned to Second Officer Howell's office. She couldn't imagine what she might have done wrong, and she felt rather as she had years earlier, when her housemistress had sent for her because she'd been seen out of school without her gloves, a heinous offence.

She knocked on the door and waited. Then, hearing a peremptory 'Come', she turned the handle and stepped inside, coming smartly to attention before a slender woman of maybe forty or so. 'Eight four three one nine two Ordinary Wren Dowland, ma'am. You sent for me.'

'Yes, Wren Dowland. At ease.'

Penny adopted the 'at ease' stance.

'You know, don't you, that we have to read all outgoing mail?'

'Yes, ma'am.' She wondered what she might have written that was classified.

'You've been corresponding with a naval officer.' She consulted her notes and said, 'Lieutenant C. R. Newing, RN.'

Her question was answered. 'That's right, ma'am. We live in the same village. In fact, we're neighbours.'

'Oh?'

'We didn't know each other before I joined the Wrens, but we met outside my grandfather's boatyard when I was on leave after basic training.'

'Oh, your grandfather owns a boatyard, then?'

Penny wasn't sure where this was leading, so she fired her only gun. 'Yes, ma'am, he's Rear Admiral Clement, except he's retired now, which is why he bought the boatyard.'

'Oh, I see.' Miss Howell was immediately impressed. 'And is Lieutenant Newing known to your grandfather?'

'Yes, ma'am.' It was essentially true, and Penny was an essentially truthful person.

'You see, for the sake of discipline, relations between Wren ratings and naval officers are discouraged, but…. How often do you and this officer… see each other?'

Penny tried not to smile at 2/O Howell's thinly-concealed embarrassment. 'We saw each other recently in Portsmouth, ma'am. He was at HMS *Kestrel*, but he's been posted, so I don't know how long it will be before we'll see each other again.' She added, 'He's a pilot in the Fleet Air Arm, so he could soon be at sea in an aircraft carrier.'

'Yes, he could. Look, this whole thing sounds innocent enough, so I'm going to take it no further.' She consulted the document in front of her again and said, 'You were at Hedgeworth School for Girls, I see.'

'Yes, ma'am.'

'And you left with an excellent report.'

'Give or take the odd reprimand, ma'am.'

'Oh?'

'Being seen out of school negative gloves, singing inappropriate words to the School Song during Morning Prayers, and reading after Lights Out. Just high spirits, ma'am.' She realised by the time she reached the end of her sentence that, if Miss Howell had a sense of humour, she regarded it as a personal secret to be shared with no one.

'Oh, I see. Tell me, have you considered applying for officer training?'

'No, ma'am.'

Her unhesitant reply seemed to prompt genuine surprise. 'Why not?'

'It's never occurred to me, ma'am. I've been too busy training to be a telegraphist, and I think, when I pass out, I'd like to use the skills I've learned. PO Telegraphist Stanhope is an excellent instructor, ma'am, and I feel confident that, with his preparation and my enthusiasm, I'll make the grade.'

'I'm sure you will, Wren Dowland. In the meantime, if you have second thoughts, you can always put in a request to see me.'

'Thank you, ma'am. I'll remember that.' She wasn't at all interested, but she had no wish to sound ungrateful.

'Actually, you could be using your skills sooner than you anticipate.'

'Could I, ma'am?'

'Have you heard the news?'

'If I'm honest, ma'am, I haven't. As I told you, I'm concentrating on my training.'

'Well, the enemy have invaded Holland, Belgium and France. I think we're all going to be busy before long.'

11

OVERTURE AND BEGINNERS

When Clive and his crew landed at RAF Manston, they weren't surprised to learn that they would be operating temporarily under the umbrella of RAF Coastal Command. The latter, inevitably the Cinderella of its own service, was hard-pressed for aircraft, and was bolstering its strength with a collection of obsolete types as well as those and their crews borrowed from the Fleet Air Arm.

The arrival of the Swordfish prompted a degree of good-natured banter, with references to their elderly biplane image and dated equipment, but the newcomer's versatility and exceptional bombload quickly earned the hosts' surprise and respect.

Initially, the Swordfish were required to patrol the Channel, as they had at Worthy Down, but they were given a new role, four days later, when they were ordered to attack an enemy tank column on the road between Calais and Gravelines. Realisation that the enemy were so dangerously close to the French coast lent a heightened sense of urgency to the mood of the crews as they took off from Manston.

The flight was remarkably short, and the squadron soon found itself over the target. The tanks and their transporters were escorted by lorries with anti-aircraft weapons in quadruple mountings, but there was no sign, so far, of enemy fighters. That was one blessing, and an important one.

In turn, each of the Swordfish banked to the left and dived on the column, releasing its bombs at 1,000 feet. As they climbed again, each air-gunner fired on the escorting lorries, aiming for the machine-gun crews, but they were hampered in their efforts by the smoke and debris caused by the bombing. They were reassured, however, by the knowledge that the enemy were labouring under the same impediment.

On their return to Manston, they were allowed a short break while the aircraft were refuelled and re-ammunitioned, because they were to carry out a second attack. It seemed that the enemy had despatched another column, and the Swordfish were to carry out a second strike, again without a fighter escort.

With that disquieting news, they took off again and headed for the enemy column's last reported position.

It became obvious from some distance that their fears were now realised, and that an umbrella of fighters was in place over the column. The Swordfish peeled off, as they had earlier, and dive-bombed the column, each pulling out of its dive at 1,000 feet and jinking from side to side to avoid anti-aircraft fire as well as fire from enemy fighters. Clive saw three Swordfish go down, but he was unable to identify them. With all the smoke and fire, as well, it was impossible to gauge their success, but they returned to Manston with the knowledge that whatever they'd achieved had been at a severe cost. When they landed, they learned that their total loss had been five Swordfish. The loss of fifteen members of the squadron, some of whom were close friends of the survivors, was truly devastating, but another immediate concern was that the enemy were almost at the French coast.

* * *

Despite 2/O Howell's portentous words, instruction continued unhurried and uninterrupted at Portsmouth's Signal Training Centre. Meanwhile, Penny's confidence was growing rapidly. An occasional 'BZ' from PO Tel Stanhope was encouraging enough, but a second summons from the Second Officer brought her even more surprising news.

'PO Telegraphist Stanhope is extremely pleased with the class as a whole, Wren Dowland, but he tells me he is delighted with your progress.'

'Really, ma'am?' She knew he was pleased with her work, but this was even better.

'Yes, coming from an experienced RN petty officer, that is praise indeed. He says you have demonstrated, so far, that you have a clear understanding of every aspect of the course.'

'That's very kind of him, ma'am.' After the initial surprise of the compliment, she was actually struggling to understand what was so special about her efforts. Surely, the whole point of the course was to enable understanding and ability.

'I want you to think hard about applying for officer training. Wren Dowland. You've been very modest, but Petty Officer Stanhope says you have the ability to see the job in its entirety, and that means you would be wasted as a Wren Tel. What have you to say?'

Hopelessly bemused, Penny said, 'I'm reminded of *Twelfth Night*, ma'am.'

2/O Howell blinked. '*Twelfth Night*? What on earth do you mean?'

'If you remember, ma'am, Count Malvolio says, "Be not afraid of greatness. Some are born great; some achieve greatness, and some have greatness thrust upon them." Having said that, ma'am, who am I to complain? I suppose His Majesty found himself in a similar predicament three years ago, except that his responsibility is considerably weightier than ours.'

'It is,' agreed Miss Howell, 'and I'm sure he didn't complain.'

Penny wondered how she could be so certain of that, but she kept the thought to herself and said, 'Neither shall I, ma'am.'

'Then you agree to have your name put forward?'

It seemed that she had little choice. 'Yes, ma'am.'

'You'll need to complete the course, naturally enough, and then you'll have to undergo officer training at the Royal Naval College at Greenwich. I'm sure you won't experience any difficulty.' Glancing down at Penny's service document, she said, 'And I imagine you'll always be able to call upon your grandfather for advice.'

'That's always been the case, ma'am.' Some things were reassuringly constant.

* * *

At the end of his leave, Wilf Gregory reported to HMS *Nelson*, where he completed his joining routine and was reunited with the shipmates with whom he'd crewed the stricken HMS *Wenlock*.

'It looks like they're keeping us all together,' he remarked.

'Aye, said Albert Fisher, pessimistic as usual, 'but what have they got in store for us?'

They discovered the answer to that question the next day, when a petty officer came to the mess. 'You've all to report to Lieutenant Commander Edwards in Number One Mess, Frobisher Block at four bells of the forenoon watch.'

Wilf asked, 'What's happening, PO?'

'I've no idea, but I'm coming with you, so I expect we'll all find out this forenoon.'

Naturally enough, conjecture was rife, but the occupants of the mess reported, as ordered, and found themselves part of a larger party of more than a hundred ratings. A lieutenant commander entered the mess, and everyone came to attention.

'Stand easy, everyone,' he ordered. 'I'm Lieutenant Commander Edwards, and I'm sure you've all thought of a thousand possible reasons for this gathering, but what I'm going to tell you now must go no further than this mess. Is that understood?' There was an affirmative murmur, and he went on. 'The war in France is going less well than we expected. In fact, the British Expeditionary Force has been caught with its pants well and truly round its lower limbs and will have to be evacuated by sea. You will form a landing party, commanded by Captain Tennant, who will be with us shortly. We shall then be taken by destroyer to the French port of Dunkirk.' He stopped to let the news sink in. 'You will be divided into smaller parties,' he continued, 'each under a leading seaman, and your task will be to shepherd the retreating soldiers of the BEF to the pier, to be embarked in the waiting destroyers and returned to these shores. You will each be issued with a rifle and ten rounds of ammunition. The reason for this is that it may be necessary for you to deal with uncooperative and possibly hostile soldiers. They've had a very hard time in France, they'll be tired, hungry and thirsty, and I imagine they're feeling pretty blood-minded. I shouldn't be surprised to find that some of them are also the worse for alcohol. I'm not suggesting, however, that you shoot them, drunk or sober.' Here, he paused to allow some laughter. 'However, it may be necessary for you to enforce discipline with a show of strength. Having said all that, your chief weapon will be orderliness and self-discipline.' Looking around the mess, he asked, 'Is that understood so far?' Again, there was a loud murmur to the affirmative. 'You will eat at eighteen-hundred, you will then draw weapons, ammunition and webbing equipment, and then you will proceed to the dockyard, where you will embark in HMS *Wolfhound*. I shall be going with you, but let me say, anyway, good luck, all of you.'

*   *   *

A briefing of a somewhat different kind had taken place at RAF Manston, during which the assembled aircrews were told about the imminent evacuation. The few fighters available to Coastal Command would be required to intercept the enemy bombers, which would inevitably attempt to bomb the BEF and the evacuating fleet into oblivion. The Swordfish would patrol the Channel in order to prevent U-boats and E-boats attacking the fleet. Clive had never seen an E-boat, but he was sure he would recognise one when he saw it. The Swordfish would carry a mixture of depth charges for use against U-boats, and the small, 20 lb Cooper bombs, which they would deploy against any E-boats they found. It seemed ironic that the Swordfish, which was primarily a torpedo-bomber, should begin the war as a dive-bomber *cum* anti-submarine aircraft, but circumstances dictated, and those circumstances were, at the very least, unusual.

12

THE CURTAIN RISES

Wilf Gregory stepped into the hotel that was to become Captain Tennant's headquarters, to find planning and organisation of the highest order. Lists of names were read out, two dozen at a time, each party being assigned to a leading seaman. There were six parties in all, and Wilf took charge of Party Charlie.

The assembled parties were then given their terms of reference, including the rules of engagement.

'Don't go looking for trouble,' they were told, 'but be prepared for it. Go into the town and round up anything in khaki. Bring them down to the pier and hand them over to the parties on duty there.'

It sounded easy enough, but Wilf doubted it would be. For one thing, the town was under continuous air attack. He waited until they were dismissed, and then mustered his men. 'Right, Naval Party Charlie, follow me.' He led them into the street. 'Use the walls for shelter,' he told them. 'They'll shield us against some of the shrapnel, at least.'

One of them asked, 'What if the building gets a direct hit, Hooky?'

'You'll probably go up with it, but don't worry, you won't know anything about it.' He flinched when a bomb fell about 100 yards away. 'That's one that's not going to hurt you,' he said.

'Pongos, Hooky,' said one of the party, pointing to where a group of soldiers was emerging from a bomb-wrecked building.

'Come on, then.' Wilf led the way towards the apparently aimless troops, some of whom carried rifles, while others seemed to have lost or discarded theirs. Some brandished bottles of wine, presumably looted from abandoned French cellars.

'Who's in charge?' Wilf's question seemed to pose a problem for the inebriated troops, but then his eye settled on a man bearing a lance corporal's stripe. Realising that he was under scrutiny, the NCO said hurriedly, but not too clearly, ''S noffink to do wiv me. I'm not resp… rep….' He gave up and repeated, ''S noffink t' do wiv me.' Pointing to Wilf's good conduct badge and mistaking its significance, he said, 'You're a corporal. You take charge.'

'All right.' He paused as the scream of a diving Stuka made speech inaudible. 'Come with us and we'll take you down to the pier.'

One of them said, ''D you hear that? They've got a pier at this seaside place. Why didn't we think…?' The rest of his sentence was cut short by a bomb blast that caused shrapnel and other fragments to shower the area where they were standing.

Wilf forbore to tell him that it was because they were out of their minds on looted wine and various other beverages. Instead, he checked to see if anyone was hurt, and then, having ascertained that no one was, said, 'Come on, then, let's move.'

Recognising the voice of authority, which had very likely been absent from their lives for some time, the men shuffled off readily beside the naval party.

When they reached the pierhead, a naval lieutenant was shepherding the latest arrivals on to the pier. 'Well done, Leading Seaman,' he said. 'You soldiers form an orderly queue and follow those men.' He pointed to the long line of weary-but-impatient evacuees already on the pier. 'Oh, no!' His exclamation was prompted by a direct hit by one of the Stukas on a destroyer currently embarking men at the end of the pier. A fire was already burning fiercely, and the ship was keeling over to seaward, with soldiers leaping or diving into the sea.

'Come with me, lads.' Wilf knew better than to let his party stand around watching a disaster such as the one currently taking place, and he led them in search of more khaki-clad vagrants. His heart went out to the crew of the stricken destroyer, but he had a task to perform

* * *

Clive hoped his present had reached Penny in time for her 21st birthday. He'd posted it in good time, so it should have reached her already. He was actually searching for U-boats and E-boats, so it wasn't a good idea to spend too much time worrying about the post, and he was reminded of that when he felt Bill tapping his shoulder. He looked round and saw that his observer was pointing below, so he followed the gesture and saw two small craft at three o' clock. He looked around the sky for enemy fighters. Happily, there were none, so he went down to investigate. Although he'd never seen an E-boat, he reckoned that the two craft below looked small enough to qualify as torpedo boats. A quick glance over his shoulder told him that both Bill and Kit Carson were looking through night glasses. They would know the identity of the ships before he did.

At around 1,000 feet, Bill spoke to him through the Gosport tube. 'It's okay, they're ours.'

Clive pulled out of his descent and climbed again to resume the search.

* * *

Penny opened the cardboard box addressed to her in Mrs Hogben's laboured hand and took out the cake she'd baked. It smelt wonderful, and it must have taken lots of precious ingredients that would soon be in short supply. She calculated that if she cut it into quarters, and then each quarter into three, there would be a piece for each member of the class and Petty Officer Stanhope, too. It was just as well Daphne and Annabelle were no longer members of the class.

There were expressions of delight as well as birthday greetings when she handed out the cake, and PO Stanhope was particular taken aback to be included in the celebrations.

'Thank you, Wren Dowland,' he said on receiving his share of the cake, 'and congratulations on reaching your majority.'

Betty from Burnley asked excitedly, 'What else did you get?'

'Lots of things.' It was true, although they weren't all immediately apparent that morning. Her father had invested twenty-one pounds in National Savings on her behalf, which was a lot of money and a secret best kept to herself while she was in the company of girls who were less well-off. Also, her grandfather had told her in his letter that he was holding his present until she went home on leave, so she had that to look forward to. Her current excitement, however, was Clive's present, a locket in the shape of a heart. She couldn't wear it when she was in uniform, but she wouldn't always be in uniform.

'That's beautiful,' said Betty. 'He must love you an awful lot.'

'Oh, I don't know about that, but we're quite chummy.'

With the cake out of the way, it was time to start work. The war would not wait.

* * *

An officer at the pier told Wilf, 'Most of this lot were sent to France almost untrained. They could march and they could shoot – after a fashion, but we must get them away before we can begin to embark the frontline troops, the men who are fighting a rear-guard action to make this evacuation possible.'

'I don't think "possible" is quite the word, sir,' said Wilf, looking towards the ill-disciplined and ill-tempered occupants of the pier.

'I'm inclined to agree. We just haven't the boats to transfer them to the ships out there. Still, you're doing a fine job, Gregory. Keep it up.'

'Thank you, sir. Aye, aye, sir.' He and his party moved off again.

It wasn't long before they located more arrivals, who turned out to be drunken, sullen and mutinous.

As usual, Wilf asked, 'Who's in charge?'

'Who wants to know?' The challenge came, not from an NCO, but from a bedraggled private soldier, who made threatening movements with his rifle.

'Isn't there an officer about?'

'Officer?' The man laughed, as did several others. 'We ain't seen a fuckin' officer for days. The bastards are all lookin' out for 'emselves.'

'You'd better come with us to the pierhead.'

'Who says?' The scruffy soldier appeared to be spokesman for the rest, who clearly looked to him for a kind of leadership.

'Lower your weapons and come with us,' insisted Wilf.

'Fuck off, sailor boy.'

It was time for Wilf to assert some authority. 'Naval party Charlie,' he ordered, 'load and make ready!'

There was a clatter as two dozen ratings worked the bolts of their rifles. For the first time, the soldiers looked warier and less mutinous.

'Choose your targets and take aim,' said Wilf. 'The country doesn't need mutinous riff-raff like this lot.'

Two dozen sailors took aim at the gathering, and the defiant one suddenly came to his senses. 'All right,' he said, 'we'll come. There's no need to get trigger-happy.'

'You'll come with us like proper pongos,' said Wilf. 'Fall in, three deep!'

Hurriedly, the motley gathering fell into three ranks.

'Squad, by the right, quick march! Left, right, left, right....' He was still shouting orders when he delivered them to the pier party. 'Squad, halt!'

An officer asked, 'What's all this about, Leading Seaman?'

'They didn't want to come, sir, so I thought a bit of discipline might oil the wheels.'

'You're absolutely right. Well done.'

A nearby explosion caused the soldiers to look around them for shelter, but Wilf shouted, 'Stand fast! You're going on the pier to join a ship, so you'd better start behaving like men, not frightened sprogs.'

'Really, Leading Seaman,' said the officer, 'I think you should be doing my job. Still, carry on.'

'Aye, aye, sir.'

* * *

It was forenoon on the 28th before Clive sighted the enemy. He was approaching Zeebrugge when Kit spotted an E-boat and communicated the fact to Bill, who alerted Clive. The Nazi ensign was in plain view.

'Here goes.' Clive put the Swordfish into a dive, firing his single machine-gun as he went, until, at 1,000 feet, he released four Cooper bombs. As he pulled out, he heard Bill shout, 'You got the bastard!'

Clive looked back and saw the burning wreckage of the E-boat astern of them. It was never good to see men killed or in the water, but it was one E-boat that would never reach the evacuation fleet, and that knowledge gave him some satisfaction.

* * *

Inevitably, a bomb hit the pier, hurling the men waiting on it into the sea. Wilf knew they wouldn't all be able to swim, and it was awful to see them struggling in the water and drowning, too far away for anyone to help them. It was the second hit on the pier; the first had been bridged with makeshift materials, but now the soldiers would have to wait even longer before the breach could be made passable. Meanwhile, yet more would-be evacuees were arriving.

'Leave them here,' an officer at the pier told Wilf.

'Aye, aye, sir.' He led his men into the town again in search of more soldiers, while his own eyes told him that the seafront was overcrowded with them. Whalers from the destroyers were ferrying men as quickly as they could, but the rising surf was making the task almost impossible.

There were more explosions in the direction of the pier while Wilf and his party were gathering their charges, and they learned, on reaching the pier, that it was now virtually unusable.

'If the French would only let us use the old mole,' said one of the officers, 'we might be in with a chance. We're also desperately short of shallow-draught vessels. We can only hope they'll arrive soon.'

Wilf was also aware that food and water were being rationed. Men who'd not eaten for days were having to queue for the most basic items. The situation was giving rise to ugly scenes, which meant that the armed seamen were needed all the more to keep order.

* * *

At home, Arthur fumed with frustration and indignation. He'd been to Dover, where he'd seen the awful spectacle of an exhausted, defeated army being shepherded to waiting trains, and all that time, he'd felt useless.

'*Chloe*'s going to be needed,' he told Walter. 'You and I could crew her, if you're game.'

'Just try leaving me on the shore, sir.'

'That's the spirit, Chief. Speaking of which, I think we should add some to our rations, purely for medicinal purposes, of course.'

'You're right, sir. Them pongos might need a drop of medicine.'

Arthur lit his pipe and sighed deeply. 'I just can't understand how the situation was allowed to develop. At the end of the last war, the

Grand Fleet, the BEF and the new Air Force were each under the command of an incompetent half-wit – one of them was in my term at Dartmouth – and now it seems the Army still hasn't learned its lesson.' Drawing on his pipe, he said, 'Of course, it's not just the Army. The blasted politicians are equally to blame.'

'As we are for putting them in office, sir.'

Arthur dismissed the idea irritably. 'A minor detail, Chief. The buggers must shoulder the blame themselves.'

The telephone rang in the office, and Arthur went to answer it.

'Ellis's Boatyard, Sandbrook. Clement speaking.'

'Admiral Clement, it's Ernest Briggs, sir, at the Sailing Club.'

'Yes, Briggs?'

'I've had word that volunteers with boats registered with the Admiralty are to muster at the Lord Warden Hotel on Admiralty Pier, Dover, by six o' clock tomorrow morning, sir. We can only guess at what's required of us, but every owner has volunteered his boat. I know you're not a member, sir, but are you prepared to take yours?'

'What a damn' silly question, Briggs. Of course I bloody-well am.'

'I thought it only polite to ask, sir.'

'Yes, well, of course. I'll see you at Dover Harbour.'

Returning to the slipway, he said to Walter, 'Someone's finally got his organising hat on, Chief. They want us at the Lord Warden on Admiralty Pier by oh six hundred tomorrow.'

His announcement encountered the merest lift of an eyebrow. 'Count me in, sir. It's good to be able to do something useful.'

13

THE MAIN EVENT

If Arthur longed to see evidence of organisation, it confronted him when he and Walter reached Dover Harbour. Many small craft were already at sea, having been fuelled and provisioned earlier, and now someone called through a megaphone for Sandbrook Sailing Club members to report to the Lord Warden Hotel.

'I suppose we're honorary members,' said Arthur, joining the rest.

In the hotel foyer, he found a queue for a desk manned by a lieutenant commander, RN. At an adjacent desk, a leading storeman and another rating were issuing steel helmets and warm clothing, presumably to civilians who'd volunteered to take their boats to France. By this time, Arthur was in no doubt about the nature of the emergency.

When his turn came, the naval officer looked at him and blinked. 'Aren't you Admiral Clement, sir?'

'Rear admiral, retired.'

'Welcome aboard, sir. What is the name of your boat?'

'*Chloe.*'

The lieutenant commander found her name on his list. 'As you've no doubt guessed, sir, the BEF has been pushed back to the port of Dunkirk and must be evacuated. Shallow-draught vessels are required to ferry evacuees from the beaches to the destroyers off-shore. Are you prepared to take your boat over there and help with the evacuation. sir?'

'Of course I am.'

'I knew you would be, sir, but I had to ask. What about your crewmember?'

'I'm ready to go, sir,' said Walter. 'Chief Shipwright Artificer Gregory, sir.'

'Good for you, Chief.' Turning to Arthur, he said, 'I have to ask

93

you to sign T One Two Four Articles, to say that you're Merchant Navy sailing under Royal Navy orders.'

'Very well.' Arthur took the pen, dipped it in the inkwell provided and signed the form.

'If you go to the next desk, you'll be issued with steel helmets, warm clothing and rations.'

'Thank you, Lieutenant Commander.'

'It's my duty and my privilege. Goodbye and good luck, sir.'

'Thank you.' They joined the queue at the next desk. When their turn came, they received a duffel coat each, a steel helmet, a seaman's jersey and several days' rations. They declined the offer of seaboots, as they had their own.

'Petrol and drinking water are being issued on Admiralty Pier, sir,' said the leading storeman, 'and a rating will be assigned to you.'

'Will he, by Jove?' Arthur was less than impressed, but he returned to *Chloe* in readiness for her to be filled up with petrol.

A mobile petrol bowser and its crew were busily dispensing petrol to each boat, and *Chloe*'s turn finally came. The attendant filled the built-in tank and the two jerry cans provided by Arthur. As he withdrew his nozzle, Arthur screwed the cap back on the tank and looked around the pier. 'If the rating doesn't turn up soon,' he told Walter, 'we'll go without him.'

A few minutes later, a rating came to *Chloe*'s bows and introduced himself. He was young and fresh-faced, and he carried a clipboard. 'I'm Leading Seaman Palmer,' he said. 'Who's the owner of this boat?'

'I am,' said Arthur.

'Will you be coming with her?'

'We both will.'

'Very well. Has Lieutenant Commander Banks explained what's happening?'

'Yes.'

'Good. The town is under constant bombardment, so it's very dangerous over there. Are you still prepared to go?'

'Of course we are.'

'In that case, I'm here to guide you between the minefields and get you there safely. After that, you'll be in the lap of the gods.' He took two containers of drinking water from one of the harbour workers and placed them on the after buoyancy tank.

'*Chloe* will be in my hands,' Arthur told him, 'but you're welcome to come for the ride.'

'This is Rear Admiral Clement,' said Walter, no doubt wishing to avoid an unpleasant situation.

'I'm sorry, sir,' said Palmer. 'I didn't know that.'

'There's no reason why you should. This is Chief Shipwright Artificer Gregory, by the way, Palmer. You're in exalted company, although I have to say in all honesty, as well as modesty, that we're both retired.'

'I see, sir.' There wasn't much else he could say, so he watched as an elderly destroyer flashed a signal, and said, 'That's for Sandbrook Sailing Club. HMS *Woodlark* is going to lead us across the Channel. If you're ready, sir, we'll get under way.'

Walter put the engine astern, and *Chloe* left the pier, turning tightly to port so that she could leave the harbour by the Western Entrance.

Arthur asked, 'Who is Flag Officer Dover, nowadays, Palmer?'

'Vice-Admiral Ramsay, sir. He's also Officer Commanding Operation *Dynamo*, as this evacuation is called.'

'I thought things were beginning to look up.'

Palmer naturally made no comment. 'We're going to take Route Zebra, sir. That's straight across the Channel to a point east of Calais and then along the coast to Dunkirk. There are three routes avoiding the minefields, sir.'

'I'm grateful for that information, Palmer.'

When all the boats were in position, the destroyer gave a single hoot and got under way with the boats following.

'I imagine it's an unholy shambles over there,' said Arthur.

'There are officers and ratings in Dunkirk organising the embarkation, sir,' Palmer assured him.

'Glad to hear it.' Things really were looking up.

'I see this whaler's been converted to sail, sir,' observed Palmer.

'Yes, I hope you're not going to point out that she's less than thirty feet long.'

'I wouldn't dream of it, sir. I'm sure you know the length of a Montagu whaler.'

'Quite.' After a few minutes, Arthur asked, 'Have you done any sailing, Palmer?'

'I did some at *Ganges* and *Raleigh*, sir.'

'Good. You may get another opportunity before we're done. This engine isn't as reliable as it might be. Of course, in my day, we all trained under sail.'

'Of course, sir.'

Looking astern, Walter said, 'One of the boats has left station, sir.'

Arthur looked and saw a large dinghy with its sails spread. It was tacking away from the formation and leaving it behind. 'It's *Per Mare*, that bloody fool Harper,' he said. 'He's not a sailor, he's an ex-Royal Marine.' Conversationally, he went on. 'It's ever since that damned fool Kipling wrote his bloody silly poem. Now the buggers genuinely believe they're soldiers and sailors too.'

Someone on the bridge of *Woodlark* called through a loudhailer, '*Per Mare*, keep in station!'

No one heard Mr Harper's reply, but he was clearly reluctant to obey orders. Leading Seaman Palmer smiled to himself, possibly at Arthur's remarks, although he maybe had a few thoughts of his own about maverick amateur yachtsmen.

While it was on his mind, Arthur donned a webbing belt and holster. In response to Palmer's glance, he said, 'Thought I'd better bring my revolver along in case of recalcitrant pongoes. You never know.'

Palmer smiled. 'You've dealt with them before, then, sir.'

Woodlark's captain hailed *Per Mare* again, but to no effect. Arthur shook his head at Harper's foolishness and answered Palmer. 'This is my second evacuation, Palmer. The previous one took place at Gallipoli.'

'Really, sir? My dad was at Gallipoli.'

'Army or RN?'

'RN, sir. He was a quarters armourer in HMS *Hestia*, sir.'

'The devil he was!' Arthur laughed delightedly. '*Hestia* was my ship, my second command after *Chloe*.'

'Ah, then this boat is named after your first ship, sir?'

'That's right.'

'Well, I've got to get home, now, sir, if only to tell my dad we've both sailed under the same captain.'

'You do that, Palmer.' Having initially resented the leading seaman's presence, Arthur was now warming to him. 'How long have you had your leading rate?'

'Two years and three months, sir.'

'You should do well.' For the moment, Arthur was distracted. 'That bloody fool Harper's overhauled *Woodlark*. If he's not careful, he'll get himself lost.'

'Or killed,' said Palmer. 'There's only a narrow channel between the minefields.'

* * *

'Take them down to the mole, Gregory,' said the lieutenant at the pier. 'We've got clearance to use it, now.'

'Aye, aye, sir. What's happening here, sir?' Army vehicles were rolling through the town, now, heading towards the beach at La Panne.

'They're creating a makeshift jetty. By driving their vehicles into the sea, they're making it possible for troops to make their way to deeper water, where shallow-draught craft can embark them.'

'What a brilliant idea, sir.' Wilf had already seen motor anti-submarine boats operating off-shore.

'It was General Alexander's idea, Gregory. Anyway, off you go and unload your people at the mole.'

'Aye, aye, sir. Follow me, lads.' Wilf led them towards the ancient mole, which was already performing exceptional service in getting troops away. By this time, bombing had become so much a fact of life that men were crossing open ground confidently, and he had no difficulty in herding the two dozen or so to join the line of men already waiting their turn. There were still acts of mutiny, however, and Wilf had no hesitation in threatening them with the ultimate consequence. He knew he'd never have to carry out the deed, as long as he made the threat confidently enough. Even so, it was hard work for the naval parties. All they could do was follow orders and give an example of smartness and self-discipline to a force that had all but given up hope.

Wilf was delivering another group of soldiers to the mole when he heard a growing murmur of excitement.

'Look,' said one of them, pointing to seaward, 'more boats.' His announcement was accompanied by the shouts and cheers of the others on the mole, but Wilf didn't know what to think. For all he knew, the latest arrivals might be enemy craft sent to attack the evacuation fleet, and it wasn't until the leading vessels drew closer that he realised some of them were under sail.

An officer called out, 'Leading Seaman, over here.' He looked remarkably cheerful in spite of the arrival of yet another wave of Stukas.

'Yes, sir?'

'You can start taking them down to La Panne, now. You'll find a makeshift jetty of lorries there. We're going to load the next lot on to the civilian craft, and they'll take them out to the ferries and destroyers.' Almost as an afterthought, he said, 'You're doing a grand job. Carry on.'

'Thank you, sir. Aye, aye, sir.' He looked around for his men. 'Naval Party Charlie, to me.' Then, having assembled them, he led them again into the ruined town in search of evacuees.

* * *

Dunkirk was completely obscured by smoke, but what remained of the BEF could be seen clearly on the beach and in the sand dunes behind it. A destroyer stood at the eastern mole hurriedly embarking troops while other ships made for home at high speed, their decks packed with soldiers from the crowded beaches. Coasters, tramp steamers, colliers and assorted merchant ships waited gamely in deeper waters until they also could take their turn at the mole, while the most wonderfully bizarre collection of vessels worked close inshore. There were Thames barges under sail, drifters, lobster boats, pleasure boats, paddle steamers from seaside resorts, tugboats, sailing yachts and dinghies, cabin cruisers and boats of every description, not all of the minimum length prescribed by the Government – Arthur wasn't the only boat owner with a mind of his own – but they were all needed.

'I don't know how we're going to shift that lot,' said Leading Seaman Palmer, raising his voice against the screams of the Stukas, 'but we'd better make a start as soon as we can.'

With the aid of a loudhailer, *Woodlark* directed the boats to the beach at La Panne, instructing them to use the half-submerged lorries as a jetty and to bring their evacuees to the nearest available ship. It was the greatest wonder they heard the order, as the air raid was in full force, but Arthur took over *Chloe*'s wheel and negotiated a channel between the upperworks of the sunken ships, grimly aware of the losses the Navy had suffered so far. As he approached the emergency jetty, he saw soldiers scrambling towards them over the vehicles, and he said to Palmer, 'We can take two dozen each trip. No more than that, or they'll capsize her.'

'Aye, aye, sir.' Palmer picked up a hook, ready to steady the boat against the lorries or to fend off unwanted passengers.

When the beleaguered troops were within hailing distance, Arthur shouted, 'I can take twenty-four!' He took *Chloe* up beside a swamped three-tonner, and the soldiers, some of whom had already been turned away from the now-departing boats, eagerly made their precarious way over the steel and canvas jetty.

'Twenty-four,' repeated Arthur.

Palmer counted them as they boarded. 'One, two, three— make for the middle of the boat, four, five....' When the twenty-fourth man was on board, he held up his hook to deter the others. 'No more this trip. We'll be back.'

'Well done, Palmer,' said Arthur. 'Half ahead, Chief.' He brought the boat about and headed for the nearest destroyer.

'We ain't 'alf glad to see you, sir,' said one of the soldiers 'We thought we was stuck there for the duration.'

'After this,' said another, 'I fink I'll join the Navy. They're the only buggers what knows what they're doin'.'

'You may be right at that,' said Arthur, chuckling to himself. 'Full ahead, Chief.'

'Full ahead, sir. Aye, aye, sir.'

The soldiers exchanged glances, perhaps wondering who these ageing civilians were, who spoke like sailors, but they made no comment, being sublimely happy for the moment, to be off the beach.

* * *

Wilf and his men were having a rest from their otherwise non-stop exertions. The greatest temptation was to fall asleep, but they knew they would be needed shortly.

Two officers, a captain and a commander, were talking quietly. The captain, presumably the Officer-in-Charge, said, 'We've got to get the rag, tag and bobtail out before the rear-guard start arriving, and now that the civilian craft are here, if I dare say anything, we're in with a fighting chance.'

'So we are, sir,' said the commander. 'As long as those chaps are sensible, and they don't get in the way of the fleet, they should be all right. I'm just afraid that some of them will be hit by destroyers and capsized.'

'They'll have to take their chance.'

The two left the room, and Wilf was unable to hear the rest of the conversation. It was the most wonderful thing that so many civilians had volunteered to do that, and that someone had planned far enough ahead to make it possible. He wondered if Rear Admiral Clement was among the volunteer boat owners. It was more than likely, and it was just as likely that Wilf's dad would be with him. He tried not to think about it. Instead, he looked at the big clock in the hotel foyer and said, 'Come on, lads, we've got work to do.'

* * *

Having transferred his twenty-four passengers to HMS *Woodlark*, Arthur returned to the jetty, where he called once again, 'Two dozen! No more!'

The men stumbled forward and descended, one by one, to fill up *Chloe*'s seats. Palmer counted twenty-four. 'That's all,' he said. 'We'll be back.'

One of the soldiers who'd been refused said, 'You've easily got room for another three or four in there.'

'No more,' said Arthur. 'You'd capsize her.'

'Bollocks!' The man started to descend.

'Stop there!' Arthur cocked his revolver and pointed it at him. 'I'll shoot the next man who tries to board this boat.'

'You wanna decide whose side you're on,' said the man, hanging back all the same.

'You need to ask yourself the same question. If you're still here when we return, and if you're prepared to behave like a civilised human being, we'll take you then. Take her away, Chief.'

'Aye, aye, sir.'

Arthur turned the boat and headed again towards the waiting destroyer.

* * *

According to the returning Hurricane pilots, most of the Luftwaffe seemed to be converging on the Dunkirk beaches, so it was all the more surprising that the Kriegsmarine appeared to have deserted the English Channel. Clive and his crew had sunk the only E-boat they'd seen, and they were unlikely to spot any U-boats, as they would dive at the first sighting of an air patrol. Still, no enemy naval forces was good news, so Clive wasn't too disappointed. He continued to search.

* * *

A crew of three meant that Arthur could organise a series of watches, although darkness made evacuation difficult at night, and he eventually decided it was necessary to wait for daylight, which brought with it the additional benefit of a downturn in the weather and, consequently, relief from the almost incessant bombing.

As soon as daylight made it possible, Arthur and his crew resumed their task. On two more occasions Arthur had to threaten mutinous evacuees with his revolver, but most of them were either too tired or too grateful to be difficult. One restless spirit among them, however, enquired from the stern of the boat, 'Who does that old geezer fink 'e is, shoutin' orders an' wavin' 'is revolver abaht?'

'That's Rear Admiral Clement, son,' Walter told him quietly, 'and he's a crack shot with that pistol, so mind your manners.'

Some soldiers had been in the water far too long, and *Chloe*'s crew soon found that they had a case of shock among the boat's occupants. As he sat, slumped against the timbers, shivering, none of his companions seemed to notice, but Palmer removed his duffel coat and handed it to the man beside him. 'Get it round him, quick,' he said. 'He's in a bad way.'

'Maybe a drop of something might warm him inside,' suggested Walter.

'No, Chief,' said Palmer firmly. 'It's the last thing he needs.' Arthur looked at him enquiringly, and he said, 'Spirits would cause a rush of cold blood to the heart, sir. That really would kill him.' Self-consciously, he said, 'I did the first-aid course quite recently, sir.'

Arthur smiled and nodded. 'I'm glad you came, Palmer,' he said.

With some difficulty, the shocked soldier was helped on board HMS *Sabre* in time for the destroyer's fifth departure.

'I remember the 'S' Class from the last war,' said Arthur. 'That old lady's doing a magnificent job.' Watching Palmer don his duffel coat again, he said, 'I think we should pipe "Up Spirits". It'll help us on our way.' He opened a bottle of rum and passed it to Palmer and Walter, who both took a grateful swig.

'It's a treat to have "neaters", sir,' said Palmer, returning the bottle to Arthur.

'Well, it's fair to say you've earned it.' Looking at the soldiers on the jetty, he said, 'And it looks as if we've not done yet. All the same,' he said, huddling into his coat against the drizzle, 'it's good that we're spared the company of the Luftwaffe. Long may the foul weather last.'

* * *

For Clive and the rest of his squadron, the overcast sky and rain were a mixed blessing. Swordfish were the only aircraft capable of flying in those conditions, so they were confident that the Luftwaffe would be temporarily grounded, but it also made the task of patrolling the Channel more difficult. At times, the cloud was impossibly low, which meant that to fly beneath it gave the crew little chance of sighting anything. It was better to fly higher, taking advantage of breaks in the cloud to scan the wider areas of the Channel, and it was potluck that, through such a break, they spotted a surfaced U-boat.

He and Bill had evidently seen it at the same time, because Bill's shout almost coincided with Clive's realisation that it was an enemy submarine. The two gun towers, one on each side of the conning tower, identified it as a Type XI U-cruiser, a particularly powerful and well-armed U-boat.

It seemed that, with the noise of its diesel engines as it charged its batteries, the crew on the conning tower were not yet aware of the aircraft's presence, because their first reaction came with one of the conning tower party pointing excitedly towards the Swordfish and the others disappearing quickly down the hatch. The U-boat was diving as Clive carried out his attack. Approaching from astern, he followed its course and released both depth charges. The Swordfish bucked as it was relieved of its load, and Clive levelled out to circle the area. An excited tapping on his shoulder and a shout from Bill alerted him to a patch of oil on the surface. Clive continued to circle the position, and less than a minute later, the U-boat's bows broke surface and hung, suspended for what seemed an age before subsiding slowly, stern-first beneath the waves. Its disappearance was followed by a massive release of oil and air that was clearly visible from 1,000 feet. Swordfish 2C had done what was necessary, and many lives had possibly been saved in the long run, but Clive and his crew resumed their patrol with the disquieting knowledge that the U-boat's crew had paid for that benefit with their lives.

* * *

It wasn't often that a junior rating was able to appreciate the overview involved in a major operation, but Wilf couldn't help but admire the inspired organisation that was making the evacuation a success. He knew, by the sheer numbers being taken either from the mole or from the makeshift jetty, that it was successful. The word from above was that the first of the rear-guard would be arriving before long. Wilf and his fellow leading hands were assured that most of the drunken malcontents were now in England or, at least, on their way there, leaving room for the fighting men to be evacuated. In a rare, spare moment, Wilf asked one of the officers how the Army came to have so many of the other kind.

'Last-minute conscription and inadequate training,' the lieutenant told him. 'Those ill-disciplined characters you had to deal with had been sent to France with only the most basic training. I suppose we have to blame the politicians for that, but, when you think about it, the conditions that gave rise to this war were also created by politicians.'

With a tired smile, he said, 'It's just as well the nation can depend on you and me, Leading Seaman Gregory.'

'That's right, sir.' Wilf looked up at the wall clock and said, 'Naval Party Charlie, on your feet. We've got work to do.' As he led his party into the town yet again, he thought about the lieutenant's words. His final observation had been a light-hearted one, but Wilf couldn't help feeling braced by it. The evacuation couldn't go on forever. Sooner or later, they would run out of soldiers to evacuate, and then, when it was finally over, he could enjoy the satisfaction of knowing that he'd been a part of something indisputably magnificent. Meanwhile, he had to help keep the numbers moving and, to aid the process, a new system was in place. Instead of naval parties searching the town for soldiers, they were operating checkpoints, where they could guide the evacuees to the beaches.

By late afternoon, the first of the rear-guard began to arrive. Weary but unbowed, a unit halted beside Wilf's party, and he had no need, on this occasion, to ask who was in charge, because a sergeant identified himself without prompting.

He asked, 'Which way to the sea, Jack?'

'Carry on along this road, Sergeant, and you'll find the next naval party. They'll direct you to the beaches.'

'Thanks, Jack. Come on, lads.'

Wilf watched them go, wondering what they might have made of some of the earlier arrivals. They would certainly have provided an example.

*　*　*

Arthur and his crew had now lost count of the trips they'd made to and from the beach. Certainly, the stream of humanity seemed endless, and the only way to do the job was in blinkers. The toil would end when the job was done.

One bright spot occurred when Palmer had climbed the scrambling net to speak to a petty officer on the upper deck of the destroyer. He descended again with a parcel of sandwiches from the galley.

'I hope you gentlemen like corned beef,' he said, opening the parcel, 'because it was all they had to spare.'

* * *

Towards the end of the week, the Luftwaffe redoubled its efforts, as if to make up for the day lost to the weather, and four destroyers, as well as a number of civilian craft, were sunk. By that time, however, a growing optimism began to emanate from within HQ. Air raids were as fierce as ever, and troops continued to arrive in vast numbers, but controlling them was infinitely easier than it had been at the start. They had begun waiting in the sand dunes above the beach, where there was at least some semblance of cover. Meanwhile, at the makeshift military hospital, doctors and orderlies worked doggedly, patching up wounds and carrying out amputations. As one rating in Wilf's party remarked, 'Just for once, everybody's pulling their weight.'

'That's right,' said Wilf, 'that's what it's all about, everybody pulling his weight.'

Later, they went out to resume their duties during a particularly heavy air raid, and two of Wilf's party were hit by shrapnel. He sent one of them back to HQ with a field dressing on his thigh, but the other was bleeding heavily from a torso wound. Wilf stayed with him, holding a field dressing desperately to his wound while he waited for a stretcher. The stretcher arrived too late to save the wounded rating, a boy of eighteen, killed while helping to save his countrymen.

* * *

By the end of the week, the job was done. Despite the efforts of the Luftwaffe, an as yet unknown number of men had been evacuated, the last of the French rear-guard were being embarked, and what was left of the volunteer fleet was able to leave the beaches. For various reasons, many of them had left earlier, but it was a point of honour for Arthur not to leave before the end. He and his crew were weary but satisfied as they carried their last boatload to HMS *Sabre*.

When they reached the ship's side, the scrambling nets had already been hauled up, and a sub-lieutenant called down to them, 'I'm sorry, sir. We're chock-full. Can you make your way back with them?'

'I should hope so,' said Arthur, surveying the weary collection of Green Howards, Durham Light Infantry and French troops.

'Good luck,' called the sub-lieutenant. With visible pride, he said, 'This is our tenth crossing.'

'Well done. Good luck.' Arthur turned to his crew and said, 'At least the Luftwaffe decided to take the day off. Let's follow the convoy.'

To mark the occasion and for the sake of passenger morale, he brought out the rum and passed it round. The French didn't seem terribly impressed with it, but the British soldiers appreciated it to the full. It also amused them to be borne back to England by a rear admiral, albeit a retired one.

Apart from those prone to seasickness and a few Frenchmen emotional at leaving their mother country behind them, everyone was in good spirits, despite the tiredness they shared, and there was a general air of optimism until they reached the point east of Calais, where they joined the swept channel that ran north-west to Dover. That was when the engine spluttered weakly and stopped.

'We're out of fuel, sir,' said Walter matter-of-factly. The soldiers looked to Arthur in alarm, but he was unperturbed.

'Lend a hand, Palmer,' he said, releasing the main spar and throwing the end of the halyard to him. 'With the wind sou'westerly, we'll be sailing on a broad reach.' As Palmer hauled on the halyard to hoist the mainsail, Arthur busied himself with the foresail.'

'Aye, aye, sir.'

'You know what to do, don't you, Chief?'

'Aye, aye, sir.' Walter knew he had to maintain the same course as the others.

'That's right. We don't want to stray from the swept channel.' Memories of the wreckage of Harper's *Per Mare* were painfully fresh in his mind. Its occupants had suffered Palmer's worst fear, hitting a mine only five miles out of Calais.

'I can't believe this,' said one of the Green Howards. 'We're sailing, just like they did in the olden days. Errol Flynn would have been in his element, don't you think?'

'Ah, well, you see,' said Arthur, 'every sailor of my generation was trained under sail.'

'I bet the Navy knew what it was doing, even then,' said the Green Howard.

'Give or take the occasional blockhead, I suppose it did.'

106

It was clear that the recent debacle was on the soldier's mind, and he confirmed it when he asked, 'Do you think things'll be any better under this Churchill fella, sir?'

'Well, they can't be any worse, can they? And there's also the fact that Churchill has always been ready for a scrap, which was never Chamberlain's first option. It's true to say that Churchill's made a bugger of various jobs, but I can't think of anyone better able to inspire the nation.' He thought a moment, and said, 'He should be all right as long as he listens to the advice of those who know better. He's inclined to be headstrong, as I recall.'

It was very pleasant, sailing back to Dover in the company of men who appreciated what he was doing for them. It was so pleasant, in fact, that he decided to celebrate the fact by splicing the mainbrace. Reaching for the rum, he asked, 'Who's for another tot?'

The Frenchmen shook their heads, while the Tommies looked upon their sailor-hero with increased gratitude.

As they returned to the starting point of their adventure, Arthur took stock of the situation. The Green Howard's question had set him thinking. It would take time for a routed, ill-equipped army to be turned into the fighting force the country needed. On the other hand, the Kriegsmarine was being taught a lesson of the bloodiest kind off the Norwegian coast. Thank goodness, as the man had said, the Navy seemed to know what it was doing.

14

JUNE

MAKING THE GRADE

To Penny's relief, Clive remained at Manston for the time being. At least she knew where he was, even though she had no idea what he was doing. The papers and newsreels were full of the Dunkirk evacuation, and mention of civilian-owned boats of all shapes and sizes set her in mind, naturally, of her grandfather. Knowing him as she did, she had no doubt he would have wanted to be involved in the operation. Her mind was set at rest when a letter from him arrived at the barracks.

Dearest Penny,

How is the course progressing? I hope you're still enjoying it and that you're set to pass with flying colours.

By this time, you'll have heard about the evacuation. I know the news people have made some characteristically extravagant claims, and you've possibly wondered about the civilian participation that's captured their imagination. The fact is that the Admiralty appealed for owners of shallow-draught vessels to ferry the evacuees from the beach to the destroyers waiting offshore, and Gregory – I believe you know him as 'Walter' – and I took Chloe across to lend a hand. We had the pleasant company of a leading seaman called Palmer, who acquitted himself so well that I've written a letter of commendation to his senior officer. Just for good measure, I've also written to young Ramsay, now a vice-admiral, congratulating him on an excellent operation and mentioning Palmer at the same time. It was a massive undertaking, and we were pleased to play a small but essential part in it.

Another bit of news is that Gregory's son Wilfred, now a leading seaman, is at home, not from the sea, but from the streets of Dunkirk, where he and about a hundred-and-fifty other ratings kept order and shepherded the evacuees to their various embarkation points. The whole operation was immaculately well organised, and I'm delighted that the service acquitted itself so splendidly, both at sea and ashore.

I understand your father's joined the Local Defence Volunteers. No one's been commissioned yet, so he's had to muster as a private, second class, not that it's prevented him from turning out in his old uniform, complete with Sam Browne belt, nor from sporting his revolver, for that matter. Full marks for spirit, I say!

Your mother's also keeping well, and she tells me Joan is, too. I haven't seen Joan since your last leave, but she seems happy enough with that Air Force fellow. No comment, there, of course.

Mrs Hogben wishes to be remembered to you, although I'm sure you'll never forget her. She showed me your letter of thanks for your birthday cake. It meant a great deal to her. Good girl! I've got your present wrapped and ready for your next leave. I hope you'll like it.

Work hard and keep well. We'll see each other soon.

Yours, with all my love.

'Grandpop' XXX

Penny had to tell everyone, including PO Tel Stanhope, about her grandfather's adventure. Naturally, there were some who found it difficult to believe, but she realised that not everyone was gifted with imagination, and she knew the truth, so who cared what anyone else thought?

The matter was temporarily forgotten that afternoon, when PO Stanhope enlivened a practical procedure exercise with some entertaining signals. One that always made Wrens giggle was 'INT QRM', which meant 'Are you being interfered with?' It was some time before the girl in question was able to collect herself and send, 'QRM', confirmation that she was, in fact, being interfered with. Another fit of giggling occurred when PO Stanhope sent a deliberately corrupted signal, emulating poor reception. It read: 'Pro... M...a ....rd for b....m s..ape.'

The recipient of the signal requested a repetition of the text and was surprised to read, 'Proceed to Malta Dockyard for bottom scrape.'

'What's wrong with that?' PO Stanhope was as straight-faced as usual. 'In peacetime, we often had our bottoms scraped.'

It was too much for a class of young girls, some barely out of school, and it was a while before order was restored, and the PO was able to explain that the barnacles that grew on a ship's bottom could slow it down considerably, and that they had to be scraped off. All was well until he sent the signal, 'Can you accommodate another one in your berth?' He assured them that such messages were tame stuff compared with those encountered by male ratings under instruction. 'No,' he told them, 'they'd shoot me if I used them with a class of Wrens.' By that time, they all thought he was wonderful, and no one wanted him shot, so they pressed him no further.

* * *

On the eighth of June came the news that HMS *Glorious* had been sunk by the battlecruisers *Scharnhorst* and *Gneisenau*, and Clive and Bill, among others, were devastated. The small number of survivors meant that many of their old squadron as well as others in the air group must have gone down with her. Her two escorting destroyers, *Acasta* and *Ardent* had also been sunk. *Scharnhorst* was reported to have been seriously damaged in a torpedo attack by the destroyers, but that was little consolation.

'If only those two could meet one of our battleships,' said Bill as they walked out to the waiting Swordfish.

'They're too crafty for that,' said Clive. 'They only come out when they know there's no risk of meeting anything their own size.'

Walking beside them, Kit Carson waited for a break in the conversation to ask, 'Where are we going, sirs?' As ratings, telegraphist/air-gunners were excluded from briefings, which meant that they only ever learned the details of a sortie from the pilot or the observer.

'Believe it or not, Carson,' said Clive, 'we're patrolling the English Channel again, to make the U-boats keep their heads down.'

'It's been decided,' said Bill, 'that Channel patrols are so exciting and enjoyable, they've given us this one as a reward for the E-boat and the U-boat we sank. Don't let anyone tell you there are no perks in being a Swordfish crewmember.'

'I see it as one on-going perk, sir.'

'That's what I like to hear,' said Bill, swinging his pack into the after cockpit and climbing in after it, 'a contented air-gunner. We've got to keep him happy while he's got a gun in his hands.'

'The same goes for these chaps,' said Clive, grinning at the ground crew. 'That crank is a fearsome piece of equipment.'

'Just wait 'til we start winding, sir,' the man with the crank told him. 'That's when it gets fearsome.' He laughed. 'For us, anyway.'

At a signal from Clive, the ground crew began rotating the huge propellor to draw fuel into the nine cylinders, after which the man with the crank climbed up on to the lower wing and inserted it into the inertia starter. Another man joined him to heave laboriously on the crank until the flywheel inside the engine cowling gathered momentum, charging the current required to start the engine. At the optimum moment, the clutch engaged, and power flowed into the engine, which coughed twice and then started. Clive waved his thanks to the ground crew, giving them the 'chocks away' sign as he ran up the engine. He gave it time to warm up before taxiing to the end of the runway, where he had to wait for permission to take off.

After a minute or so, a green Very light soared from the balcony of the control tower, and Clive opened the throttle, increasing speed all the time as he moved down the runway, finally lifting off effortlessly in spite of the three depth charges the aircraft was carrying. Within minutes, they were over the sea, climbing and ready to carry out another anti-submarine patrol.

* * *

Arthur was surprised. The letter from the Admiralty was dated the thirty-first of May, and it was now the tenth of June. The postal service was usually prompt and reliable, so he could only imagine that the letter had hung around for at least a week in somebody's 'Pending tray. Still, the Admiralty had been quite busy during the past two weeks, so he was amused rather than critical. The content of the letter, however, was a more serious matter. It seemed that Ellis's Boatyard was under consideration as a site for the assembly of prefabricated coastal craft, and that a civil servant would be calling on the yard on Monday, the tenth of June at eleven pm.

Arthur consulted the large office clock, which told him it was five-and-twenty minutes past nine. There was time to get organised. Leaving his office, he entered the long, covered workshop with its four slipways. Just two fishing boats were receiving attention, and that was good. It meant that he could demonstrate both capacity and readiness. As far as he could recall, the MLs of the previous war were about 110 feet long overall, and if the new breed were similar, there would be no problem accommodating them.

He found Walter at the far end of the workshop and beckoned him over.

'Yes, sir?'

'The Admiralty has need of us again, Chief.'

'Really, sir?'

'Yes, but not at sea this time. Someone's coming today to see about using the yard to build MLs. There must have been a foul-up in communication, because I only got the letter this morning.'

'MLs, sir? That's asking a lot.'

'Not from scratch, Chief. Come to the office, and I'll show you the letter.' As they walked to the office, Arthur explained. 'Fairmile Marine are prefabricating parts that can be delivered by lorry to various yards around the country, where they'll be assembled. It's going to mean calling on men we've laid off in the past, and our chaps will have no difficulty with the work. The letter assures me that these things could be assembled by a workforce that doesn't know a stem from a stern gland.'

'I wish I could tell Wilfred, sir, but I suppose it's classified information.'

'It's better treated as such, Chief. We don't want the Luftwaffe paying us a visit.'

'No, sir. You know Wilfred's at home, now, don't you?'

'Yes, I remember your telling me.'

'They reckon he's worked hard enough to deserve another spot of leave so soon after the last one.'

Arthur put the letter down on his desk and said, 'Of course, he led one of the landing parties they put ashore at Dunkirk to marshall the pongoes, didn't he?'

'That's right, sir. Him an' his men were exhausted by the time the last destroyer brought them into Dover.'

'He's a chip off the old block, Chief. You're right to be proud of him.'

'Thank you, sir.' Walter shuffled his feet, grateful for the compliment but self-conscious as well. Happily, a distraction occurred to him. 'How is Miss Dowland faring in Pompey, sir?'

'She's going from strength to strength, Chief, and thank you for asking. As a matter of fact, she's been recommended for officer training.'

'Good for her, sir, and quite right, too, her being the granddaughter of a flag officer.'

'Oh, it takes more than that, and thankfully, young Penny seems to have what it takes.' Looking at his pocket watch, he said, 'We should find out before long whether or not we have what it takes, at least, as far as the Admiralty are concerned, because the civil servant should be with us soon.'

* * *

Penny's class were told earlier than expected that they'd completed the course successfully and that their draft chits would follow In the meantime, they were to enjoy a short period of leave. In what time remained before she had to catch her train, Penny wrote a quick note to Clive.

This is just to let you know that I've passed out as a telegraphist – but not for long! I'm about to board the train for home but, after five days' leave, I'm to report to the RN College at Greenwich for officer training! No arguments!

I can hardly wait to see Grandpop again, and particularly after his deeds of derring-do at Dunkirk, but what are the chances of your getting leave as well? Maybe it's too much to hope for, but it would be wonderful to see you again, and I shall see you again sometime, eventually. I'm determined about that.

Anyway, from tomorrow until Wednesday, I'll be at my home address.

Please take care.
Yours with lots of love and best wishes,
Penny XXX

She posted the letter at Portsmouth and Southsea Station before boarding the London train.

* * *

On their return from patrol, Clive and Bill were met by a grinning Squadron Leader Hedges, the Station Adjutant.

'I suppose, by rights, you two should be awarded the DFC, as you've been operating under RAF command, but we have to make allowances in your case.'

'What are you talking about, sir?' asked Clive.

Hedges could contain himself no longer. 'You're both to receive the Distinguished Service Cross,' he told them. 'Congratulations!'

'Thank you, sir.' Clive, and then Bill, shook hands with him.

'I've no doubt it has something to do with the E-boat and the U-boat you sank, but it was a quick turn-round. The old man only sent in his recommendation three weeks ago. By the way, your air-gunner's going to get the DSM, as well.'

'Have you seen him yet?' Carson had gone ahead of them to his hut.

'No, I just missed him.'

'We'll tell him, sir, and then we'll thank the CO for his recommendation.'

'Good for you. Well done, again.'

They walked over to the long hut, where Carson was accommodated, to give him the news. As Clive and Bill were both professional officers, the DSC would help them in their respective careers, but Carson's DSM was just as well-deserved. As they walked to the hut, Clive resolved to write to his parents and to Penny as soon as he could.

15

HOME IS THE SAILOR

Wilf Gregory had slept for most of the first twenty-four hours he was at home, but he realised on opening his eyes and adjusting to the fact that he was in his own bed, that if he didn't make the necessary effort soon, he would waste what remained of his precious leave.

There was no one else at home; his dad would be at the boatyard, and his mum had most likely gone to the shops, so he buttered some bread, smeared it with jam, and ate it quickly before taking a towel from the linen cupboard and his swimming trunks from the chest of drawers. It was a fine, sunny day, perfect for a swim in the sea, and he'd been looking forward to it at odd times during the past fortnight.

There was an alley that served as his shortcut to the beach; it separated the terrace where he lived from the coastguard cottages and, although he'd grown up in Sandbrook with the Channel as a familiar neighbour, he still felt a quickening of his spirits when he walked between the two close, brick walls that led to the coast road.

He stopped dead at the end of the alley, feeling unbelievably stupid. Although he'd heard talk about the threat of invasion, somehow, he'd never connected it with Sandbrook, and it should have been obvious that his hometown would be among the most vulnerable. At all events, the truth was there before him, in the unwelcome shape of barbed wire, ugly, looped and menacing, extending as far as he could see. Disappointed and embarrassed, although there was no one there to witness his foolishness, he returned via the alley to Hythe Road. He would call at the public baths, where he would have to pay an extra penny for soap, but at least he had his own towel, which would save him another penny.

He walked to the end of the road and turned left on to Albert Street, which led to the public baths.

The woman at the turnstile was the same one he remembered from years back, or so it felt. She seemed pleased to see him. ''Morning, Jack,' she said. It seemed that civilians, as well as members of the other armed services, still found it necessary to address naval ratings by that name.

'Good morning. I'd like a slipper bath, please.'

'Have you got your own soap and towel?'

'I've got a towel.'

'It's a penny for the soap. That's fruppence, altogevver.'

Wilf dug into the pocket of his webbing belt and took out a threepenny bit.

'Thanks.' She operated the lever that dispensed tickets and handed one to him along with a tiny piece of carbolic soap. 'Just one thing 'fore you go inside, Jack.'

'What's that?'

'Will you turn round so I can touch your collar?'

'Okay.' It was little enough to ask, so he turned and allowed her to touch the blue jean fabric of his square collar. He had no idea when the practice had begun, but many people, especially women, still liked to touch a sailor's collar for luck.

'Thanks, Jack. Enjoy your bath.'

'Thanks.' He went through the door marked 'Slipper Baths' and showed his ticket to the attendant, a man with a large paunch, who entered a green-painted cubicle and proceeded to run the statutory five inches of water. When he was satisfied that it was no deeper than regulations allowed, he pointed to the anchor on Wilf's left sleeve and said with a waggish grin, 'Popeye has his tattooed on his arm.'

'He's a Yank,' Wilf told him. 'He doesn't know any better.' He went into the cubicle, closing the latch behind him, and undressed. If nothing else happened that day to please him, and he wasn't optimistic, he was determined to enjoy his soak.

He draped his clothes over the wooden chair provided and lowered himself into the water, which was hot but bearable. Resting his head on the end of the bath, he allowed himself a luxurious soak for about two minutes. It was his first bath since a very hurried one in his quarters in

Dunkirk, and it was an oasis of peace.

When he was rested, he soaped himself all over with the tiny piece of carbolic he'd been given, wondering why the stuff, however large or small, was hopeless at creating suds. Finally, he rinsed himself and climbed out. He'd just finished drying himself when he heard the attendant say, 'Time you were out, Popeye.'

'I'm just getting dressed, Wimpey.'

'Hey, less of that.'

'All right. Don't call me "Popeye", then.'

The attendant made no response, which meant he was either out of earshot, or he was ill-equipped to bandy witticisms. Wilf finished dressing, rolled up his towel and made for the exit. A cup of tea beckoned. It would be his first that day, but he wasn't ready to go home yet, so he decided to push the boat out and visit the teashop at the corner of Albert Street and Hythe Road. He'd had neither the time nor the opportunity to spend money during the past fortnight, so he reckoned he was due for a treat, even if it was only a cup of tea and a bun of some kind.

When he reached the teashop he realised he was the only customer and, wondering if that made him somehow special or just a nuisance, he took a seat at the first table he came to.

It seemed that the bell that had rung as he entered the shop had alerted a waitress, who looked around the room and, seeing him, came over, notepad in hand. 'Good morning, Jack,' she said. 'What can I get you?'

'Hello. I'd like a pot of tea and... Have you any currant buns or anything like that?' Her waitress's cap was a distraction, but he was sure he knew her from somewhere. She was rather attractive, too.

'Yes, we have Chelsea buns. What sort of tea would you like? I'm afraid we've only got Assam and English Breakfast.' She added apologetically, 'It's the same everywhere, they say.'

'I missed my breakfast this morning,' he said, 'so I'd better make up for it now. I'll have English Breakfast, please.'

Peering at him, she said self-consciously, 'I hope you don't mind me asking, but aren't you Wilfred Gregory?'

Realisation dawned, and he said, 'Esme Daniels. I thought I recognised you.'

'It's been a long time, Wilfred.'

'Eleven years,' he confirmed. 'I was too shy to talk to you when we were at school.' Glancing discreetly at her wedding ring, he said, 'I thought some lucky lad would snap you up, and I was right.'

She lowered her long eyelashes and said quietly, 'Somebody did. I married Len Farrell.'

'I remember Len.' The lad he remembered was pleasant and popular, but he was always in trouble at school for laziness. He always knew he'd go into the family business, so he saw no point in working at school. 'His family were fishermen, I remember.'

She nodded. 'Len was lost at sea. It happened in the big storm in nineteen thirty-six.'

He could have bitten out his tongue. 'I'm sorry, Esme,' he said. 'I really am.' They couldn't have been married long when it happened, and his remark about somebody snapping her up was out of place.

Awkwardly, she said, 'Thanks. I'll get your order.'

Left to ponder his clumsiness, he was quick to see the irony of it as well. He'd been too shy to speak to her when they were at school, and now, when shyness was little more than a memory, he'd blundered in and said the wrong thing. He waited in painful embarrassment until Esme returned with his order.

'A pot of English breakfast tea and a Chelsea bun,' she announced, taking each item from her tray and placing them on the table.

'Esme,' he said, 'I'm really sorry I was so… you know… about you getting married, I mean….' Now he couldn't say what he wanted to say. It was getting worse all the time.

'You didn't say anything wrong, and you weren't to know.' Changing the subject deliberately, she said, 'I'm afraid the icing's a bit thin on the bun. You've got to blame the war, I suppose.'

'I haven't had anything to eat since last night, so it'll suit me fine.'

She looked around her, possibly to ensure they were alone, and asked, 'What have you been doing to go without breakfast?'

'Sleeping. I didn't get much sleep at Dunkirk. There was a lot going on.'

'Oh, were you at Dunkirk, Wilfred? Hang on a sec. You can't go through the morning on a Chelsea bun.' She disappeared, presumably into the kitchen, leaving him to wonder what she had in mind.

She returned after a few minutes with two slices of buttered toast.

'There,' she said, 'it's on the house. I'd get you some jam, but there'd be bother if I got caught.'

'Thanks, Esme. That's really good of you.'

'It's the least I can do.' Looking around warily again, she said, 'I should eat that toast, if I were you, before the boss sees it and charges you for it. She wouldn't be too pleased with me, either.'

'The last thing I want to do is get you into trouble,' he said, making a start on the toast.

Her eyes wandered shyly over his uniform, and she said, 'I heard you'd joined the Navy.'

'That was eleven years ago. I joined as soon as I left school '

'The uniform suits you.' She looked as if she might be nerving herself to say more. Eventually, she said, 'Can I ask a favour?'

'Of course you can.' Anticipating her request, he said, 'You want to touch my collar for luck, don't you?' It was a fair bet, because everyone else wanted to.

'If you don't mind.' Now embarrassed, she stroked the blue fabric. 'Is it meant to be ironed like this?'

He imagined she was looking at the three, equidistant, concertina creases in his collar. 'Yes, that's just as it has to be.'

'What does this mean?' She was pointing to the embroidered anchor on his left sleeve.

'That's a killick, the badge of a leading hand, and this one,' he said, showing her the category badge on his right sleeve, 'says I'm a gunlayer-armourer. That means I operate small-calibre anti-aircraft guns.' She was obviously interested in the uniform, so he showed her the lanyard. 'They used these to fire cannon, back in the olden days, but they're just decoration now. The black silk,' he went on, touching the folded scarf, was a sign of mourning for Lord Nelson, but they kept it as part of the uniform in his memory.'

'It's a lot for you to take care of.'

'Not really. We're used to it, and if you have pride in your uniform, you're happy enough to take care of it.' He left unmentioned the fact that any rating found with his uniform in less than pristine condition would find himself in the rattle. Meanwhile, hopefully under the cover of her curiosity, he was admiring her dark-brown, wavy hair, her clear complexion and deep, brown eyes. She looked even better than he remembered her eleven years earlier. At least, he thought she did. Trying not to look at her too obviously, he noticed a poster on the wall behind her and, having particularly good eyesight, learned that a dance was to be held on the following evening at the Temperance Hall in Sandbrook, to raise funds for.... At that point, Esme moved her head and obscured the poster, but he'd read what he wanted to know. 'Are you going to the dance at the Temperance Hall?' he asked.

For a moment, she seemed amused, and then she said, 'I haven't been to a dance since before I was married, and it's not the kind of thing I can do now I'm on my own.'

'I'm sorry, Esme. I've put my foot in it again.'

'No, you haven't—' She was interrupted when the door opened and two women entered the shop. She left him so that she could attend to them. By the time she returned he'd eaten the toast and the bun and was pouring a second cup of tea.

'What did you want to say about a dance?' she asked.

'I don't know if I should be asking you this.' He wondered if he would ever stop feeling foolish.

'I've been a widow nearly four years, Wilfred,' she told him patiently. 'You don't have to treat me as if I'm still fragile.'

'No, fair enough.' He nerved himself and asked, 'Will you come with me to the dance tomorrow night?'

She hesitated, possibly surprised by his request, although she must had suspected that was what he had in mind. 'I'd like that very much. Thanks.'

Now that she'd agreed, he felt enormously relieved. It made a welcome change from feeling embarrassed. 'Right, I'll call for you tomorrow,' he said, looking at the time on the poster, 'at half-past six. Where do you live?'

'Thirty-five Victoria Terrace. I moved back in with my mum and dad after I lost Len.'

'It was probably a good idea,' he said, wishing he could think of something more sensible to say. He'd met lots of widows; it was difficult to avoid them, the previous war having created so many, but a woman widowed at twenty-one was still a shock.

'I'll look forward to it, Wilfred. It's been nice, meeting you again, but I'd better get on.'

'All right. In that case, I'll pay my bill.'

* * *

That evening, Wilf listened to his dad talking about the events of the day at the boatyard and, eventually, his mum asked, 'And what have you been up to, Wilfred.' She always used his full name.

'I went for a bath, and then I went to the teashop for a cup of char and a wad.'

'A what?'

'A cup of tea and a bun or a sandwich,' his dad translated.

'There must have been something special about it,' said his mum, ''cause you're looking very pleased with yourself.'

'I met an old... acquaintance... from school,' he said. He couldn't really call Esme an old friend, because they'd never exchanged more than a few words until that morning in the teashop.

'Who did you meet?'

'Esme Daniels.' Correcting himself, he said, 'She's Esme Farrell, now.'

'Oh yes,' said his mum in the hushed tone she reserved for personal tragedies, 'that poor girl, widowed when they'd barely tied the knot.'

'She's living with her mum and dad again.'

'She'd have to. She wouldn't be able to keep the cottage on a widow's pension.' By way of explanation for her husband's benefit, she said, 'They rented one of the fishermen's cottages in Albert Street.' Returning her attention to Wilf, she asked, 'How's she keeping, then?'

'All right. She's a waitress at the teashop. That's where I saw her.' With a mischievous smile, he said, 'She gave me two rounds of buttered toast on the quiet, because she thought I needed feeding up.'

'Oh yes?' His mother's curiosity was well alight. 'Go on, then. What happened after that?'

He told her happily, 'We're going to a dance at the Temperance Hall tomorrow night.'

'Well I never.' For Walter's benefit, she said, 'She was widowed easily three years ago, so it's respectable enough.'

'Nearly four years,' confirmed Wilf. 'I wondered if it would be all right asking her to go to the dance, and she said it was.'

16

A Mixed Reception and Two Kind Ones

Louisa Dowland greeted her younger daughter without undue ceremony and led her out to the station yard. 'I see you're still not in uniform,' she remarked as observantly as usual.

'No, Mum. As a matter of fact, my current uniform hasn't long to go before I replace it with one from the naval outfitter in Savile Row.'

'Oh, and who's going to pay for that?' she asked, opening the car door for Penny to put her bag in.

'Some of it will be free issue, but I'll pay for the rest. Grandpop says he'll pitch in if necessary.'

'You do surprise me.' She took her seat behind the wheel and started the engine. 'He'll spoil you to death.'

'Don't you want to know why I'm getting a new uniform?'

'I've no doubt you'll tell me sooner or later.'

'I've a jolly good mind to keep you in the dark,' she said playfully.

'Oh, Penelope, must you be so childish?' As the car left the station yard, she said, 'I have some news for you, about Joan and Charles.'

'I'm all agog, Mum. If you think I'm grown-up enough to hear it, tell me the worst.'

'Really, Penelope.' She drove a little further and, presumably unable to contain herself any longer, said, 'The news is that they're expecting a baby, probably after Christmas.'

'Tremendous news.'

'I thought you'd be surprised.'

'That's one word for it.' When she'd fully absorbed the news, she said, 'It's more of a shock, really, those two, of all people, getting up to that kind of thing.'

'You know how I feel about coarseness, Penelope,' said her mother icily.

'Yes, and those two share your feelings, which is what makes it all such a surprise.'

'I refuse to discuss it with you while you're in this silly, childish mood. When we arrive, I think you'd better go and unpack your things. Hopefully, you'll come down in an improved, more sensible, frame of mind.'

Just then, Penny saw a motorcyclist pull up opposite the driveway to the Newing residence. She could scarcely believe her luck. He was wearing goggles, but she recognised him. As they passed him, Penny smiled and waved, receiving a delighted wave in return. 'I'll certainly be in an improved state of mind,' she promised, her heart now beating faster than ever.

* * *

Clive retrieved his cap from the pillion and walked into the kitchen, where his mother was preparing vegetables.

'You're looking particularly pleased with life,' she observed.

'Life is good.' He kissed her to prove it. 'I'm going to make one telephone call, and then I'll tell you all about it.' Leaving her guessing, he went to the telephone in the hall and dialled Penny's number. It rang for maybe five or six seconds and then a woman's voice came on the line. The voice wasn't Penny's, so he imagined it must belong either to her mother or her serious-minded sister.

'Hello,' he said, 'I wonder if I might speak to Penny, please.'

The voice, which sounded less than friendly and was most likely that of her mother, asked, 'You wish to speak to *Penelope*?' In emphasising Penny's correct name, she gave the impression that the Dowland family frowned on diminutives.

'If at all possible. Yes, please.'

'And who shall I say is calling?'

'Will you tell her, please, that it's Clive Newing?'

'Penelope has only just returned home and is unpacking her things, Mr Newing. I'll see if she's free to come to the telephone.' There was a dull thud as the heavy receiver encountered a surface more yielding than either itself or Penny's mother, and Clive waited.

After a very short time, Penny came on the line. 'Clive?' She sounded excited.

'Hello, Penny. I saw you arrive.'

'I know. How long have you been home?'

'Since yesterday.'

'Wonderful. I wrote to you. You won't have received it yet.'

'I had a letter from you on Tuesday.'

'No, I wrote since then, to tell you everything, that I was coming home on leave and that... my other news.'

Clive made sense of that sentence and said, 'I wrote to you yesterday to tell you the same.' He added, 'Also my other news, but tell me your news first.' It was only right to let her have first go.

She said gleefully, 'I have to report to the RN College, Greenwich, for officer training.'

'Good for you, Penny. I'm delighted.'

'Your turn, Clive.'

'All right. I've been awarded the DSC.' Modestly, he added, 'Bill, my observer, got one, too, and Kit Carson, our TAG, is getting the DSM.'

'That's wonderful. I'm ever so proud of you, but you're speaking in code, Clive. What is a "tag"?'

'A telegraphist air-gunner. I can't remember his proper Christian name, but his surname's Carson, so he's called "Kit".'

'I don't get it, but never mind. It's wonderful that you've got the DSC. Have they said what it's for?'

'Now, Penny, it's not the done thing to ask or to tell.'

'Never mind. The wonderful thing is that we're both on leave at the same time.'

'Isn't it? I imagine you'll want to be with your family this evening, so shall we meet tomorrow?'

'I'm not sure about the first bit,' she said cryptically, 'but yes, let's do that. Have you anything in mind?'

'Let's take a picnic and go somewhere... anywhere.'

'Yes, let's.'

'I'll pick you up at, oh, ten-thirty, and I'll bring you home to change.

because we'll go out to dinner. I don't often have an opportunity to welcome a new Wren officer to the ranks.'

'I'm not commissioned, yet, Clive. Don't tempt Providence.'

'Oh, it's a foregone conclusion, I'm sure. I'll see you tomorrow, then.'

'Wonderful.'

''Bye.'

''Bye.'

Clive returned to the kitchen, sitting at the table where his mother was working.

She asked, 'Was that the girl you saw on your last leave?'

'Yes, and I saw her again in Pompey.'

'Where?'

'Portsmouth. She was training with the Wrens at Victoria Barracks. She's going on to Greenwich, next, for officer training.'

'Good girl.' She smiled her special smile, the one that came with a blink that told him she understood how he felt.

Clive returned her smile and watched her peel the potatoes for dinner. He'd known boys at school who'd been embarrassed when their parents arrived to collect them at the end of term, but he'd never had that problem. His friends used to tell him how pretty his mother was. 'Pretty' wasn't the right word for a woman of her age, of course, but no one knew that at the time, so he was no less pleased by their reaction. He was just as proud when his parents came to the passing-out parade at Dartmouth, and his mother earned the admiring looks of his fellow-midshipmen, not to mention those of some of the instructors. They would no doubt find a more appropriate word than 'pretty', but the effect she had on them was just as telling.

'What will you find to do with her?'

'Tomorrow? We're going to take a picnic and go down the coast, somewhere. We'll find a place.' He was sure they would.

'The beaches are all wired off, now.'

'I know. I went into Sandbrook this afternoon. It's the ugliest thing imaginable, that expanse of barbed wire. They've mined the beach, as well.'

She finished the last potato and rinsed it with the rest. Then, thinking of pleasanter things, she said, 'A picnic will be nice. I'll find something for you to take.'

'Thanks, Mum.' He hadn't been angling for that, but he appreciated her help.

'What else will you do?'

'I'm going to bring her back so that she can change, and then we'll find somewhere to eat and, hopefully, dance.'

'What a romantic soul you are, Clive, and quite right, too.' The thought seemed to act as a reminder, because she said, 'I haven't told you, have I? Audrey's seeing someone now, a junior doctor. She seems rather keen on him.'

'Poor man. She'll wind him round her little finger, the way she treats them all.' Whilst he was very fond of his sister, he had no illusions about her talent for manipulation.

'Don't be unkind. Actually, he's waiting to hear from the War Office. He's volunteered for the Royal Army Medical Corps.'

'Has he, by jingo? That'll keep the Old Man happy.'

Half in fun, his mother said, 'Don't let your dad hear you call him that.'

'He'd prefer that to some of the names his patients call him '

'Don't, Clive. That's unkind.' Nevertheless, she was amused. 'Actually, if you're not going far tonight, he may let you use the car.'

'Do you really think so, Mum?'

'Give me a chance to speak to him.'

He stood up and pushed the chair under the table. 'Mum,' he said, joining her, 'I don't deserve you.'

'You're quite right, you don't, especially when you're so rude about your dad and your sister.'

'I take it all back for your sake.' Wrapping his arms round her, he gave her a heartfelt hug. 'It's good to be home again.'

'It's lovely to have you home, and we're very proud of you.'

'Aw shucks, Ma.'

'Who says that?' she asked, laughing.

'It was probably Tom Mix or Buck Jones. One of those cowboys.'

'Away with you.'

* * *

'Penny,' said Arthur when she'd released him, 'when did you arrive home?'

'About an hour and a half ago.'

'If only I'd known. Your birthday present is at the house. Still, we can rectify that later.'

'I'm looking forward to that, Grandpop. As a matter of fact, I'm out of favour at home.'

'Again, and so soon? You surprise me.' He swung his office chair round to give her his full attention and asked, 'What have you been up to now?'

Counting on her fingers, she said, 'Failure to wear uniform when on leave, playing childish games, and failure to greet the news of my sister's interesting condition with due reverence. More will follow, I feel sure, but I committed those three within minutes of stepping off the train.'

'You're a hopeless case, Penny.' He flicked a switch down on his intercom, and a female voice answered.

'Mrs Enright,' he said, 'will the tea ration run to a final pot of the day?'

'I believe so, sir.'

'Excellent, then please do the honours. My granddaughter has arrived unexpectedly.'

'Very good, sir.'

Penny waited for him to flick back the switch, and said, 'I wrote to you and told you I was coming on leave, Grandpop.'

'I know. I meant that you'd arrived earlier than expected.' With that cleared up, he said, 'Congratulations, by the way, on the next stage in your naval career.'

'Thank you.' Wistfully, she said, 'I'm told that there are officers and ratings who don't take Wrens, and particularly Wren officers, seriously.'

He nodded sympathetically. 'I'm sure that's true, Penny, but time will tell. As Wrens go on freeing men for the fleet, as they say, and proving themselves invaluable, as I believe they will, attitudes are bound to soften, as they did during the last war.'

'I hope so.'

'But,' he said, changing the subject, 'how, exactly, did you respond to the news of Joan's... condition?'

'Oh, I just said how surprised I was.'

'Was that all?'

'Not really. I said I was also surprised that two people as serious-minded as those two, had actually done something so frivolous.' Seeing her grandfather raise his eyebrows, she said, 'I'm sorry to embarrass you, Grandpop, but that was just the way I saw it.'

He smiled in spite of himself. 'You can hardly be surprised at your mother's reaction. It wouldn't be the kind of response she would expect from her young, unmarried daughter.'

There was a knock, and Arthur's secretary came in with a tray of tea things. 'Good afternoon, Miss Dowland,' she said, 'and congratulations on being selected for promotion.' Her grandfather had evidently spread the word.

'Thank you, Mrs Enright. How are you keeping?'

'Very well, thank you, Miss Dowland.'

'Just leave the tea things, if you will, Mrs Enright,' said Arthur.

When they were alone again, Penny returned to the subject of Joan's news. 'I imagine what I said shocked her. I received a curt reprimand about coarseness, but I'm sure the more heinous offence was my failure to be completely overwhelmed by my celebrated sister's latest achievement.'

Arthur smiled at her assessment. 'I daresay you're right,' he said, dismissing the subject, 'but what other news have you to tell me? You must have lots.'

'Yes, I have. Do you remember Clive Newing, the pilot we met before I went to Pompey?'

'I do.'

'He's been awarded the DSC,' she told him proudly.

'Oh, good man. I'm sure it's well-earned. He was in Norway, as I recall.'

'And France, patrolling the Channel. We may call in tomorrow – we're going on a picnic – and he'll be able to tell you more, except I doubt he will, because he's so modest. He tells me it's bad form either to ask or to tell.'

'He's absolutely right, and I'm delighted for him. It'll do his career no harm at all.'

* * *

The exclamation from the scullery told Wilf that his mother had found herself unexpectedly short of something, and when she emerged, she confirmed his suspicion.

'Wilfred, will you be a good lad and go down to Mr Wickham's, the greengrocer's for me? I'm out of carrots, so I hope he has some left. A couple of pounds will do, if he has any.'

'Okay, Mum. Where's the ration book?'

'Vegetables aren't rationed, silly. They're just not always easy to get. Here.' She gave him a shilling piece and, seeing him hesitate, said, 'Turn left from here, and it's just a little way down this street and on this side.'

'Right.' He reached for his cap and squared it off before leaving the house.

Wickham's greengrocery was, as his mother had said, only a short distance down the street, and he was soon there.

The bell tinkled gently as he opened and closed the door, summoning a man possibly in his thirties, whom Wilf took to be Mr Wickham. He walked with a pronounced limp as he approached the counter.

'Yes, Jack, what can I do for you?'

Distracted for the moment by the familiar earthy smell that greengrocery had, Wilf made himself concentrate. 'Have you got two pounds of carrots, please?' he asked.

'That's about all I have got. Here,' he said, putting a bunch of carrots on the counter, 'there's just over two pounds there, and they're the last in the shop.'

'Thanks.' Wilf was handing over the money when the doorbell tinkled again, and he was surprised to see Esme. She carried a shopping bag of groceries. 'Hello,' he said, 'fancy seeing you again.'

'You never know who you're going to see when you go shopping,' she told him drily.

'Good afternoon, Mrs Farrell,' said the shopkeeper. 'What would you like, supposing I've got it?'

'Just half a pound of carrots, please, Mr Wickham.'

'I'm sorry. I've just sold the last of the carrots to Jolly Jack, here.'

Her look of disappointment was followed quickly by one of philosophical acceptance, but Wilf wasn't going to see her leave empty-handed. 'Take these two,' he said, handing them to her. 'I've got plenty for my mum and dad and me.'

'Oh, I couldn't.'

''Course you can. Go on, take them.' Without waiting for an answer, he dropped them into her shopping bag. They felt near enough to half a pound.

'It looks like you've got yourself a knight errant there, Mrs Farrell,' said the greengrocer.

'Let me pay you for them,' she said.

'Don't you dare. If I start selling greengrocery, Mr Wickham will have me run out of town.'

'That's right,' agreed Mr Wickham. 'Just call it a noble deed and enjoy the carrots.'

'Oh well, thank you.' Esme still looked awkward.

'Will you let me walk you home and carry your bag for you?'

'Won't it take you out of your way?'

'Only a few yards.' He reached for her bag, and she handed it to him shyly.

'Mind you go straight home, you two,' said Mr Wickham playfully.

They left the shop, and Esme said, 'Mr Wickham's always nice to me. I think he feels sorry for me. It's a bit embarrassing, but it's better than the way some shopkeepers are. Some of them can be downright miserable, as if it's their customers' fault things are in short supply.' As they walked along, she said, 'It's really good of you to do this, Wilfred.'

'I'm just repaying your kindness this morning,' he told her. There was no need for him to tell her he enjoyed every second he spent in her company.

They passed Esmeralda Street, and it prompted Esme to say. 'I used to get tormented at school when we first started there, because of my name being Esmeralda. Parents just don't think when they name their children, do they?'

'I don't see anything wrong with it. It's a nice name, but so is "Esme".'

'Do you think so?'

'It's my favourite name.' It had enjoyed that status since his visit to the teashop that morning, but having said what he had, he felt suddenly awkward, and he covered his gaucheness by asking, 'Will you have enough with just two carrots?' He remembered her saying she lived with her parents.

'Yes, they're only to go into a stew.'

They turned into Victoria Terrace and came to Esme's door, where she took her bag from him. 'Thanks ever such a lot for the carrots, and there was no need to carry my shopping, but thank you, anyway.'

'It was no trouble, Esme.'

'I'm glad, and I'm looking forward to tomorrow night.'

'So am I. I'll see you then. ''Bye.'

''Bye.'

He ran home with the carrots, because he knew his mother needed them, but he was glad he'd walked Esme home.

When he arrived, his mother asked, 'Have you been standing in the field, watching them grow, Wilfred?'

'No,' he said, giving her the carrots and her change. 'I'd just got served when Esme came into the shop, wanting carrots, believe it or not, and these were the last in the shop. I had a good two pounds – Mr Wickham gave me good measure – so I gave her two carrots.' He'd been unable from childhood to hide his feelings, and before he could stop himself, he said, 'I couldn't bear to see her disappointed, Mum.'

Her eyes had softened, and she said, 'You did the right thing, Wilfred. Didn't he, Walter?'

Wilf's father sat in his armchair, pleasantly amused by Wilf's story. 'I say your heart's in the right place, Wilf. I'd have taken pity on the poor girl myself, if I'd been there.'

'She said Mr Wickham's always nice to her because he feels sorry for her. She finds it embarrassing sometimes.'

'Yes,' said his mother, 'and she paid an awful price for that sympathy. Mind you, Henry Wickham knows all about that. He's been lame from birth with that withered leg of his, poor man.'

It seemed to Wilf that, with so many unfortunate people about, it was just as well there was also a lot of sympathy. Also, seeing Esme again had been a bonus. He, too, was looking forward to the dance.

17

'MAGIC ABROAD IN THE AIR'

When Clive arrived, Penny was ready for him, wearing a flowered, lightweight summer dress. 'Where can I put this?' she asked, holding up a tin box.

'What is it?'

'My contribution to the picnic.'

'Oh, well done. Stow it in one of the panniers.' He pointed to the pannier on the offside and, as she unbuckled the strap, he noticed her wristwatch. 'What a truly exquisite watch,' he said. 'It's just right for you.'

'Thank you. It was Grandpop's present on my twenty-first birthday. I'm also wearing the locket you gave me.' She pointed to the heart-shaped locket.

'I've got something else for you. I'll give it to you this evening. Depending on what you're wearing, you may want to add it to the ensemble.'

'I'm intrigued.'

'That's not all you are,' he said, switching off the engine and kissing her discreetly. 'Can you remember what to do?'

'Thank you, and yes, I have to tuck my skirt in fore and aft.'

'That's right. I'll look the other way while you do it.'

'You're an officer *and* a gentleman.'

'Dashing and debonair,' he confirmed.

'I wouldn't go that far,' she said, mounting the pillion. 'Can we go via the boatyard, just to have a quick word with Grandpop?'

'By all means.' He checked that her feet were on the footrests and then kicked off the engine. It was good to feel her arms around his waist again as they rolled down the drive to join the main road.

The journey to the boatyard took only a few minutes; the distance was negligible and there was very little traffic. Clive pulled up and held the Norton steady while Penny dismounted. As soon as she stood beside him he joined her and stood it on its centre stand. Taking his cap from a pannier, he set it at a discreet angle and followed her into the boatyard, where they found Arthur in his office.

'Come in, both of you,' he said when Penny tapped on the door and opened it.

'Hello, Grandpop. I've brought Clive to see you, as you asked.'

'Splendid. Congratulations on your DSC, my boy.' Arthur shook his hand enthusiastically.

'Thank you, sir. It was a team effort, and I'm happy to say that my observer and air-gunner both received their just reward.'

'Generously spoken. I gather you were involved in the evacuation.'

'Grandpop and one of his men took *Chloe* to Dunkirk,' said Penny proudly.

'Yes, you told me. You have my fullest admiration, sir.' Clive had heard about the civilian involvement and had been less than surprised to hear that the admiral had taken part, but his response was no less genuine. 'We were behind the scenes,' he said modestly, 'patrolling the Channel to ensure the Kriegsmarine kept its nose out of the proceedings.'

'And you were successful, apparently.'

'We were lucky, sir.' Clive was essentially a modest man, and what he said was true enough. 'We sank an E-boat, and then on another occasion, a U-boat, so I suppose you could say we were exceptionally lucky.'

'Splendid work! If those two had got among the destroyers, things might have been very different. Look, the sun's peering over the yardarm. Will you both join me in a celebratory drink?'

Clive looked at Penny and said, 'That is most generous of you, sir.'

'Yes, please, Grandpop. Just goffers for me, please.'

'Goffers for Penny, and what will you have, Lieutenant? I can offer you gin or whisky.' His smile was an admission that he was asking a silly question.

'Gin, please, sir.'

'I'll join you with that.' Opening his drinks cabinet, he poured orange blossom cordial for Penny and two gins. 'Help yourself to water, Lieutenant.'

'Thank you, sir.' Clive took the jug of water and added the tiniest drop to his drink.

'That's right,' said Arthur. 'Water should be a threat rather than a punishment.' Holding up his glass, he said, 'Here's to your DSC. Congratulations.'

They drank the toast, and Clive said, 'If I may, sir, I'd like to drink to the next stage in Penny's career.'

They drank to that, and Penny made her contribution. 'Everyone who made the evacuation of the BEF not only possible, but the success it was.'

Having indulged his granddaughter, Arthur said, 'We've toasted everyone but the ship's cat. It really is time to call a halt to the mutual admiration.'

Laughing, they agreed with him and finished their drinks.

'Have an enjoyable day, both of you, and I hope to see you again before too long, Lieutenant.'

'I'd like that, too, sir.' He shook Arthur's hand. 'Goodbye, sir.'

'Goodbye.'

Penny took her place on the pillion and asked, 'Where are we going?'

'I don't know, yet. Not far, because petrol's a constraint.'

She made no reply, so he imagined she was happy to let their destination remain a surprise. Accordingly, he kicked off the engine and headed inland for a few miles, enjoying the Garden of England at its best and coming to a halt when they reached Monks Horton.

'This is quiet enough,' he said, switching off the engine. 'There's no point in going up the coast now that it's all mined and wired off.' He waited for her to dismount so that he could do the same.

'I worry about your petrol, Clive.'

'There's no need to worry,' he assured her. 'It's lasting well. I filled the tank before I left for the Med. That was before the war. Anyway,' he said, taking her in his arms, 'how much more devoted can a chap be, than to share his last pre-war tank of petrol with the flower of his dreams?'

'You're just a poet at heart.' She nevertheless looked around her nervously.

'There's no one about.' He kissed her, feeling her relax as he did so. After a minute or so, he released her and opened the near-side pannier, from which he took a folded car rug. She helped him lay it on the grass verge.

'You're terribly organised,' she said. 'How many times have you done this?'

'Counting today?'

'Yes, I suppose so.'

He proceeded to count on his fingers, finally arriving at a total. 'About nine times in all,' he said confidently. Then, seeing her expression falter, he explained, 'The other eight were with my family when my sister and I were young and innocent. At least, I was.'

'You had me worried. I thought you'd had a Bluebeard past.'

'I know. I'm sorry, I didn't mean to worry you.' He drew her towards him again and said, 'Of course, I've been on several banyans as well, but they don't count, as they were all-male parties.'

'What's a banyan?'

'A beach picnic with food roasted over an open fire. On such occasions, officers and men alike forget themselves and join together in ribald song. You'll have to forgive me if I don't give you a demonstration, because, if you heard me sing, you'd never forgive me, and if you heard some of the words we sang, you'd be horrified.'

'You're daft, Clive.'

'In that case, let's do something sensible. Would you like a cup of tea?'

'I'd love one.'

'No sooner said than done, milady.' He opened the near-side pannier again and retrieved a Thermos flask, two mugs, milk and sugar. 'Do you have sugar in tea?' he asked.

'No, thank you.'

'Neither do I.' He returned the sugar to the pannier, removing his tunic and draping it over the saddle.

'What else have you got in there?'

'That's about all.' He thought again and said, 'There's my revolver.'

'Are you serious?'

'Very. I'll use it to defend you if the Nazis come. Of course, I'll only be able to shoot six of them before I run out of ammunition, but you can blame Their Lordships for that.'

'Who are they?' she asked innocently.

'Their Lordships of the Admiralty. You'll run across them soon enough.'

Shaking her head in despair, she said, 'You get dafter.'

'No, I'm quite serious.' He poured tea from the Thermos as he spoke. 'Even so,' he said, 'in the interests of your peace of mind, a change of subject is probably in order.'

'Yes.' She looked thoughtful and asked, 'What did you sink as well as the U-boat?'

'An E-boat, and it wasn't just me. Bill and Kit Carson were involved as well.'

'Bill is your…?'

'Observer. Carson is my air-gunner.'

'Right. Is "Kit" really his name?'

'No, we call him that because his surname's Carson. Kit Carson was a famous character in the Wild West.'

'Ah.' One part of the puzzle apparently remained. 'What's an E-boat?'

'It's a torpedo boat, very fast and well-armed. "E" stands for "Enemy", because most naval officers can't remember "*Schnellboot*", which is what the Nazis call them.' By way of an excuse, he said, 'As things stand, we have an awful lot to remember, without adding silly German names to the list.'

'You don't take anything seriously, do you?'

'There are some things,' he said, kissing her to show he was serious, 'that have to be taken seriously.' Unbidden, the sinking of HMS *Glorious* and the loss of a great many friends sprang to mind, and he dispelled the thought as quickly as he could. 'I try not to waste serious thought on matters that don't really call for it,' he said.

'I see.' She returned his kiss and, because it had been on her mind, she said, 'In a sense, you and I have something in common.'

'I hope so.'

'I mean, according to Grandpop, there are senior naval officers who take neither Wrens nor the Fleet Air Arm seriously. He's more enlightened than them, of course, but he hears things.'

He considered the matter. 'You know, there'll be a lot of noses put out of joint before long. Senior officers in shore establishments will have to admit that they just can't function without Wrens, and the realisation will keep them awake at night. There'll also come a time when a key target will need to be engaged at a range beyond that of any battleship's guns, so carrier-based aircraft will have to do the job, and the good old "Stringbag" is ready and waiting.'

'Is that the aeroplane you thought was the most exquisite thing you'd ever seen?'

'Until I saw you dressed overall,' he confirmed.

That made her think. '"Overall" is a strange word,' she said. 'If you'd seen me in the bluette, the overall I had to wear in basic training, you wouldn't have given me a second glance.'

'Fiddlesticks.' He searched quickly for an appropriate compliment and found one. 'I'd find you irresistible,' he said, 'in oilskins, a sou'wester and seaboots.' With that assertion, it seemed that their conversation had run its course, because, by unspoken agreement, they kissed at length.

* * *

Wilf's mother watched her son press his number one uniform and asked for the second time, 'Are you sure you don't want me to do anything, Wilfred?'

'Quite sure, Mum, thank you.'

'Leave him to it, Mary,' said Walter. 'He's doing a good job.'

'I could have polished his shoes,' she insisted.

'You're a good shoe polisher,' said Walter diplomatically, 'but Wilf knows how they have to be.' Mischievously, he said, 'I hope Esme's a good dancer, Wilf. You won't want her treading on your toes after you've lavished so much spit and polish on those shoes.'

'I can take avoiding action, Dad.' He placed his concertina-folded bell bottoms on a chair and hooked his white front over the tapered end of the ironing board, ironing it flat. Next, he took his collar and reinforced the creases in it.

'Why do they have to be like that?' asked his mother.

'Regulations, Mum. That's all I know,' said Wilf, eyeing the creases in his collar before placing it with his trousers. His immaculately-pressed jumper hung from the picture rail, on a hanger.

When his uniform was ready to be worn, his mother, now resigned to the fact that her services were currently not required, said for the third or fourth time, 'We're very proud of you, Wilfred.'

'Thanks, Mum.' Her sentiment was due largely to a letter that had arrived for Wilf that day. He was a shade embarrassed by its contents, but he'd nevertheless allowed his mother to sew his father's spare ribbon on to his number one jumper. His numbers two and three could wait until his return to Portsmouth, when he would have access to a naval stores.

* * *

Now changed into his best uniform, Clive reversed up Penny's drive and parked outside the house. Penny must have seen or heard him arrive, because she opened the door and greeted him before he had time to ring the bell.

'Penny,' he said, 'you've put my beloved Swordfish to shame again. You look wonderful.'

'Thank you,' she said, accepting a discreet kiss, 'but I'm sure your aeroplane can do lots of things I can't.' She took her seat in the Wolseley and arranged her skirts so that he could close the door. When he was in his seat, she said, 'It's very kind of your father to let you use the car again.'

'This is my mother's doing. She's very persuasive, but my father gave way in the end because he couldn't bear the idea of my taking you out in anything less civilised. He's an old-fashioned soul.'

'You told me that last time. I bet he's a lot kinder than you make out.'

'He can be quite chummy when he hasn't got a pair of forceps in his hand.'

'Oh, you.' She gave up, knowing that behind his cynical façade Clive must be on good terms with his father. Changing the subject, she said, 'Your mother's lovely, isn't she?'

'You've noticed. Most people do.'

'I'm not surprised.'

'You wouldn't believe how, when I was at school, the masters' attitudes towards me changed on open days. They'd beat me within an inch of my life and treat me shamefully throughout the year, and then my mother arrived, and suddenly they couldn't be nice enough.' He shook his head in mock-disapproval. 'As they say in the American pictures, they were suckers for a pretty face. They forfeited any respect I ever had for them.' He pulled up at the bottom of the road and then turned towards Folkestone.

'Where are we going?'

'The Grand Hotel.'

'Wonderful.' Presently, she asked, 'Did your sister inherit your mother's looks?'

'Yes, along with my father's threatening manner, I'm afraid.'

'Clive,' she said, exasperatedly, 'I've been in your father's chair, and I can say confidently that he's not at all threatening.'

'Ah, but you see, he's a sucker for a pretty face, too. That's why he married my mother.'

With a heavy sigh, she said, 'You're hopeless. I wish you'd be serious, just for a minute.'

'All right,' he relented. 'Most people would say my sister is pretty, although I don't think she's quite as pretty as you.'

'Are you still being serious?'

'Yes, the minute's still ticking. To summarise, you and my sister are both pretty.'

'Thank you.'

'My mother, as you say, is beautiful, and my father isn't, but he's an all-round good hand, which compensates for a great deal.'

'Well done, Clive.' Penny sounded delighted. 'I knew you could be sensible.'

'I spend a lot of time being sensible, as I told you this afternoon. You must allow me a little time off.'

'I'm sorry, I forgot.'

'You're forgiven, Penny. I'll forgive you for anything. Let's have a glorious, frivolous evening. It'll help me to be serious when I need to be.' It was a timely suggestion, as he'd just turned into the carpark of the Grand Hotel.

* * *

When Esme opened the door, Wilf was suddenly tongue-tied and, afraid of looking silly, forced himself to speak. 'Esme, you're....' He was still searching for the right thing to say. Eventually, he said hopelessly, 'I was going to say, "As pretty as a picture", but you're prettier than that.' Now he felt foolish. Usually capable and confident, he was struggling to say what he felt. She looked so appealing in a dark-green, button-front dress that he was unusually speechless.

She smiled at the compliment. 'Thank you, Wilfred. You look very smart, too. Will you come in for a minute? My mum and dad want to meet you.'

'Yes, of course I will.' Removing his cap, he followed her past the blackout curtain and into a sitting room, where two middle-aged people sat, presumably waiting to meet him.

'This is Wilfred,' said Esme.

He shook hands with them. 'How do you do, Mr Daniels? How do you do, Mrs Daniels?'

'I believe you've known Esme for some time, Wilfred,' said Mr Daniels.

'That's right. We were at Wellesley Road Elementary School at the same time,' explained Wilf, 'but we only met again yesterday, at the teashop.'

'We just wanted to meet you,' Mr Daniels explained, 'because this is the first time Esme has been invited out since she lost Len.'

It seemed to Wilf that Esme's parents were extremely protective, and he was glad for her sake that they were. 'I know,' he said. 'Don't worry, she'll be safe with me.'

'I'm glad to hear it, Wilfred.' Mr Daniels shook his hand again.

'Enjoy yourselves,' said Mrs Daniels.

They took their leave, and Wilf offered Esme his arm, as he'd seen others do. It was a special moment for him, and felt that he was just recovering the power of speech, but Esme's mind was still on the conversation that had just taken place. 'They worry about me too much, you know,' she told him.

'I expect they can't help it.' That brief exchange had also given him cause to think. 'Have you any brothers or sisters, Esme?'

'No, there's only me. What about you?'

'I only had a brother. He died when he was three.'

'Oh, Wilfred.' She squeezed the arm she was holding. 'That's awful.'

'It was,' he agreed, 'but the reason I asked was, your mum and dad have seen the most terrible thing happen to their only daughter. It's not surprising they want to protect you.' Although he was too shy to say so, he felt much the same urge, and he'd only begun to know her properly since their meeting in the teashop.

'You're very thoughtful, Wilfred.'

'Am I?' It was news to Wilf, but being the down-to-earth chap he was, he was a stranger to self-appraisal. One thing he knew, however, was that he'd never been happy with his full Christian name. 'Everybody except my mum calls me "Wilf",' he said. 'Will you?'

''Course I will, if you want me to.' She laughed. 'I remember how I felt when I was being tormented about my name.'

They stopped at the kerb before crossing the High Street. 'I wish I'd known,' he said. 'I'd have stuck up for you.'

She laughed again. 'We were only five, maybe six, but I really believe you would.' She surprised him then by changing the subject and asking, 'Are you good at dancing?'

'I must be. I've got badges for it.' He showed her his good conduct badge. 'This one's for the foxtrot, and this one,' he said, pointing to the crossed rifles on his forearm, 'is for the waltz.'

'I don't believe you. What are they for, really?'

'The stripe is for staying out of trouble – I should get another one next year – and the one with the rifles on it is the Good Shooting Badge.

'I'm impressed. What's this one?' She was pointing to the ribbon his mother had sewn on so proudly that morning.

'That's the DSM,' he told her modestly. 'The letter came only this morning, telling me I'd been awarded it.'

'What does it stand for?'

He was embarrassed now. 'It's the Distinguished Service Medal.' Borrowing a remark his father had once made, he said, 'They had one left over, and they didn't know what to do with it, so they gave it to me to make me look smarter.'

'I don't believe you. Did they send you the medal as well as that ribbon?'

'No, there has to be a bit of a ceremony for that, when a senior officer, probably the Commodore of Portsmouth Barracks, will hand them out officially. This isn't really my ribbon,' he said, patting it with his free hand. 'It's one of my dad's that he doesn't need anymore.' He added, 'He got his in the last war.'

'So you and your dad are both heroes.'

'I'm not a hero, Esme. I just did what I had to do in Norway, so they've rewarded me for it.' He was trying desperately to think of something to say that would relieve him of his embarrassment, and he was thankful when they arrived at the entrance to the Temperance Hall, where they could already hear the band playing 'South of the Border'. Wilf showed the tickets to the official on the door and took Esme to the cloakroom, where they left her coat and hat and his cap. 'Let's grab this table,' he said, finding one that was vacant. What would you like to drink?' As its name suggested, the Temperance Hall was an unlicensed venue, so only soft drinks were available, and wartime restrictions meant that the range was more limited than usual.

'If they've got orange blossom, I'd like that, please. If they haven't, anything orangey would be nice.'

'It's a pity they can only sell goffers.'

'What are they?'

'Non-alcoholic drinks.'

'Oh, I'd never heard them called that before. I don't drink, anyway. I never have.'

It seemed to Wilf as he made his way past several dancing couples, that her tragic circumstances ensured that she hadn't had many opportunities to acquire bad habits.

There was, as yet, no queue at the bar, and he returned with an orange blossom cordial and an orange squash. It was better than nothing, and it was just potluck that the only dance that week was at a place run by teetotallers and frequented, apparently, by superstitious females. 'We haven't been here two minutes,' he said, 'and I've had my collar touched by half the girls in Sandbrook.'

'Do you mind?'

'Not really. The way things are, people need all the pleasure they can get. Good luck to them.' He was distracted when the bandleader announced 'A Nightingale Sang in Berkeley Square'. He asked, 'Would you like to dance?'

'Yes, please.'

He took her hand and led her on to the floor.

'This is the first time I've danced since I was… eighteen, I think.'

'Is it?' She seemed to be managing all right in spite of her lack of practice.

'Len didn't go in for this sort of thing. His favourite pastime was drinking.'

Wilf made no comment. Fishermen were generally regarded as ardent drinkers. They worked hard, often in difficult and dangerous conditions, and they naturally needed their relaxation. Len was presumably no different from most. He tried not to think about him, although it wasn't difficult when he was dancing with Esme. It was wonderful just to be in physical contact with her as they danced to the song that had won the affection of a whole generation. The vocalist sang, '*There was magic abroad in the air*', and that certainly seemed to be the case, at least from Wilf's point of view. It was a beautiful song at time when people treasured good things more than ever before.

At the end of the number, they applauded the band and the singer, who was no doubt doing her best.

'Do you remember the last day at school?' asked Esme when they returned to their table.

'The party? Yes, I remember it. We had dancing then, but it was Old Tyme dancing – the veleta and the military two-step.' He shook his head at the awfulness, as it seemed to him. 'The teachers were from another century.'

'I expect they would be. When you think of it, our mums and dads are.'

'Yes, it was a daft thing to say. I don't know why I said it.'

'You didn't dance with me, did you? I remember seeing you dance with Rosamund Healey.'

Wilf closed his eyes in embarrassment. 'Oh, Esme,' he said, 'why did you have to remember that?' Rosamund was the most unfortunate girl in the year and possibly the school, awkward and unpopular because she was so plain. 'She was crying because none of the lads wanted to dance with her. I just felt sorry for her, that's all.'

'I know, and I admired you for doing what you did.'

'I didn't know that.' Suddenly, he felt better about it.

'Did the other lads make fun of you?'

'For a while. The worst one was Alan Jackson. He didn't know when to stop.'

'Oh, that's awful. Now I think about it, I remember how horrible he could be.' Seemingly without thinking, she squeezed his hand. 'How long did you have to put up with that?'

'Only about two or three minutes, and then I took him outside and knocked seven bells out of him.'

'I don't blame you.'

'Would you have danced with me then, if I'd asked you?' He had to know.

''Course I would, you daft thing.'

'I wish I'd known that. I'll make up for it tonight.' The band had started another favourite from the previous year, 'They Can't Black-Out the Moon'. 'Would you like to dance again?' he asked.

'To make up for nineteen twenty-nine?' She smiled. 'Yes, I think we'd better.'

He took her in hold and they moved around the floor as if they'd always danced together. That was how it seemed to Wilf, and another thought that occurred to him was that, whilst the senior officer in charge of the evacuation at Dunkirk had recommended him for the DSM, an honour that had taken him completely unawares, a greater reward by far after the turmoil of Norway and Dunkirk was an evening spent with the girl he'd been too shy to speak to, let alone dance with, at the Wellesley Road leavers' party. He couldn't credit his good fortune.

* * *

Penny asked, 'Will you still be based at Manston?'

'No, it's back to Worthy Down for us, although it's bound to be a temporary posting. Just for now, though, the Channel's our first line of defence.' He laughed shortly.

'What's funny?'

'If you remember, there was a move, before the war, to dig a tunnel between England and France. The Government will be glad they gave up on that.'

'Oh don't, it doesn't bear thinking about. Let's dance instead.' The band were starting 'Red Sails in the Sunset'.

Taking her in hold, Clive said, 'I find this one difficult.'

'Do your best. That's all anyone can ask.'

'You sound like one of the masters at school.'

'None of our mistresses would have said that. They insisted on much more than our best.'

'I don't think I like the sound of your school, Penny.' He was actually trying to concentrate on fitting the foxtrot steps to the complex rhythm of the song, a task that he felt called for advanced mathematics as well as prodigious coordination.

'Our school motto was *"Contendunt virilliter ad excellentiam"*.'

'That's quite a mouthful. Go on, I'll buy it.'

'"Strive manfully for excellence".' She laughed. 'Can you imagine a hundred and eighty girls striving manfully?'

'Not without over-exciting myself, I must confess.'

'You're struggling with this dance, aren't you?'

'Yes.' There was no point in denying it.

'Slow, quick-quick slow, quick-quick slow....'

'I like it when you're masterful, even without striving.' Even so, it came as a relief to him when the number ended and they could take their seats.

'The problem is the triplet on the second beat,' said Penny. 'Taking two steps to a figure of three isn't the easiest thing to do.'

'Now you're being technical. Have you had musical training?'

'Yes, I strove manfully at the piano for more than ten years. I'd play more when I'm at home if I thought it would annoy my mother and my sister, but so far, I've seen no evidence of it.'

He sighed heavily. 'And you complain when I talk about my family.'

'Your parents are lovely, and for all I know, your sister probably is. If you ever feel like doing a swap, let me know.'

'All right. Anything you want to do is fine by me.' He could hide his feelings no longer, and he decided that it was a good time to give her the present. Taking a small, flat jewellery box from his pocket, he gave it to her.

'Is this the mystery gift?'

'Yes, it is. Open it,' he suggested, 'and the mystery will be solved.'

She removed the lid and stared at the brooch. It was a replica of an officer's cap badge, and it was mounted on a slender bar with a pin catch. 'It's lovely,' she said. 'You really shouldn't have. It's gold, isn't it?'

'Only fourteen carat.'

'But it's still exquisite. Thank you, Clive.' Looking around, she said, 'If we were alone, I'd kiss you, but that'll have to wait.'

'That's what it's about. It's a sweetheart's badge.'

'Really?' She seemed genuinely surprised. 'I've seen something similar among my grandmother's things.'

'They come in various forms, but they all say the same thing.'

'Don't keep me in suspense, Clive.'

He took a large breath. 'When I come home on leave and spend time with you, I feel like Robert Browning.' He hesitated, completely unused to baring his soul and therefore feeling quite unequal to the task. 'At least, Robert Browning expressed himself rather better, being a poet.'

She frowned in concentration, but clearly failed to see the point of the allusion. 'However manfully I strive on this occasion,' she said, 'I fail to understand. Do you mean you want to set a ladder beneath my window so that you can abduct me, the way he did with Elizabeth? Honestly, I can think of ways that don't involve ladders or upstairs windows.'

'If I had to, Penny, I'd do exactly that. What I was really trying to say in my prosaic, naval officer's way is that when we're together it's as if "God's in his Heaven – all's right with the world."'

She nodded and smiled. 'You're beginning to make sense.' She pinned the brooch to her dress and closed the catch, taking her hands away to show it to him.

'Do I have to spell it out?'

'Yes, I'd like you to do that. Spell it out in your prosaic, naval officer's way. However, for maximum effect, I'd like to hear you say it on the dance floor during a romantic number.' The song just beginning was 'Deep Purple.' She gave him her hand and let him lead her into the dance. 'It's a straight, split-common time, two uncomplicated beats in a bar,' she assured him, 'no triplets.'

Relaxing now to a rhythm he found undemanding, even if her description might have been in Greek, for all it meant to him, he kissed her softly on her neck and whispered the words she wanted to hear.

* * *

The dance ended inevitably with the waltz song 'Who's Taking You Home Tonight?' By this time, Wilf and Esme were dancing closer than ever. It had happened quite naturally, unconstrained by the austere influence of the hall and its trustees, and now the event was about to end. Reluctantly, they broke apart to applaud the band and singer. Though lacking in some respects, the latter had compensated for her lack of ability with a degree of zeal that alone deserved acknowledgement.

'It's been absolutely wonderful,' said Esme when they collected their things from the cloakroom. 'I haven't done anything like that for... donkeys' years.'

Wilf was conscious that it was the second time she'd said something of the kind, so he knew the evening had made a profound impression on her. As they left the blacked-out hall, he looked up at the clear sky and said, 'It's a pity we can't walk along the seashore.'

'Yes, it would be a bit prickly with all that barbed wire.'

'Not to mention the mines.'

'What are mines?' Her curiosity was almost childlike at times.

'Little bombs that they hide under the shingle. If somebody trod on one, he probably wouldn't live to regret it.'

That seemed to set her thinking. 'You must have seen some awful things at Dunkirk,' she said.

'Yes, and some good things, wonderful things. The evacuation was organised by experts. We lost a lot of ships, but even so, the "Andrew" did everybody proud.'

'Who's Andrew?'

'Sorry. I meant the Navy. It's what we call it. It wasn't just the Navy, though. There were others as well, lots of them, ordinary civilians like my dad and the retired admiral he works for. They took the admiral's boat and ferried evacuees from the beach to the destroyers.'

'Does your dad really work for an admiral?'

'A retired admiral. I was wary of him at first – what rating wouldn't be? But I'd no need to be. He's a good hand.'

'What you said about ordinary people taking their boats sounds unbelievable.'

'You had to be there,' he agreed. 'We had the job of taking soldiers from the town and herding them on to the mole, a sort of concrete breakwater they had to use after the pier was destroyed by bombing. Most of them were drunk and mutinous, and we had to threaten some of them at gunpoint before they started behaving themselves, but then, when we'd got all of them away, the rearguard, the soldiers who'd been holding the line, arrived. They were different again, proud and behaving like proper soldiers.' The memory was still fresh for him, and he found himself reliving it. 'The best sight of all,' he told her, 'was the Coldstream Guards. They didn't just file along the mole like the rest of them. They shouldered arms and marched to the destroyer that was waiting for them, as smart as only the Guards can be. It was a wonderful sight, and I'll never forget it.'

They were at the end of Esme's street, almost at the door, but Wilf stopped and led her into the nearest alley. 'Esme,' he said, 'I have to go back to Pompey on Friday.'

'Where's that?'

'Portsmouth. Can I see you again before I go?'

''Course you can. If you're leaving on Friday, it'll have to be tomorrow, won't it?'

'Yes, that's the only time there is. If I come for you at a quarter past six, we could maybe go to the pictures.'

'They're showing *Wuthering Heights* at the Picture Palace,' she said, further enthused. 'I haven't seen Laurence Olivier for ages, and Merle Oberon's in it as well.'

Wilf didn't care what the film was or who was in it. He just wanted to spend more time with Esme. 'All right. Would you like to do that?'

'Mm.'

'Thanks for coming tonight.'

'I've had a smashing time, Wilf.' She inclined her face for a goodnight kiss, and he moved forward unsteadily until, possibly sensing his awkwardness, she cupped his waist with her hands, as if in invitation. Still unsure of himself, he brushed her cheek with his lips, relishing the smoothness of her skin and the naïve intimacy of the occasion. He hesitated then, faltering, but conscious of her hands around his waist, her kissed her again. Like most people, he was aware of the convention that restricted intimate contact on a first assignation to a chaste kiss on the cheek, but he found himself drawn nevertheless to her slightly-parted lips. Again, she made no move to avoid him, and he kissed her fully, taking her in his arms. To his delight, far from objecting to his attentions, she seemed eager for them to continue, and he indulged himself in the exquisite softness of her lips.

After a moment of extended bliss, she said a little breathlessly, 'I have to go now. Thanks again for a lovely time.'

'Thanks for coming with me. I'll see you tomorrow at eighteen... six-fifteen, then?'

'Yes.'

He kissed her again and walked the short distance with her to her door.

18

FIRST CHOICE

Clive left for Worthy Down, and Penny packed her bag in readiness to report to the Royal Naval College, Greenwich on the following day, but not before she'd paid another visit to the boatyard. As ever, her grandfather was delighted to see her.

'Are you all set for your next adventure?' he asked.

'Packed and ready to go,' she confirmed.

'You're looking very happy, Penny. I can only imagine you both had an enjoyable day.'

'Day and evening,' she told him, opening her cardigan to show him her brooch.

'My word,' he said, 'that takes me back.' He admired it in detail, finally saying, 'He's a fine chap. If you're happy, so am I.'

'Oh, what a difference. Joan's been sniffy about it, I imagine because Charles never gave her anything like this, and Mum told me not to get carried away.' Remembering their conversation about Robert Browning, she said, 'I almost wish he would carry me away, except that I want to make a success of serving in the Wrens. After that, I'll gladly run away with him.'

He laughed good-naturedly. 'Bide your time, young lady. Don't do anything in a hurry.'

'I wouldn't do anything to embarrass you, Grandpop,' she said, hugging him.

'I know, but you'll have to excuse me, because I have to see Gregory about something.' Remembering, he said, 'His son Wilfred's been awarded the DSM, by the way.'

'Oh, good for him. Tell Walter I'm delighted, will you?'

'Of course. Meanwhile, I wish you the very best at Greenwich, and I expect to hear all about it in your letters.'

'Oh, you shall.' She stood on tiptoe to kiss him goodbye.

* * *

Clive reached Waterloo just as the twelve-oh-five to Portsmouth was about to leave. Boarding the train by the nearest door, he made for the first-class compartments. On his way, he came across an able seaman with a kitbag and a walking stick. He was trying to arrange the kitbag so that he could use it as a cushion to sit on, but he stopped briefly to salute Clive.

'Don't worry about that,' Clive told him. You've got enough problems. Can't you find a seat?'

'No, sir. All the third-class compartments are full.'

'Come with me. I'll find you a seat.'

The surprised sailor could only say, 'Aye, aye, sir.'

Clive led him along the corridor to a first-class compartment with three empty seats. Its passengers were all in civilian clothing. He opened the door and said, 'I'm bringing this man in because his injury makes it impossible for him to stand in the corridor.' He indicated an empty seat, and the sailor took it gratefully. Having recovered from their surprise, the other occupants continued to read their newspapers.

'It's kind of you to do this, sir,' said the rating. 'I was on crutches until two days ago.'

'Not at all. Where did this happen?'

'Dunkirk, sir.'

'And they've drafted you already.'

'Only to barracks, sir, awaiting draft.'

The compartment door opened, and the ticket collector said, 'Tickets, please.'

The other occupants offered their tickets to the collector, who punched them. He did the same to Clive's before asking, 'Have you got a first-class ticket, young man?'

The rating showed his ticket.

'This is a third-class ticket. What are you doing in a first-class compartment?'

'I brought him in,' Clive told him. 'He can't stand in the corridor in that state, and all the third-class seats are taken.'

The ticket collector shrugged. 'That's beside the point, sir. If he hasn't got a first-class ticket, he's not allowed to travel in this compartment. Come on, Jack. Off you go back to third-class, and don't try to pull any more fast ones.'

'Stay where you are,' said Clive, conscious that all eyes were now on him and that the rating was about to struggle to his feet. 'If it worries you so much,' he told the ticket collector, 'I'll give him my ticket and I'll stand in the third-class corridor, but if I have to do that, make no mistake, I shall write to the London and South-Western Railway, and tell them how one of their ticket collectors treats the men who are fighting for this country. This rating was seriously wounded in the Dunkirk evacuation, and I think he deserves better than to be treated as a fare dodger. It's up to you if you don't want to remember the name Newing for altogether the wrong reason.'

'Absolutely.' One of the other passengers lent his support, and the others nodded or murmured in agreement.

The ticket collector licked his lips. 'Well, sir, if you put it like that, I think I can stretch a point in this case.'

'A wise decision, Ticket Collector. If I were you, I'd punch his ticket and leave the poor man in peace.'

When the official had closed the door, the rating said, 'Thank you, sir. I didn't want to make any trouble.'

'There was none. You said you were heading for barracks. Are you going to HMS *Nelson*?'

'Yes, sir.'

'I imagine there'll be transport laid on from Pompey and Southsea Station.'

'Yes, sir.'

'Good, because I think you've suffered quite enough already.' He sat back and reflected on his leave, which had been more than usually enjoyable.

* * *

153

Once again, Wilf called for Esme, and they walked together to the Picture Palace, where Wilf surprised Esme by buying two balcony tickets.

'I've never been up there,' she said.

'It's nicer than downstairs,' he assured her. His main concern was to avoid the couples who frequented the rear stalls and whose activities would have been too embarrassing for words.

They took the stairs past the showcased still photographs of forthcoming attractions, and followed the usherette's torch beam to a vacant double seat. The supporting film, a western had just begun, but so far it didn't look all that promising. Wilf didn't mind; all that mattered to him was that he was with Esme. He reached for her hand, and she took his readily. He was content to hold her hand through the rest of the film.

The next item was the British Movietone News and, as Wilf had feared, they were still showing footage of the Dunkirk evacuation. The camera panned along a line of tea-drinking, sandwich-wolfing soldiers, each grinning and winking at the camera and using his free hand to give the absurd thumbs-up sign. Wilf lowered his head, closed his eyes and waited for it to go away.

'Are you all right, Wilf?' asked Esme, immediately concerned for his welfare.

'Fine,' he said, patting her hand. Happily, the newsreel turned to other matters of public interest, and he was able to watch, uninterested himself, but no longer nauseated.

At length, the lights came up, and so did the 'Girl With the Tray'.

'Can I get you an ice cream or something?' he offered.

'No, thanks, not so soon after I've eaten.'

It was a fair point. He reflected that the Girl With the Tray was an old joke. When he and his friends were youngsters, the ice cream seller in those days was a lady of generous frontage, and every time they saw a woman with a large bosom, someone would make a reference to the Girl With the Tray. It was a tired joke that refused to die, although it certainly wasn't something he would ever dream of mentioning to Esme.

'Why did you close your eyes when they showed the film about Dunkirk?' she asked.

'It wasn't what it looked like,' he explained. 'The newsreel people paid those blokes to smile and give the thumbs-up. It was an insulting way to treat exhausted men. They only wanted to eat and find somewhere to sleep, but Movietone News treated them like a freak show.'

Esme showed her sympathy as she usually did, by squeezing his hand. It was just one of the qualities that made her so delightful.

Eventually, *Wuthering Heights* began, they were told, on the bleak and windswept Yorkshire moors. Wilf had never been to Yorkshire, although he'd known a few Yorkshiremen in the service. They came from Sheffield, Leeds and other towns and cities that sounded very bleak indeed, so he accepted the setting and was soon absorbed by the story. He took Esme's hand again, stroking it occasionally with his thumb, but never enough to distract her from watching the film.

Compelling performances by Laurence Olivier and Flora Robson gave way to a flashback that established the vivid childhood relationships between Cathy, Heathcliff and Hindley, drawing Wilf and, if her rapt expression were an indication, Esme as well, into a rhapsody of make-believe. Wilf had never read Wuthering Heights – he'd scarcely read a book since leaving school – so he'd no idea how faithful the film was to the original story, but he didn't care. It was the perfect antidote to the mayhem and suffering he'd seen in recent weeks and, in spite of his normally down-to-earth nature, he couldn't help but be drawn in by the extravagantly romantic dramatisation.

The end of the film came all too soon and, after the National Anthem, they made their way to the exit. A drink wasn't a good idea, as Esme didn't drink, so Wilf thought quickly and said, 'As it's a clear night, why don't we get as close to the beach as we can, and walk along the bit we're allowed to walk on?'

'That would be really nice.'

They took one of the alleys that led to the coast road, and Esme clung to him, saying, 'I wouldn't normally come through here. It's too scary for words.'

'Nothing's going to happen to you while I'm here.'

'It's not just that. I just find it dark and scary.'

He put his arm round her and led her towards the patch of starlit sky that marked the end of the alley.

'That was a wonderful film,' she said.

'Yes.'

'I nearly cried at the end when the man mentioned the two sets of footprints in the snow.'

'Did it upset you?'

'No, silly. I nearly cried because it was so romantic.'

Unable to fathom her reasoning, Wilf could only accept it.

'I hadn't been to the pictures since....'

'You were eighteen,' he prompted.

'Len wasn't interested in anything like that. As long as he could have a drink, that was all he needed.' Suddenly she asked, 'Do you drink much, Wilf?'

'Not very much.' It was true. Wilf seldom drank in quantity. Lieutenant Soames had ordered the mainbrace to be spliced on arrival in Scapa Flow, and the combination of extreme tiredness and the double tot of rum had rendered Wilf almost helpless.

'I suppose it's all right if it doesn't cause problems. Does it make you bad-tempered?'

'No.' It seemed an odd question, but he decided not to pursue it.

'Just look at those stars,' she said, changing the subject abruptly as they emerged. 'They don't care that there's a war on. They'll go on twinkling whoever wins.'

Wilf couldn't imagine that a star was capable of taking sides, but he'd no wish to argue with her. 'I expect they have more important things to occupy them,' he said.

They turned to walk along the wired path. 'Esme,' he said, 'will you write to me?'

''Course I will.'

'I know your address. Mine's HMS *Nelson*, Portsmouth, but you need my official number and I haven't got anything to write it on.'

'I've got my diary and pencil,' she said, opening her bag. 'Here it is.' She took the slim pencil from its sheath and opened her diary at the back. 'Ready.'

'Leading Seaman – just write "LS" – W. T. Gregory. Have you got that?'

'Yes.'

'JX one eight two seven five nine. Have you got that?'

'JX one eight two seven five nine,' she confirmed.

'You're a quick writer.'

'I have to be,' she said, returning her diary to her bag. 'Customers get shirty if we take too long to write their order.' She took his arm again. 'What's your middle name?'

'Thomas.'

'That's all right. Mine's Cynthia.' She wrinkled her nose and said, 'My mum and dad just didn't think when they were choosing names.'

'"Cynthia" is all right, but I like "Esme" better.'

'You told me it's your favourite, didn't you?'

'Yes.' He wondered what she was going to say next.

'Do you mean that?'

'Yes.'

'It wouldn't be everybody's first choice.'

It was the last night of his leave, time was running out, and Wilf was conscious of a burgeoning sense of urgency that he'd never previously known. 'You're my first choice, Esme,' he told her, 'and the name came with you.'

Again, she asked, 'Do you really mean that?'

'If I didn't mean it, I wouldn't have said it.' The same urgency that had prompted his frank disclosure now made him take her in his arms and kiss her.

'That's the nicest thing anybody's said to me since....'

'Since you were eighteen?'

'No, before that.' They kissed again, and she said with a degree of contentment that was clearly evident, 'I feel so safe with you.'

Wilf was reminded of an earlier conversation. He asked, 'When Len had been drinking, did it make him bad-tempered with you?'

'Yes.' After a little more thought, she said, 'It's hard to stop loving somebody, but it gets easier when you stop liking them.'

Wrapping his arms round her, he held her close, unable to fathom how anyone could hurt her, and knowing he never would.

She emerged from a long and meaningful kiss to ask, 'What's the time?'

He peered at the luminous dial of his wristwatch and said, 'It's nearly twenty-two forty-five.'

'What?'

'I'm sorry. It's a quarter to eleven.'

'I should be getting back.' Her regret was clearly evident.

'All right.'

They returned arm in arm the way they'd come, along the wired fence and through the alley.

When they were almost at Esme's door, they stopped again where they had the previous evening, and they kissed until the time came for Esme to go indoors.

'I'll write to you,' she promised.

19

APPOINTMENTS AND DRAFTS

Wilf was returning from breakfast, when a regulating petty officer saw him and said, 'Leading Seaman Gregory. I was just coming to find you. You're wanted in the draft office.'

'Thanks, RPO.' He turned and walked to the draft office, wondering what the service had in store for him. He would soon find out. He was in a good mood, having just received a letter from Esme, and he hoped the draft wasn't bad news.

When he arrived, the petty officer at the first desk shuffled through his papers and found the appropriate draft order. 'Leading Seaman Wilfred Thomas Gregory JX one-eight-two-seven-five-nine,' he said.

'That's right, PO.'

'You're from Kent, aren't you?'

'Yes, PO.'

'Good news, then.'

'Is it Chatham, PO?' That really would be good news.

'No, it's a new place they're setting up at Dover harbour as a base for coastal forces. They haven't commissioned it yet, but when they do it'll be called HMS *Wasp*. You're to report to the main gate there by seventeen hundred today. You'll find it at what used to be the Lord Warden Hotel. A tiddley place indeed.'

'Thanks, PO.' It sounded very odd, but it had one tremendous advantage, even over Chatham, and that was that it was only fifteen miles or so from home and Esme.

'That's all I can tell you, but you'll find out what's what when you get there. Here are your documents and travel warrant. Carry on.'

'Thanks, PO.' He set off back to the messdeck to pack his kitbag.

When he arrived, he found a rating who was struggling with his bedding. A walking stick stood propped against the locker, and the lad was obviously in some difficulty. He realised then that he recognised him from *Wrathful*. 'Craddock,' he said, 'what are you doing here?'

'Hello, Hookie. I don't know. You know how they move blokes around for no reason. Maybe it's because I'm unfit for duty.'

'What happened, mate?'

'I copped a load of shrapnel at Dunkirk. I've been on sick leave and I'm just loafing until somebody decides what to do with me.'

'Here,' said Wilf, picking up a mattress cover and unfolding it, 'let me give you a hand-out to make a "biscuit" with your bedding.'

'That's big of you, Hookie. You won't believe this, but when I got the train down from Waterloo, there wasn't a seat to be had.'

'I can believe that, Craddock.'

'No, the thing is, I was trying to make the best of things on the corridor, and this officer comes along, a lieutenant in the Fleet Air Arm. He says, "Come in this compartment, sailor, and sit down." Well, it was a first-class compartment, but he insisted, an' when the ticket collector came round wantin' to chuck me out, the officer didn't half give him a bottle. He said, "This man's been wounded, fightin' for 'is country, an' this is how you treat 'im." I couldn't believe it.'

'Well, good for him. Pass us that pillow, Craddock.'

'He told the ticket collector his name an' all, when he was layin' it on the line. I've good cause to remember it. It was Newing, Lieutenant Newing.'

'Chuck us your counterpane. Now I think of it, there's a Lieutenant Newing in my hometown – well, the posh part. He's a pilot. I've seen him about the place.'

'Well, wherever he lives, he's a good hand.'

Wilf wrapped the folded counterpane immaculately around the biscuit of bedding and walked over to his locker. 'I've got a draft to Dover,' he said. 'That's where I'm off now.'

Craddock frowned. 'There isn't a naval establishment in Dover,' he said.

'Not yet there isn't, but there soon will be.'

* * *

Wren officer training, or the 'Knife and Fork Course', as it was known, at Greenwich occupied only a few weeks. Many described its purpose as simply to instruct Wren ratings in the art of behaving as officers and ladies. For many, including Penny, it was a total nonsense, but rules were there to be obeyed, and she and the rest of her intake went about their duties cheerfully, because that was the only way the service allowed.

The time came for them to collect their new uniforms. A leading airman photographer, suitably chaperoned, as all male personnel had to be, took the official photographs for the benefit of the newly-commissioned officers' families or, in Penny's case, her grandfather and Clive. There was a passing-out parade and ceremony with a brief period of leave before each officer reported to her first appointment, which, in Penny's case, was HMS *Pembroke*, Chatham.

She arrived home to learn that her grandfather was at the Sea Cadet Centre, sailing being curtailed because of the minefield that protected the south-east coast, so she arranged to visit him the next day, reconciling herself to an afternoon and evening with her family, with Joan and Charles also present.

As she'd feared, her father was soon in conversation with Charles about financial mysteries, while her mother and Joan preferred matters relating to maternity. Penny, who was interested in neither, was relieved when the telephone rang, and she went into the hall to answer it.

'Hello.'

'Penny, darling.'

'Clive!' As distractions came, he had no competition.

'I thought I might catch you at home. I just want to pat you on the back.'

'Thank you, darling. I don't know that I've achieved all that much. It was a very short course, and it involved a lot of flannel, but I've sent you a photograph, anyway.'

'Oh, bless you. That reminds me of something else. Would you like a signed photo of Vivien Leigh?'

'Gosh, has she joined your squadron, now?'

'Not quite, but she's joining Larry in married quarters, now that they're official and respectable, although how long it'll last, I've no idea – their stay, I mean, not their marriage – he's all set to take part in another film, set in Canada, I believe.'

'That would be wonderful. Yes, please. Vivien Leigh's lovely.'

'So are you, my love.'

'Oh, Clive. You're full of it, but yours is the first friendly voice I've heard since…. No, that's not true. I spoke to Mrs Hogben this afternoon.'

'Who's Mrs Hogben?'

'Grandpop's cook and housekeeper. She's lovely.'

'I'm glad. Anyway, darling, I know you can't tell me on the phone where you're appointment is, but let me know when you write to me.'

'Of course. We can be much chattier, then.'

He hesitated, no doubt picking up the clue. 'Yes, that's true.'

'I'll let you know.'

'Time's nearly up. I just wanted to congratulate you.'

'Thank you, darling. I love you.'

'I love you too. 'Bye.'

''Bye.'

Penny put the receiver down. It had been all too brief, but it was still wonderful to hear his voice again. She rejoined the others in the drawing room.

'Presumably that was either your grandfather or Lieutenant Newing,' said her mother.

'Clive, actually. He's sending me a signed photograph of Vivien Leigh to add to the others,' she told her happily.

'What others?' demanded Joan, whose questions inevitably sounded like an interrogation, especially when directed at her younger sister.

'If you must know, Laurence Olivier and Ralph Richardson.'

'The story doing the rounds,' said Charles, adopting his familiar smirk, 'is that Olivier tried to join the RAF, but he failed the pilot's test, so he had to join the Navy instead. I gather they're not as choosey as the RAF.'

'He's too clever for the RAF,' said Penny. 'He would have embarrassed them.'

'Penelope,' said her father, who was probably impatient to resume his conversation with Charles about the financial situation, 'that was very rude. I think you should apologise to Charles.'

162

'It was also uncalled for,' said Penny's mother, closing ranks, as usual.

'Fair's fair, Mum. Charles was being unfair to someone who wasn't here to defend himself and, as Laurence Olivier was kind enough to send me a signed photograph, I took up the cudgels on his behalf.'

'I doubt if he knows you exist,' said Joan, joining the pack.

'Of course he does. Clive asked Ralph Richardson and him for those photos, and he told them who they were for. They were only too happy to oblige.' It was the first fun she'd had in ages and she was enjoying herself.

'I still say you were very rude,' said her mother.

'I was only sticking up for Laurence Olivier,' insisted Penny. 'I suspect Charles has a down on him because he's a mere pilot. He wouldn't be half so rude about him if he knew how many pennies make up an airman's wage.'

'And that,' said Penny's mother, 'will be quite enough. I don't know what's got into you since you went to that place in London, but I'll thank you to remember your manners.'

'And my place, presumably.'

'Yes,' said Joan from the ringside.

'Anyway,' said Charles, trying artlessly to change the subject, 'we haven't seen your new uniform, Penelope. Where is it, for goodness' sake?'

'It's in my wardrobe, where it will stay until I take up my first appointment.'

Her mother intervened with a deep sigh. 'Don't encourage her, Charles. She's obviously in one of her silly, childish moods. Let's talk about something else.'

'Yes,' said Penny getting up to leave the room, 'you could carry on discussing either taxation or lactation. Do be careful not to confuse the two.'

* * *

Wilf reported to the Paymaster's Office at HMS *Wasp* with his paybook and movement order.

'That's fine, Gregory,' the paymaster lieutenant told him, handing him the familiar station card. 'Your draft is to ML Ninety-Seven, and you'll find her tied up alongside Admiralty Pier. That's on this side of the harbour.'

'Thank you, sir. Where have I to report for joining routine?'

'Joining routine?' The paymaster laughed. 'You've just completed it. Things are very informal here.' Smiling at Wilf's incomprehension, he said, 'Carry on, Leading Seaman Gregory.'

'Aye, aye, sir. Thank you, sir.' Still coming to terms with a highly unusual naval establishment based in what, until recently, had been a luxurious hotel, Wilf retraced his route, leaving the building and searching the crowded moorings for his draft. He found ML97, the sixth vessel in the row. There was no quartermaster on the gangway and she appeared to be deserted. He stepped on board and called, 'Below!'

A few seconds later, a tall petty officer with a weathered complexion and a stern expression appeared at the head of a ladder and asked, 'Who are you?'

'JX one eight two seven five nine Leading Seaman Gregory, PO, come aboard to join.'

'Good, I've been expecting you.' The petty officer offered his hand. 'I'm PO Rankin, Cox'n of this ship.'

'How do you do, Cox'n?' Wilf shook his hand.

'Well, you've found ML Ninety-Seven, a Fairmile Type "A" motor launch, one hundred-and-ten feet overall, beam seventeen feet, five inches; displacement sixty tons. Her top speed is twenty-five knots and her armament is one Hotchkiss three-pounder quick-firing gun aft, two single three-oh-three Browning machine guns forrard on pedestals, and twelve depth charges. Her complement is two officers and, apart from you and me, twelve ratings, none of whom knows his arse from the officers' heads. We are the only real sailors aboard this ship, Gregory, you and me, and it is our job to play nursemaid to everyone from the Jimmy down to the youngest under-age sprog on board. The captain's RN, but the Navy's attitude towards coastal forces means it won't be long before they replace him with a Wavy Navy officer. What's your history?'

'*Excellent*, *Carlisle*, *Wrathful* and the Dunkirk landing party, Cox'n.'

'I remember now. DSM and twice mentioned in dispatches, right?'

164

'Right, Cox'n.' Wilf was afraid his superior was going to hold his record against him, but the Coxswain surprised him.

'I'm glad to welcome you aboard, Gregory. This ship and its company need experienced men, believe me. Most of them are as keen as mustard, but they haven't a bloody clue, so it's up to you and me to give 'em the benefit of our training and experience. As the one and only leading hand, you'll be expected to oversee matters of seamanship, train the gun crews and take your turn with me at the wheel. It's very important that each man knows more than one skill, because the enemy's not averse to thinning out the numbers. Okay so far?'

'Yes, Cox'n.' For all the petty officer's rapid patter, Wilf suspected he was in the company of a sound and reliable senior rating.

The PO nodded. 'Have a good look around the ship and then find yourself a bunk in number two mess, Hands to Supper is piped at eighteen hundred. Muster on board at oh eight hundred tomorrow.'

'Right, Coxswain.' Wilf set about familiarising himself with the smallest ship he'd ever served in. He needed to be conversant with its layout and every detail within it.

* * *

The pilots and observers waited to be 'told off'. Soldiers and airmen were briefed, but sailors, including officers, were told off. The term had been in use since Nelson's time and had served the Navy so well that no one could see any reason for changing it.

Their patience was rewarded when the Commander (Flying), attended by two other officers including a serious, bespectacled lieutenant, whom the aircrew knew to be a meteorologist, entered the compartment. A leading airman photographer completed the ensemble.

'Good afternoon, gentlemen.'

There was a polite chorus of 'Good afternoon, sir.'

'I realise you've done very little night flying recently, but RAF Coastal Command seem to think you're capable of anything. I suppose that's quite an accolade and, yes, we are still supporting them in their operations, which currently include strikes against the invasion barges being mustered in the Channel ports.' At this stage, one of his entourage nodded to the photographer, who illuminated the screen behind Commander (F) with a photograph showing a row of barges moored by the bows or the stern, because it was impossible to tell the difference, to a jetty. 'Blenheim bombers of Coastal Command are currently bombing such targets in Calais and Boulogne,' he told them, 'whereas this photograph was taken over Dieppe.'

'We can only imagine,' said one of the others, who Clive now recognised as an intelligence officer, 'that the barges are there only temporarily, and that in the event of an invasion attempt they would be transferred to Calais or Boulogne in order to make the shortest possible crossing.'

'It's a cheering thought,' said Commander (F) with a modest smile, 'that even the shortest crossing in those flat-bottomed barges would be likely to render their occupants so seasick as to be unfit for action on reaching the beaches.' The thought was evidently so cheering that the assembled aircrew allowed themselves a moment of laughter. When it had died down, Commander (F) continued. 'Tonight's target will be those barges at Dieppe. Swordfish One F and Two F will carry flares and a one thousand pound load of high explosive bombs. The rest will each carry a full load of HE bombs.' He and the others went on to furnish details of the operation.

20

Dead Men's Shoes

One by one, the six Swordfish aircraft took off from the tarmac runway and climbed to 7,000 feet, where they formed up and took a south-easterly course across the Channel. With a full bombload, their maximum speed was about 85 knots, which made the flight to Dieppe an hour and a half, and the return journey, for those fortunate enough to evade the anti-aircraft defences, about an hour.

The two flights continued through the patchy cloud that was forecast. A little more cover would have been welcome on such a strike, but the weather, as always, was not negotiable, and Clive, like the others, kept a lookout for enemy aircraft. It was inconceivable that the Nazis should be preparing for invasion and not protecting their fleet against possible air attack. As the force approached Dieppe, however, it seemed that the threat was not to come from the enemy's twin-engined fighters, but from anti-aircraft fire, which erupted seemingly from all directions, temporarily blinding the aircrew with its brilliance. Even so, the squadron commander, followed by Clive, chose his moment, diving on the crowded harbour and releasing flares and bombs.

As he pulled out of his dive, Clive felt a massive jolt and saw that the tip of his starboard lower wing was reduced to shreds. Bill had also seen it, because he rapped Clive on the shoulder and pointed to it. Meanwhile, Clive continued to climb between the crimson bursts of the flak and the brilliant white of the star shells. Risking a glance over his shoulder, he saw at least one Swordfish fall like a flaming torch, and search as he would, he was unable to see the squadron commander. Still gaining altitude, and with the torn canvas of his damaged wing flapping madly in the slipstream, he looked around for the others. Eventually, he levelled out beyond the range of the anti-aircraft fire and searched again. Bill tapped him on the shoulder again and pointed to two Swordfish now taking up station astern of them. The squadron commander and presumably two others must have been shot down. Bill bellowed a magnetic course via the Gosport tube, and with the familiar sickening feeling of loss, Clive set it on the verge ring of his compass and led the remaining two aircraft back to Worthy Down.

* * *

On the command, 'Let go forrard, let go aft', Wilf oversaw the casting off of the bow line and then the stern rope. Next to go were the 'springs' that inhibited movement ahead and astern while the ship was moored alongside. He had two concerns. One was that the order was carried out promptly and efficiently, and the other was that the inexperienced ratings involved managed the task without injuring themselves. When he saw that the ordinary seaman on the stern rope was nursing a burned palm and fingers, he said, 'You'll let go a bit quicker next time, won't you? Get a dressing on it. Good lad.' The injured man was one of the gun crew Wilf would be training once the ML reached open water.

By the time the ship was in a position to practise gunnery, some of the ratings were green with seasickness. The ML was notoriously lively at sea, and few of the recruits had any sea time to their credit. The best plan was to keep them busy. With one training the gun, one on the elevating gear, one loading and another 'laying' or aiming the gun, he called their attention.

'This is the Hotchkiss three-pounder, quick-firing gun,' he told them. 'It gave faithful service in the last war until it was replaced by the Vickers three-pounder, and it still packs a punch. However, it's only as quick-firing as it can be reloaded and laid. In skilled hands, it can fire thirty rounds per minute, one every two seconds. That's something to work towards, isn't it? Now, this is how you open the breech. You stand to one side, or the spent shell case will hit you where you daren't show your mother, and you won't like it. Neither will she when they send you home with your unmentionables flattened like pennies.' For the first time, they forgot their seasickness and laughed at his warning. 'It fires a fixed shell with a lyddite charge. That means that the ammunition is all in one nice, big piece, so you've no excuse for losing it, and the charge means it'll go off with a bloody big bang, so be prepared. Now, load!' He watched the rating insert a shell into the breach and stopped him before he could close it. 'All the way in.' Then, satisfied that the shell was safely loaded, he allowed the rating to close the breech. 'Now, gunlayer,' he said, pointing to the trigger grip, 'let's pretend for now that the gun's laid to your satisfaction. Shoot!'

The nervous rating squeezed the firing lever and leapt back in shock when the gun fired.

'There,' said Wilf, pointing to the splash where the shell hit the sea and exploded. 'You've just sent a nasty Nazi supply ship to the bottom of the briny oggin. How do you feel about that?'

Seasickness forgotten for the moment, they laughed at Wilf's playful delivery and set about loading and firing until the process became almost automatic.

'It's all a matter of drill,' Wilf told them. 'Laying, loading and firing is just drill, and now we're going to work on the first bit, which is laying the gun. After that, we'll just keep on practising until you're so good that Lord Nelson himself would have been proud of you.' Wilf's methods were very different from the screamed and bellowed obscenities, insults and threats he remembered from Whale Island, but he reckoned his new, hostilities-only charges would respond better to encouragement than to bullying. It was one aspect of naval training that was probably due for an overhaul and, in any case, gunnery training aboard ML97 was his domain and no one else's.

* * *

'Of course, we shan't know for at least a month which of our aircrew have been taken prisoner,' said Commander (F).

Clive said, 'I saw one crew that didn't stand a chance of getting out, sir.'

'Do you know which aircraft it was, Newing?'

'No, sir,' said Clive wearily, 'All I could see were flames.'

'Anyone else?'

'I saw one, sir,' said one of the observers. 'Whether or not it was the same as Newing saw, I've no idea, sir, but it was like something in a Brock's benefit. I've never seen anti-aircraft fire like it.'

Clive nodded. That had been his impression, too.

'Well, as senior flight commander, Newing, you will now take over the remaining sub-flight.'

'Aye, aye, sir.' Clive tried to sound keen.

'I'll let you know as soon as I can how effective the strike was. In the meantime, you'd better all secure and get some rest. Dismiss, everyone.'

The depleted group of pilots and observers headed for their quarters to climb into their bunks and indulge in merciful sleep. Now charged with leading the survivors, however, Clive found sleep elusive. Instead, he took out his pen and notepaper, and began writing a letter.

Dearest Penny,

I hope you're settling into your new appointment, although it's early days yet. Still, there's no harm in wishing you well.

What a leave that was! You know, I catch myself thinking what a shame it is that I couldn't bottle the day and evening we spent together, so that at odd times I could remove the stopper and enjoy it all over again. Looking at it sensibly, however, I'm reminded that the contents of bottles tend to lose their potency after a while, whereas memories never really fade, and they can be evoked at any time. One such memory that I intend to keep forever is that of dancing to 'Deep Purple', when I overcame my prosaic, tongue-tied, naval officer's way and told you how I really felt. If it's at all possible, I'll find a way of seeing you before I go to my next posting, whenever and wherever that turns out to be. Meanwhile, in the words of the song, 'Button up your overcoat....' Take great care, and we'll be together again. I'd write more, but I'm afraid my eyes are closing. I'll write again soon when I can stay awake.

All my love,
Clive XX[n]

* * *

During the afternoon, Wilf conducted a training session on the Browning .303 machine guns. With enemy vessels operating in the

Channel, they might be needed sooner than the new entries realised. Repeatedly, he took them through reloading, deflection shooting – because most of their efforts would be against moving targets – and the clearing of jams, until they were reasonably confident. As with the three-pounder, only frequent and regular practice would turn ratings who until recently had been factory workers, farm labourers, bank clerks, schoolteachers and postmen into proficient gunners.

Eventually, it was Wilf's turn to try his hand at a skill he thought he'd left behind in seamanship training, when the call came for him to join the cox'n in the wheelhouse. It was imperative that, as the only leading seaman in the ship's company, he could take over the wheel immediately, should it become necessary.

'I haven't taken a wheel for years, Cox'n.'

'You'll be fine. Report to the bridge,' the cox'n told him.

'Wheelhouse, bridge.'

The captain's voice answered down the voice pipe, 'Bridge.'

'Leading Seaman Gregory taking over the wheel, sir.'

'Good. Steer zero nine three, Gregory.'

'Zero nine three, sir.' Wilf checked the course on the compass. 'Course is north nine three east, sir.'

'Very good.'

After a while, the order came to change course to zero eight five.

'Zero eight five, sir. Course is north eight five east, sir.'

'Very good.'

The cox'n nodded encouragingly. 'Always repeat the order and then report that you've carried it out,' he said. 'That way, if there is a mistake, it's the skipper's and not yours.'

'Right-o, Cox'n.'

A new voice came down the voice pipe. 'Bridge – wheelhouse.' It sounded as the youthful first lieutenant was now being put through his paces.

'Wheelhouse, sir.'

'Half ahead together.'

'Half ahead together, sir.' Wilf put his hand on the engine room telegraph, swung it both ways to attract the PO Mechanic's attention and turned it to 'Half Ahead'. The engine room answered, and Wilf reported, 'Engines are half ahead together, sir.'

'Very good.'

They continued on their way, and the cox'n said, 'The skipper will take over soon, because we're about to enter harbour.'

Sure enough, the captain spoke again. 'Slow ahead together. Port fifteen.'

Wilf made the necessary changes and answered, 'Engines are slow ahead together. Fifteen of port wheel on, sir.'

'Very good. Hard a-port.'

'Hard a-port, sir. Wheel's hard a-port, sir.'

Wilf was expecting the cox'n to take over the wheel, but he simply kept a careful watch, nodding when Wilf carried out each order. Eventually, with the ship in its berth, the captain called down, 'Finished with engines. Well done Gregory.'

'Thank you, sir. Finished with engines, sir.'

'Well done,' said the cox'n. 'I was going to take over and bring her in, but you looked so confident, I decided to leave you to it.'

'Thanks, Cox'n. It was a reminder of how those sprogs on the guns must have felt earlier. It doesn't do any harm to be reminded about these things.'

The cox'n grinned. 'I reckon the Jimmy was sweating a bit, an' all. The poor kid can't be much more than twenty-one.'

It was a nerve-wracking business, but it was the same for everyone. At any time, key members of the crew could be killed or wounded so that they were unable to carry on, and it was essential that there were others trained and ready to step in.

* * *

The first of the prefabricated motor launches had arrived at the boatyard and, with the aid of the seemingly exhaustive instructions that came with it, Walter had detailed various workmen to each role.

'It's just like a Meccano set, really,' one of them said.

'Except Meccano has holes in it, an' that's the last thing the Navy wants,' said another, helping his mates set up one of the formers that would help create the shape of the hull.

'My lad's serving in one of these, now,' Walter told them. He'd received Wilf's first letter from Dover that morning.

'How does he feel about it?' asked Arthur, who couldn't resist joining the group in the workshop.

'He seems happy enough, sir, but he could only tell me about it in general terms because of security.'

'Of course. I imagine he'll be a lynchpin in a ship of that size.'

'He's the only killick, sir and, apart from the captain, he and the cox'n are the only proper-trained sailors in the ship's company, although I reckon the Wavy Navy will come into its own, as it did in the last war.'

'Let's hope for the best, Chief.'

Walter cast a critical eye on the way the former was lined up and, satisfied that the men knew what they were doing, stepped back again. 'How's Miss Dowland making out in her new draft, sir?' Realising his mistake, he said hurriedly. 'I mean her new appointment, sir.'

'Of course you do. I've no idea, Chief. I've yet to hear from her, but I've no doubt she'll be fine.'

* * *

Some would say that Penny had been thrown in at the deep end. In the temporary absence of a Wren second officer, she'd been made Duty Officer in the WT Office, but she was happy enough. As long as she had a PO Wren to tell her where things were kept and give her the inside information about certain ratings, she was confident that she could manage the job adequately. PO Telegraphist Stanhope had given her that confidence, and she was ever grateful to him for his superb training. Since the fall of France, the war seemed to have assumed a new urgency. There was no more silly talk of a 'phoney war', and she was ready to play her part.

21

LEARNING THE ROPES

The ship's loud hailer clicked and the captain addressed the crew. 'We're ordered to rendezvous with a convoy off Eastbourne and escort it to Ramsgate,' he told them. The greatest threats are from U-boats and aircraft. The Luftwaffe have been making a nuisance of themselves with our Channel convoys, so keep a sharp lookout.'

'If the convoy is attacked by Stukas,' Wilf told the ratings on the Browning machine-guns, 'don't waste ammunition by trying to hit them when they're diving. You don't stand a chance.'

'What then, Hookie?' asked Brewer, one of the keenest of the ratings clustered on the deck.

'Wait until they've dropped their bombs and, always provided they haven't hit us, go for the buggers when they're climbing. That's when they're slow, awkward and at their most whatsit....' He couldn't think of the word he wanted.

'Vulnerable,' suggested Brewer.

Wilf was impressed. 'If you turn out to be as good with a Browning as you are with words,' he said, 'you'll be all right, Brewer. What was your civvy job?'

'I was a newspaper reporter.'

'I'd be inclined to keep quiet about that, if I were you, or the skipper might have you writing his reports for him.' He went aft to speak to the ratings on the depth charges. With the U-boat threat, they would also need to be alert. Wilf was rapidly becoming used to his role as what amounted to bosun's mate. He found it surprisingly satisfying.

* * *

Esme's employer, Mrs Parker, had seemed strangely distant of late, although Esme had never found her particularly friendly. At closing time, however, she emptied the till as usual, but then called Esme over and gave her a week's wages.

'Yes,' she said in answer to Esme's look of surprise, 'I know it's not Saturday, but I'm having to close the shop. With so many people leaving Sandbrook it's not worth my while staying open.'

'Thank you, Mrs Parker.' It was all Esme could think of to say. In the space of a moment she'd lost her job, and there was very little likelihood of her being able to find alternative employment in the town, as the teashop was the only one of its kind in Sandbrook.

'I'm sorry I have to do this, because you've been an excellent worker, and I hope you find something soon.' She'd obviously given the matter some consideration, because she went on to say, 'One place you could try is the British Restaurant in Folkestone.'

'Thank you, Mrs Parker. I'll try there.' The British Restaurants were a new development, a means of providing working people with unrationed, wholesome meals at cost price. Working in one of them in whatever capacity would be better than no job at all.

The next morning, she caught an early bus into Folkestone, walked into the British Restaurant, and asked to see the person in charge of the kitchen.

A large woman of florid countenance came to the door to ask what she wanted.

'I'm looking for work,' Esme told her. 'I was waiting at table at the teashop in Sandbrook, but now it's closed I need a job.'

The woman gave her a rough smile but shook her head. 'There's no vacancies here,' she said.

Esme couldn't disguise her disappointment. 'Thank you for seeing me,' she said. 'I'm sorry I've taken up your time.'

'That's all right, dear. Just a minute.' It was as if she'd remembered something, and she disappeared into the kitchen, leaving Esme on the doorstep. She re-emerged after a few minutes, with an encouraging smile, and said, 'They want somebody in Dover. If you get along there now, you might be able to grab the job before somebody else does.'

'Thank you. I will.'

She hurried to the railway station for the twenty-minute journey to Dover.

* * *

After a little less than three hours, the MLs rendezvoused with the convoy and took up station on either beam. The escort consisted of the elderly '*S*' Class destroyer HMS *Sandfly* and themselves. With ten unarmed merchantmen to protect, it was the first time they'd felt important, and that feeling was to be reinforced very soon.

Within twenty minutes of their rendezvous, the senior officer flashed, 'Aircraft approaching from south. Open fire when in range.'

They waited and, sure enough, a group of dark specs appeared to the south. As they made their approach, Wilf identified them as a force of Stukas with a fighter escort of Messerschmidt BF109s.

'Remember what I said,' he told the machine-gunners. For the time being at least, the three-pounder would simply hurl explosive into the sky, hopefully causing the enemy aircrews some disquiet. As far as the MLs were concerned, the main defence would rest with the Brownings.

As soon as the Stukas came within range, the captain gave the order to open fire. *Sandfly* and ML98 were already firing, but Wilf told his men to hold their fire. Bombs came showering down, some near-missing the merchant ships and, as the Stukas pulled out and began to climb, he shouted to them to open fire. The starboard gunlayer was aiming too close to the aircraft, his bullets falling astern of it, and Wilf rushed over to correct his aim. At that point, another Stuka began to pull out, and he returned to the port Browning, where Brewer was making the same mistake. Taking a shoulder strap in each hand, he turned the surprised gunlayer further to port and shouted, 'Fire!' He was a little too late, and the bullets fell astern of the Stuka. As the next one released its bombs, however, he positioned Brewer to fire a deflection ahead of the climbing aircraft. 'Go on,' he shouted, 'give him the rest of the magazine!' Brewer fired and was rewarded when he saw the Stuka's tailplane disintegrate. 'Good lad,' shouted Wilf, 'you got him!' Realising that the magazine was empty, he turned to the loader and shouted, 'Reload!'

Meanwhile, the stricken dive-bomber hit the surface, but it was only when the attack was over that Wilf noticed the two enemy airmen in the water. They were the only casualties, the merchantmen having avoided the bombing, and scrambling nets were thrown over the side to pick them up.

The order came, 'Leading Seaman Gregory to the bridge!' Wilf thought he knew what the captain had in mind, and his suspicion was confirmed when he reported to him.

'Leading Seaman Gregory, I'm naturally delighted that the port Browning got a Stuka, but I was less than pleased that you took so long to respond to my order to open fire.'

'I'm sorry, sir.' Wilf explained his tactic, and the captain looked at the first lieutenant. As he did so, he grinned broadly. 'Well,' he said, 'we live and learn. It makes perfect sense, of course.'

It seemed to Wilf that he was extremely fortunate to have found a captain with an open mind, but he had to make one important observation. 'The Stuka was down to Ordinary Seaman Brewer, sir, not me.'

'Point taken, Gregory. Dismiss, and well done, anyway.'

'Thank you, sir. Aye, aye, sir.'

* * *

Esme got off the train and had to ask for directions to the British Restaurant, which was fortunately not far from Dover Priory Station. In the distance, she could make out the Lord Warden Hotel, where she knew Wilf was now based. What opportunities there might be for them to meet she had no idea, but simply to be based in the same town would be exciting, as long as she could find a job there.

She knocked on the kitchen door and opened it. A woman in a wraparound pinafore saw her and asked, 'What do you want, young lady?'

'I'm looking for work, and they told me at the British Restaurant in Folkestone that you had a vacancy in the kitchen.'

The woman examined her from head to toe. Finally, she asked, 'Can you peel spuds and prepare veg?'

'Yes.'

'Right, we'll see how you get on. The last one was a dead loss. Can you start straight away?'

'Yes.'

'Okay, I'll get you a pinny and show you what to do. What's your name?'

'Esme Farrell.'

The woman looked at her ring and said, 'You're married, I see.'

'I'm a widow.'

Immediately, her voice softened. 'You poor girl. Come with me. You'll soon get the hang of it.'

* * *

There was one more attack by Stukas, during which a ship was hit and had to be abandoned before it sank. All of its crew were picked up by the escorting MLs and taken to Ramsgate.

Wilf took over the wheel from the cox'n on the way back to Dover.

'I hear the skipper had a few words with you,' said the cox'n.

'Yes, he thought I was slow to open fire.'

'That's what I heard, although he'd nothing to complain about, as it happened.'

Again, Wilf explained the lessons learned at Namsos and Andalsnes, and the cox'n was impressed. 'You were lucky with this skipper, though,' he said. 'They're not all as ready to learn as he is.'

'One thing I don't understand,' said Wilf, is why they sent a fighter escort. Our blokes couldn't have known they were coming, anyway.'

'I heard the skipper telling the Jimmy about that. One of the Jerry airmen's been a bit talkative, and it seems what they're trying to do is tempt the RAF into coming over the Channel, where they can shoot 'em down. So far, they haven't accepted the invitation.

The first lieutenant's youthful voice came down the voice pipe. 'Bridge – wheelhouse.'

'Wheelhouse, sir. Leading Seaman Gregory at the wheel, sir.'

'Half ahead together, Gregory. We're approaching Dover harbour.'

'Half ahead together, sir.' Wilf rang down the order. 'Engines half ahead together, sir.'

'Very good.'

The cox'n smiled and nodded. 'Now it's his turn to sweat,' he said. 'They grow up quick in this job.'

Wilf thought of Ordinary Seaman Brewer and the others, and agreed with him.

'Move over, Greg. Entering and leaving harbour's my responsibility when everybody pulls their weight.'

As the cox'n reported the change to the bridge, it occurred to Wilf that he was fortunate in his cox'n as well as his captain.

22

August

Last-Minute Plans

While the Luftwaffe pounded the RAF's stations by day, night strikes on the enemy Channel ports continued, carried out largely by RAF Bomber Command with help from the Fleet Air Arm units currently serving under Coastal Command. For Clive, however, that came to an end when he returned from another raid on enemy invasion barges, with only two aircraft, including his, remaining. Wearily, he reported, as usual, to Commander (F).

'They've got our measure, sir,' said Clive. 'For my money, they've been saving their twin-engined fighters for the RAF's bombers, because they know the Swordfish is slow and vulnerable to anti-aircraft fire.' He delivered the information flatly, as a man who'd just lost a two good friends and a valued air-gunner.

'I agree, Newing, and I sympathise. You'll be relieved to know that you've carried out your last strike on the Channel ports.'

'Am I getting a posting, sir?'

'You are. You and your crew will report to 815 Squadron at RNAS Hatston on the twelfth, prior to joining HMS *Illustrious*.'

Clive considered the implications. 'It's good news about the Channel strikes, sir, but our two aircraft are now overworked and shot to pieces.'

'I know. They'll remain here for training purposes. You'll be equipped with new Swordfish at Hatston.'

'Thank you, sir.' In his exhausted state, it was all he could say.

'I'll be speaking to the others in your sub-flight. For now, though, let me congratulate you on an operation well carried out. You'll have seventy-two hours leave before travelling to Orkney. Enjoy it, Newing, because you've earned every minute of it.'

* * *

Penny was on watch when a Wren telephonist came to the door of the WT Office with a message for her. She wasn't cleared to enter the office, so Penny went to the door to speak to her.

'There's a telephone call for you, ma'am, on the outside line.' The Wren spoke quietly, no doubt aware that the making and receiving of personal telephone calls was strongly discouraged. 'The caller identified himself as Lieutenant Clive Newing, ma'am.'

'Thank you, Wren Dawes.' Penny hurried to the nearest outside telephone and picked it up. 'Third Officer Dorling here. I believe there's a call for me.'

The duty telephonist confirmed that there was, and put Clive through.

'Hello, Penny?'

'Clive, you'll get me shot.' All the same, it was wonderful to hear from him.

'Listen, Penny. Can you get a stand-down?' He sounded drained. 'I've got seventy-two hours before I have to catch a train. I'll be at home from tonight. I suggest tomorrow, if you can manage it.'

'I'll try, obviously, but I haven't been here two minutes, so I don't know what they'll say.'

'Tell them your fiancé-to-be has been posted abroad. For all we know, it may be true – the abroad thing, I mean. As for the rest, we can deal with that when we meet. Ring me when you can. Must go. Love you.'

Stunned by what he'd just told her, she managed to say, 'I love you too, darling.' Then she set about requesting a stand-down. Fortunately, Sandbrook and Chatham weren't all that far apart, but it was still asking a lot. Ever hopeful, she went to find out if First Officer Norton was free to see her.

* * *

Wilf recognised Esme's handwriting as soon as the Regulating Petty Officer handed him the envelope. 'Thanks, RPO.'

'You're welcome. I hope you're as happy when you read it.'

Wilf refrained from replying. Instead, he went to the messdeck to read the letter in peace.

Using his jackknife to slit open the envelope, he unfolded the letter and read the contents.

Dear Wilf,

I hope everything is going well for you.

Guess what? We're now working in the same town. Yes, the teashop had to close because there aren't enough customers, so I got a job at the British Restaurant in Dover. Let me know when you can get some time off, or whatever the Navy call it, and we can get together.

I've really missed you since you went away, and if we can meet it will be marvellous (is that right? I'm never sure how many 'l's there are in marvellous.) Maybe I should have said, 'great', like the Americans do in the films. Anyway, I'm sure you know what I mean.

It's quite good working at the restaurant, although we get some cheeky blighters among the customers, even though I wear a wedding ring. Still, I'm pleased to be in work.

I'm glad you're where you are and not at sea. At least I know you're safe.

By the way, Mr Wickham, the greengrocer asked after you. I asked him what made him think I'd know, and he said he knew there was something happening between us, because he saw it in our eyes. Do you think he did, or do you reckon somebody's been talking?

Please write soon. I miss you.

Love and very best wishes,

Esme X

* * *

Scarcely able to believe her luck – or First Officer Norton's kindness – Penny dialled Clive's number. It rang several times, and then a woman's voice answered.

'Hello?'

'Oh, is that Mrs Newing?'

'Yes. Who's calling?'

'Penny Dorling, Mrs Newing. Do you think I might speak to Clive?'

Mrs Newing laughed gently and said, 'Last time I looked, he was out for the count, but I think he'll wake up for you, Penny.'

'Oh, if he's asleep, maybe you'd be kind enough to take a message.'

'I'd be delighted to, Penny, but he's here now. He must have heard the telephone ringing. I'll put him on.'

'Thank you, Mrs Newing.'

The voice that answered was Clive's although he still sounded half-asleep. 'Hel... hello, Penny.'

'Hello, darling.' She laughed. 'What have you been doing? You sound like Rip van Winkle.'

'Never mind that. Can you get away?'

'Yes, I'll be home by noon tomorrow, hopefully, although I have to go back on Wednesday.'

'Wonderful. I have to see you before I leave.'

'Yes, but listen.' There was something she had to know. 'Were you teasing me this morning?'

'I told you once, I never tease where feelings are concerned. I'll make everything clear when we meet. I'll come for you tomorrow afternoon, while the shops are open, if that's all right.'

'More than all right.' It was too tantalising for words.

The two-minute signal sounded.

'Okay,' he said, 'I'll see you tomorrow. Love you. 'Bye.'

'I love you too. 'Bye.' She returned to her quarters, almost childishly excited.

* * *

The captain of ML97 addressed the ship's company. 'Just for a change,' he told them, it's good news. The first item of news is that our firepower is to be enhanced by the addition of a single, two-pounder pom-pom, which will be mounted on the foc'sle. It's not as straightforward a job as you and I might imagine, and the dockyard people, in their wisdom, are making it even more complicated by preparing the deck and having the gun and its mounting delivered tomorrow, Friday.' He surveyed their puzzled expressions before enlightening them. 'You're probably wondering what is so complicated about that, so I'll tell you. Their trade union won't allow them to work weekends, so ML Ninety-Seven will be out of commission until the end of their working day on Monday.' He smiled happily. 'All of which brings me to the second item of news, which is that you will receive seventy-two hours' leave from tomorrow, at eighteen-hundred. Make the most of it, because we'll soon be quite busy.' As if on cue, a formation of enemy aircraft approached from the south, their course most likely taking them over Hawkinge and Lympne air stations. Having abandoned their efforts over the Channel, they were now bombing RAF fighter stations.

The Cox'n ordered, 'Ship's company, turning right, dismiss.'

As they went about their duties, the captain said, 'Leading Seaman Gregory report to me on the bridge.'

Wilf checked that his cap was straight and reported as ordered.

'Leading Seaman Gregory,' said the captain, 'are you familiar with the two-pounder pom-pom?'

'Yes, sir.'

'Have you operated one recently?'

'Yes, sir, when I was serving in HMS *Wrathful* off the Norwegian coast. In any case, sir, you know how they do things at HMS *Excellent*, and that's where I trained on the pom-pom.'

The captain nodded wryly. 'Once learned, never forgotten,' he agreed. 'Point taken. I'm going to leave it to you to select the pom-pom crew, and then, of course, it'll be up to you to train them on it, as well as training up a gunlayer and loader for whichever machine gun is left unmanned.'

'Aye, aye, sir.'

He appeared to study Wilf more closely, and said, 'You have quite a responsibility aboard this ship, Gregory. How do you feel about that?'

'I'm happy enough, sir. We have an excellent cox'n and a good bunch of lads. They're learning fast, and they'll do well.'

'It's good to hear you say that, Gregory. I'm particularly pleased that you're happy with the Hostilities Only ratings.'

Wilf glanced uncertainly at the First Lieutenant, an RNVR sub-lieutenant, who stood silently to the side of, and a little behind, the captain. 'My dad told me that the RNVR proved itself in the last war, sir, and there's no doubt they'll do it again.'

'Oh? What was your father?'

'He retired as a chief shipwright artificer, sir.'

'So yours is a naval family, like mine.'

'Yes, sir.'

'I'm delighted to hear it. Well, I'll leave you to get on with your duties, Gregory. Carry on.'

'Aye, aye, sir.'

As he left the bridge, he heard the captain say to the First Lieutenant, 'There goes an excellent man, Number One. The Cox'n is the mainstay of the crew, but Gregory is his right hand man.'

It was good to know he was in the skipper's good books. Things were looking up all round.

Later, when he was off-watch, he wrote to Esme.

Dear Esme,

Thank you for your letter. What a stroke of luck you getting a job at the British Restaurant. I've never heard of it. Is it very posh? By the way, I asked a PO writer in the pay office how to spell 'marvellous', and he reckons it has two 'l's, but your letter would have been just as welcome if you'd got it wrong.

I miss you, too, so it's just as well I've got some leave coming up. Don't ask me why I've got leave so soon after the last one, because I can't tell you, but I'm going to be at home from Friday night until Monday. Any time you can get off will be marvellous with as many 'l's as you like!

I don't know if Mr Wickham was pulling your leg or not. Maybe he did notice something, because I was certainly pleased to see you, and I will be even happier if you can get away some time this weekend. Do you have to work Sundays as well as Saturdays? I don't know much about restaurants. Please let me know. I can hardly wait to see you again.

Love and best wishes,

Wilf X

He folded it and pushed it into an envelope without sealing it. All outgoing mail had to be read by an officer to make sure no secrets were being given away. It was an intrusion, but Wilf could see the sense in it. He just hoped the letter would reach Esme in time.

23

TRYSTS AND PLEDGES

Watching Penny return a salute from a WAAF aircraftwoman, her mother said, 'It's a change to see you in your uniform.'

'Yes, it will be. I had to leave in a hurry to catch my train, so I'd no time to change.'

'We weren't expecting you home so soon after your last leave.'

'This isn't a leave, so much as a stand-down.'

'What on earth is that?' Penny's mother had a way of querying unfamiliar concepts as if they had no right to exist.

'It's an unofficial leave. I'm here to see Clive before he takes up his new appointment.'

'Oh, yes?' Again, her response bore the stamp of disapproval. 'Where's he going this time?'

'I don't know. He couldn't say on an insecure telephone line.' To make the point that the omission was neither her fault nor Clive's she added the reminder, ' "Careless Talk Costs Lives", Mum.'

'If you say so, dear.' She unlocked the car for Penny to get in.

'If the reason for your unexpected arrival is to see Lieutenant Newing, I don't suppose we'll see much of you.'

'No, aren't you lucky?'

'Really, Penelope.' Her mother forced the lever into reverse, causing the gearbox to protest loudly, and pulled out of her parking space.

'Honestly, Mum, aren't you just a teeny-weeny bit pleased to see me? Go on, admit it.'

'For goodness' sake, Penelope, you know I'm pleased to see you. I just wish you'd be a little less childish, that's all.'

'No can do, Mum.' It was true. Penny could never play the

precocious, premature forty-year-old, like her twenty-three-year-old sister, nor would she ever want to, even when she reached that age.

When they passed the end of Clive's drive, she looked for his motorbike, as she always did, but it was out of sight.

Watching her, her mother said, 'I'm sure you'll see him soon enough.'

'No, Mum, it'll never be soon enough.' As if to demonstrate that avowal, she waited until they were home, and then dashed into the house to telephone Clive.

This time, he answered. 'The dentist's residence. Your pain is his aim.'

'Clive, that's awful. You'll drive patients away.'

'I doubt it, Penny. The surgery's on a separate line. Have you had lunch?'

'No, I've just this minute arrived.'

'Good, I'll come over for you, or do you need time to powder your nose and things? We'll be going on the Norton, if that helps you decide what to wear.'

'Give me ten minutes.'

* * *

Penny was waiting, as usual, a little surprised to see Clive's motorbike, despite his warning. 'Is it still running on pre-war petrol?' she asked as he kissed her.

'Shh.' He put a finger to her lips. 'My dad didn't use the whole of his ration, so he siphoned some off and topped up my tank.'

'I shan't tell.'

'Before we go, Penny, I need you to tell me something.'

'Yes?' Not surprisingly, she looked as if she had an inkling of what he was going to ask.

'Am I still the one and only?'

'Of course you are.'

'Forsaking all others, keeping me only unto thee?'

Impatiently, she asked, 'What others?'

'Will you marry me?'

'Even though you've chosen the most unromantic moment to ask me, of course I will. Yes, yes, yes!'

'Good. Let's go shopping.'

'I could hit you, sometimes.'

He kissed her so that she wouldn't, and then mounted the bike and waited for her to climb on to the pillion.

'Where are we going?'

'Rainforth's in Folkestone.'

'Are you sure they're still open? A lot of shops have closed for the duration.'

'Yes, disgraceful, I call it. I telephoned them this morning. They're expecting us.' He kicked off the engine and they set off for Folkestone.

Apart from military traffic, the main road was quiet, and they soon arrived in Guildhall Street, where Clive parked outside Rainforth's.

'I still don't believe this is happening,' said Penny, accepting a hand to help her off the pillion and on to the pavement. 'I told my mother we were going to buy a ring, and she thought I was playing one of my childish games.'

'The joke will be on her when we get back. Is your father at home as well?'

'Yes, why?'

'We may as well do the traditional thing and see both lots of parents. My sister Audrey's at home as well. That was quite a coincidence. Welcome, too, as I hadn't seen her for ages.'

Penny looked uncertain. 'Are you going to ask my father for my hand in marriage? I mean, to walk in with a ring on my hand is something of a *fait accompli*, isn't it?'

'Yes, we'll tell them we've *fait*ed the *accompli*-ing and we're asking them to congratulate us. Anyway, let's go inside.' He pushed open the door and held it for her to enter the shop, where a man, possibly the proprietor, stood behind the counter.

'Good afternoon,' said Clive. 'We'd like to look at some engagement rings, please.'

'Of course. You must be the gentleman who telephoned earlier. May I offer you both my congratulations?'

'Thank you very much,' said Penny.

'Thank you,' said Clive.

'Do you have an idea of how much you'd like to spend?'

'Yes,' said Clive, 'but let's keep the conversation serious. Maybe you could show us a range or perhaps a selection.'

The man went into the back of the shop and returned with three trays of rings at a range of prices, augmenting them with one from the window. 'You've chosen a good time, if I may say so. Purchase tax on luxury items is due to be applied quite soon.'

'Let's rise above mundane considerations,' said Clive.

'Oh, quite,' agreed the man, looking a little shamefaced, while Penny tried not to laugh.

'Darling,' said Clive, 'I'm going to leave the choice to you.' He stood back and gave her a clear view of all four trays.

'Some of these are terribly expensive,' she observed.

'Whereas you're priceless.'

'You're a smooth-talking rascal as well as a generous man.' She continued to agonise over the rings.

'Would it make it easier,' asked Clive, 'if we narrowed the choice?'

'Probably.'

He pushed a tray of medium-priced rings towards her. 'Does any of these appeal to you?'

She examined the tray and pointed to one surmounted by three circular diamonds. This one is beautiful,' she said, 'but I'm afraid it's rather expensive.'

'Do you think the lady might try it on?' asked Clive.

'By all means, sir.' The man took out the ring and placed it on Penny's finger. 'As luck would have it,' he said, 'it's your size.'

'I can't believe it,' she said, blinking emotionally. 'It's the most beautiful thing I've ever seen.'

'If that's your choice,' said Clive, 'and by all means feel free to look at the others....'

'I'm just mindful of the price.'

'Forget the price,' said Clive. 'I'm feeling extravagant, having just parted with my aeroplane.'

They both stared at him, uncomprehending.

'If that's the ring you'd like, then it shall be yours.'

'Oh, thank you, darling.'

Clive wrote a cheque, and they left the shop. When they were outside, Penny asked, 'How did you sell an aeroplane, when it belonged to the Navy?'

'Who said anything about selling it? I just said I'd parted with it. It just means I'll have to christen a new "Penny" when I join my new squadron, if that's all right by you.'

Looking at her left hand, Penny said, 'Anything's all right by me. When we've had lunch, do you think we might call on Grandpop? Unless you have any objection, I'd like him to be the first to know.'

* * *

Wilf stood on the platform as the Dover train pulled in, looking back and forth until he saw Esme climb down. He went forward to greet her.

'Hello, Wilf.' Her serious expression was transformed into a smile and she accepted a kiss. 'There was no need to meet me off the train.'

'Well, I did, and now I'll walk you home.'

'I have to call at Spencer's on the way,' she said, showing him her empty shopping bag.

'In that case, I'll carry your shopping.'

'It *is* good to see you again, Wilf.'

'It's the same for me,' he told her. 'That's why I came to the station.'

Several passengers greeted Wilf as 'Jack' and touched his collar. 'I wonder if they'll ever get tired of it,' he said. 'When I get made up to petty officer I won't have a collar for them to touch. Not one like this, anyway.'

'What sort will you have?'

'Just a normal jacket collar. I'll have a white shirt and a tie as well.'

Excited, she asked, 'Like an officer?'

'Sort of, but they have four buttons up the front, and senior ratings only have three.' Rather than let her get too excited, he said, 'It won't happen for three or four years yet.'

They reached Spencer's, where Esme produced her ration book and bought the groceries she needed. For Wilf, it still felt strange to hear her addressed as 'Mrs Farrell', but he would probably get used to it.

On the way back to Esme's house, Wilf steered her into the passage they'd used on their first night out together.

'Wilf,' she said, 'it's broad daylight.' Even so, she didn't appear too concerned.

When he was sure there was no one around, he kissed her. 'I'll call for you at half-past six,' he said.

'Where are we going?'

'There's only the pictures. They haven't shut them down yet.'

'Right, I'll see you then.' She accepted another kiss before moving purposefully towards her house.

* * *

Having received the admiral's sincere congratulations and the startled and almost-embarrassed good wishes of Penny's parents, they rode to Clive's house.

'Mum, Audrey,' announced Clive, 'this is Penny and we've just got engaged.'

It was obvious from Mrs Newing's reaction that his announcement was no surprise, welcome though it was. Audrey had also been privy to the secret, but she, too, was both welcoming and in a celebratory mood. She had dark hair, like Clive, and brown eyes, and she was quite pretty, as Clive had told Penny, although not the classic beauty her mother was.

'I'll get your dad,' said Mrs Newing. 'He hasn't got a patient with him just now.'

'That's a mercy for someone,' said Clive. His sister laughed and his mother gave him a grown-up look as she went to the surgery.

She returned with Clive's white-coated and half-spectacled father, who delivered his congratulations warmly and sincerely.

'You remember Penny, don't you Dad?' asked Clive.

'Of course I do. Pit and fissure cavity, first molar, right lower quadrant. How's it holding, my dear?'

A little taken aback, Penny said, 'I've had no trouble with it, Mr Newing. It's kind of you to ask.'

'I'm joking, of course. I'm delighted to see you again, and especially so, now that you're going to take this young reprobate off my hands. What a wonderful surprise it is.' He looked at the clock and said, 'I don't think it's too early for a celebratory drink, is it? I'll have something innocuous, Katherine, if you're getting them. I have another patient to see before I can relax, and I don't want to anaesthetise her with whisky fumes.'

Mrs Newing officiated, as requested, and everyone was able to toast the promised couple.

'Where are you thinking of going this evening?' asked Mr Newing.

'I think we'll go to the Salamanca while it's still open.'

'In that case, take the car. I should be horrified if this lovely young lady were to crease her crinolines, riding on the back of that contraption of yours, Clive.'

* * *

Wilf was careful to take Esme up to the balcony again to avoid the misbehaving couples in the cheap seats. The main film was *21 Days*, a thriller starring Vivien Leigh, Laurence Olivier and Leslie Banks, but first they had to endure the newsreel, which inevitably reported a different kind of war from the one Wilf had so far experienced. They sat through the catalogue of bumptious propaganda, and eventually, the main feature began.

No one could fault the performances of the leading actors, but the story lacked an awful lot. Wilf had been hoping for a comedy or at least something fairly light, but *21 Days* failed to provide the entertainment he'd had in mind.

He mentioned it to Esme when they left the cinema, but she had no complaints.

'Until I met you again,' she said, 'I hadn't been to the pictures at all for… years, so I'm not as choosey as you are.'

'Do you fancy a walk again, like we did last time? We can still get on to the seafront. It's just a bit of a narrow path.'

'Yes, I'd like that.'

They walked towards the seafront, and Wilf asked, 'What's it like, working at the restaurant? Is it very posh?'

'No,' she laughed, 'the British Restaurants are provided by the Government to see that everybody who's working gets a square meal that doesn't cost too much. I certainly wouldn't call it posh.' She laughed again. 'You should see some of the customers we get.'

'Oh, I didn't know.'

'I don't know what you do, either. I'm just glad you're not at sea.'

He had to be honest. 'I go to sea sometimes, Esme,' he said, adding, 'but not for long.' It was basically true and maybe not quite as worrying for her as it might have been.

'Be careful, whatever you do.'

He gave her waist a squeeze and said, 'I'm always careful.'

They walked on until he heard a familiar sound in the distance. Esme had heard it, too. 'What's that?' she asked.

The sounds of automatic fire came from the south and, every now and again, flashes of tracer and exploding shells lit up the horizon. 'It's just our lads telling Jerry to keep to his own side,' he told her. Again, it was strictly true.

'I don't want you getting mixed up in anything like that,' she said, sounding like a stern mother.

'Don't think about it.' Partly as a distraction, but mainly because nature demanded it, he drew her closer and kissed her in a way he'd been longing to during almost every free moment and even between tasks on board ship.

'You put a lot of feeling into that,' she said.

'I feel a lot when I'm with you.' He felt clumsy even as he said it. He'd had no experience of sweet-talking girls, even in the light-hearted way some of his oppos went in for, and now, when he was very serious, he felt hopelessly inadequate. Unable to voice his true feelings, he kissed her again.

It was clear that she wasn't about to be side-tracked, because she asked, 'What do you feel, Wilf?'

He couldn't dodge the question. He had to say something. 'You're special, Esme. As far as I'm concerned, you're very special.'

'So are you, Wilf. Even though we haven't known each other properly for very long, that's what I feel.'

Still unable to express his feelings adequately, he kissed her again, and then the feeling of urgency returned, the feeling he'd experienced the last time they'd walked on the seafront, and he knew he had to tell her properly. 'I love you, Esme.' The words were out almost before he was ready. It was almost like the time he was at HMS *Ganges*, learning to dive, and he'd lost his balance and fallen off the board and into the pool.

'Do you?' She sounded as if she hardly dared believe it.

'Yes, I do. That's the feeling I told you about.'

'Oh, Wilf,' she said in a rush of relief and happiness, 'I love you too.'

On the horizon, MTBs or MGBs were exchanging fire with E-boats, or worse, for all Wilf knew. For now, though, all that mattered was Esme's feelings for him and his for her. The distant sky was now illuminated with shellfire and tracer, but they kissed, oblivious to it.

* * *

Everything at the Salamanca was perfect. The band they remembered was playing a new song, 'I'll Be Seeing You,' which sounded magnificent, and the restaurant and ballroom were well-attended. The singer sounded very promising; he was in RAF uniform, which suggested that, like the Salamanca itself, his services were all too fleeting. The man on the door, whose job was also doubtless in jeopardy, greeted them, saying, 'This is our last fling before we close for the duration.' Clearly a man who liked things to be right, he changed that to, 'Tonight and tomorrow night, that is.'

'We shan't be here tomorrow,' Clive told him. 'We're on a short leave because we got engaged today.'

The doorman smiled broadly in spite of the occasion. 'Oh, permit me to offer my congratulations to you both and to wish you every happiness.'

They thanked him and followed the head waiter to their table.

'Everything on the menu is available,' he informed them.

'Excellent, and quite right for the occasion. We'll have a look at it in a minute.' Cocking an ear towards the band, he said to Penny, 'They're going to play our song.'

She looked at him in puzzlement.

'One of them, anyway.' The bandleader had just announced, 'They Can't Black-Out the Moon'. 'Shall we? I mean dance, not black-out the moon. We have to be realistic.'

'Let's.' She let him take her hand and lead her on to the floor.

When they'd been dancing for a minute or so, she said, 'I thought my mother was going to have a fit when we told her we were engaged.'

'I must confess I gave my folks fair warning.'

'It was so funny,' she went on, 'seeing the confusion behind her eyes. Half of her, at least, wanted to berate me for being headstrong and thoughtless, while the rest of her realised it was a done deal, and she had to accept it gracefully. As usual, my dad followed on, so that wasn't too bad.' Performing a belated double-take, she said in mock horror, 'I just said "done deal", didn't I? So much American is creeping over here via Hollywood.'

'I wouldn't object to the Americans creeping over here and lending a hand.'

'Do you really think things are as bad as that? Grandpop's quite adamant that the Germans won't try to invade, because their navy got such a terrific walloping in the Norway campaign. He says it's just not up to it.'

'He may well be right. If we can hold them off for now, we can probably survive. As for defeating them, though, that task's going to call for outside help.'

The number reached its end, and they returned to their table.

'Do you know what we're doing?' asked Penny.

As it was clearly a rhetorical question, Clive waited to be enlightened.

'We're talking about horrible things such as war and invasion, and on the day we got engaged.'

'Right, let's black-out the war.'

'Before we do, I must tell you about one thing that's happened.'

'Be my guest.' She was looking pleased about it, whatever it was.

'We had a visit from Commander-in-Chief The Nore. I learned recently that we come under Nore Command. Anyway, he's a dear old soul. He spoke to me, and I discovered that he knew Grandpop. He told us we were doing a vital job and that the Navy couldn't possibly function without Wrens freeing men for the fleet.'

The waiter arrived, and Clive gave him their order, which included a bottle of the 1935 Saint Estèphe Medoc. 'While we can still get it,' he explained.

When the waiter was gone, he returned to the visit of C-in-C The Nore. 'Do you remember my telling you that the day would come when a flag officer would have to admit something along those lines?'

'I do, now you mention it, but let's impose a moratorium on the war, and concentrate on enjoying ourselves.'

'With immediate effect,' he agreed. Then, looking over Penny's shoulder, he said, 'I see we're about to receive a visitor.'

The visitor was the bandleader, who said, 'I believe this is a special day for you both.'

'That's right,' said Clive. The doorman had evidently told him.

'May I offer my sincerest congratulations.'

'Thank you.'

'Thank you,' said Penny.

'Perhaps there's a special song you'd like to hear, in which case, we shall certainly do our best to provide it.'

'That's very kind of you,' said Clive. Turning to Penny, he said, 'Would you like to choose, darling?'

She frowned good-naturedly. 'Now you've put me on the spot.' She thought hurriedly. 'I'm trying to think of something that's about continuity and permanence, about always being in our thoughts.'

'If I might offer a suggestion, Miss, Cole Porter's "Night and Day" seems to address that requirement.'

'What an excellent choice! Let's have that, then, and thank you again.'

'It's our very great pleasure, Miss.' He returned to the dais and conferred with the band. Parts were retrieved from a cupboard behind the band and given out, and he turned to speak to the diners. 'This is a special evening for most of us, ladies and gentlemen,' he said, 'and it's particularly special for the couple at table seven, who announced their engagement today.'

Clive winced as the bandleader pointed to them with his baton, and the other diners broke into applause, which he was obliged to acknowledge.

'They would very much like to hear 'Night and Day' by Cole Porter, so here it is, and here's Stan to sing it for us.'

The band began the introduction, and Clive led Penny on to the floor to further applause, after which they danced to the excellent band and its talented vocalist, who seemed to be singing only to them.

At the end of the evening, they drove home. Clive drew up at the top of the drive and switched off the engine.

Penny said, 'Oh dear, this is the moment I've been dreading.'

'We've a lot to look forward to. We just have to be patient,' Clive told her, getting out to open her door. 'You've got my address, haven't you?'

'HMS *Illustrious*, yes.'

'I don't know how long the mail will take. We just have to live with it.'

They walked over to the place of concealment they'd used earlier, and kissed at length.

'We're like lots of other couples,' he said. 'Thousands of people are being brave, and parting, but only for the time being.'

'I'll be brave,' she promised. They kissed again.

He looked at his watch and said, 'It's almost pumpkin time.' And then, because time was short, he said, 'I love you.'

'And I love you,' she said, 'night and day.'

24

'HMS *ILLUSTRIOUS* WILL PROCEED...'

The thermometer was showing fifty-two degrees Fahrenheit when Clive and Bill walked out to their aircraft, the second Swordfish to be known as 'Penny'. The running footsteps behind them turned out to be those of Leading Airman Carson. The two officers turned to greet him.

'Good morning, Carson,' said Bill. 'Are you warm enough?'

'Good morning, sirs. No, sir, it's a shock after Essex.'

'It'll be worse when we're airborne,' said Clive.

'We can always be sure of that, sir, but the "buzz" is that we're heading for warmer climes.' He was conscious that it was unusual for officers to be on informal terms with their air-gunners, and he appreciated the relaxed atmosphere that existed in this particular crew.

'You're old enough to know better than to listen to buzzes,' Clive told him. 'We're just as likely to be destined for Western Approaches.'

The handlers were waiting for them when they reached the aircraft, and Clive clambered into the forrard cockpit for the starting up procedure. He adjusted the mixture, and the handlers wound the large propeller six times to draw fuel and air into the carburettor. Two of them then climbed on to the port lower wing and inserted the crank. At a word from Clive they began winding, overcoming resistance and increasing the rate until, after a sufficient number of turns, Clive released the clutch that enabled the magneto to transmit electric current to the engine. With a splutter and then a roar, the nine-cylinder engine burst into life. It was hard work, but as Bill had once pointed out, at least they didn't need to worry about a flat battery on a cold morning.

Clive waved his thanks to the handlers, who jumped down and stood clear of the aircraft and its spinning propellor.

The rest of the squadron were performing the same routine and, after a period of warming up, a green flare from the tower burst overheard, the squadron commander began taxiing on to the runway, and the others waited to follow him. The handlers waved good luck and farewell, and Clive and his crew returned the gesture.

It was a very short distance from Hatston to Scapa Flow, and it wasn't long before they sighted HMS *Illustrious*, the first of a new class of aircraft carrier. Everything about her looked clean and new, although how long that would last was something no one could know.

One by one, the Swordfish responded to the signals from the carrier granting permission to land and, taking his turn, Clive made his descent, received the 'OK' signal from the Deck Landing Control Officer, and felt his hook engage with one of the arrester wires. The DLCO gave the signals to apply the brakes and cut the engine. Swordfish 2K, otherwise known as 'Penny', had landed on the ship that was to be her home for the foreseeable future.

* * *

Having reported at the main gate, Wilf went immediately to the berth to see the new pom-pom, but he wasn't the first. Petty Officer Rankin was already giving it a close inspection.

'Hello, Greg,' he said. 'Good leave?'

'Very good, thanks, Cox'n.' Pleased though he was with life, he wasn't about to expand on that. 'How was yours?'

'The usual,' he said with a mischievous grin. 'The missis wore me out and the kids kept me awake. Still, I shouldn't complain.'

Wilf was examining the mounting. 'Mark Eight, Manual,' he observed approvingly.

Rankin smiled and shook his head. 'You've got "Whale Island" written all through you, Greg,' he said, 'like a stick of Blackpool rock, but I'm glad you don't give these Wavy Navy sprogs the Whale Island treatment.'

'No, it wouldn't work. These lads have come from every kind of background you can think of. Some of them have been used to thinking for themselves and questioning the way things are done, and that's the last thing the gunnery manuals can cope with.'

Rankin laughed at the thought. 'I can see your point, Greg.'

Reminded of an incident during his early training, Wilf said, 'When I was at *Excellent*, one of the class was wondering about the chains the officers wore to secure their whistles, and he asked the leading hand of the mess, "Why do gunnery officers have chains?" The killick said, "What use is a shithouse without one?" ' Wilf shrugged. 'I reckon he was right.'

'I reckon he was,' said the cox'n, chuckling. 'We're lucky with our skipper, an' the Jimmy's all right as long as he behaves himself.'

'Yes, they're not all the same. My dad, who left the Andrew as a Chief Shipwright Tiffy, works at a boatyard belonging to a retired rear admiral.'

'Tiddley company.'

'You'd think so, wouldn't you? Well, the old boy has a converted Montagu whaler, and when the call went out for inshore craft to go to Dunkirk, he and my dad took her over there. They reckoned they ferried more than four hundred porgoes to the destroyers, and then, when they heard that the last destroyer had as many as she could accommodate, they brought two dozen home. My dad says the fuel ran out as they were leaving the French coast, and they brought the whaler back under sail.'

'Phew, that's quite a story.'

'They had to deal with mutinous pongoes, an' all, same as we had to, but the admiral didn't stand for any nonsense. He just pulled out his revolver an' said, "I'll shoot the next man who tries to board my boat." Just like that. I had to do the same kind of thing, but I had two dozen matelots with rifles to back me up.'

Rankin shook his head in amazement. 'He sounds like a good hand,' he said, 'your dad an' all.'

'Yeah, and that's not all. When I came home from Norway, I went down to the boatyard, an' the admiral gave my dad an' me a tot, an' they drank to my hook and my two "mentions".'

'No.'

'He did. As you said, he's a good hand.'

'You know,' said Rankin half-seriously, 'you're so well-connected, you should be able to get something done about this weather we're having.'

Wilf laughed and Rankin joined him. It was that kind of relationship.

* * *

A seaman was scrubbing the deck outside the wardroom, but he stopped and stared when he saw Clive and Bill about to enter.

Clive asked, 'Is something the matter?'

The seaman came hurriedly to attention and saluted them both. 'No, sir. Beg your pardon, sir, but you are Lieutenant Newing, aren't you, sir?'

'Yes.' Turning to Bill, Clive said, 'Now I know I'm in trouble.' Curious, he asked the seaman, 'Have we met?'

'Yes, sir. You found me a seat on the Pompey train from Waterloo when I was struggling with my leg.'

'Of course. I remember now. How's your injury?'

'I'm right as rain now, thank you, sir. I just wanted to thank you for your kindness, that's all.'

'Think nothing of it…. What's your name?'

'JX194889 Able Seaman Craddock, sir.'

'As I said, Craddock, you were more than welcome, and I'm delighted to see you fit again.'

'Thank you, sir.' Craddock saluted again and stood aside while the two officers returned his salute and entered the wardroom.

'Buzzes abound,' said Bill, beckoning the wardroom steward, 'but we're still in the dark about our destination.'

'It's just normal security,' said Clive unhelpfully.

'Good morning, sir,' said the steward. 'What can I get you?'

'Two pink gins, please,' said Bill. 'What's your name, by the way?'

'Newbolt, sir.'

'I'm glad to meet you, Newbolt. Are you any relation to Sir Henry?'

'I believe I'm a distant descendant, sir, but the only poetry I produce is that which proceeds from the cocktail shaker.'

'That's good enough for us,' said Clive. He waited until the steward was gone, and asked, 'Are you a devotee of Newbolt, Bill?' He'd never had his observer down as a man of poetry.

'Hardly a devotee, old man, but I was once required at prep school to recite "Admirals All" after Prayers as a punishment for a particularly bad score in Maths.'

'What a strange punishment.'

'It was an unusual school, with a strange headmaster, a mathematician who frequently punished boys by making them learn music and poetry. I suppose he imagined, if he were capable of imagining anything, that we shared his foul prejudice against the arts.'

'He was certainly strange, Bill.' Clive broke off when Newbolt arrived with the drinks. 'Thank you, Newbolt.'

'My very great pleasure, sir.' He took the hastily signed mess chit from Bill, thanking him with a similar flourish.

'Oddly enough, I can only remember a little of "Admirals All".'

'Even so, I have an awful feeling you're about to share it with me.'

His fear was realised when Bill closed his eyes and recited:

'Drake nor devil nor Spaniard feared,
Their cities he put to the sack;
He singed his Catholic Majesty's beard,
And harried his ships to wrack.
He was playing at Plymouth a rubber of bowls
When the great Armada came;
But he said, "They must wait their turn, good souls,"
And he stooped and finished the game.'

Now Clive closed his eyes as he tried not to give way to laughter. Bill, however, skipped a forgotten verse and continued.

Splinters were flying above, below,
When Nelson sailed the Sound:
"Mark you, I wouldn't be elsewhere now,"
Said he, "for a thousand pound!"
The Admiral's signal bade him fly
But he wickedly wagged his head:
He clapped the glass to his sightless eye,
And, "I'm damned if I see it!" he said.'

'There's a bit more that's not very exciting,' he said, and then there's the stirring bit.'

Clive held on gamely.

'But they left us a kingdom none can take,
The realm of the circling sea,
To be ruled by the rightful sons of Blake,
And the Rodneys yet to be.'

'Bravely done,' said Clive, finally capitulating to the laughter that had threatened from the start. 'Your heart, like Newbolt's, is squarely in the right place.'

'It was reading that sort of thing that led me to join the Navy.' Bill paused to ascertain whether or not his friend was taking him seriously again and, presumably satisfied that he was, asked, 'What stirred your imagination, Clive?'

'Frederick Marryat, I suppose.'

'*Mr Midshipman Easy*?'

'Yes, it was reading that, now I think of it, that set me on the road to Dartmouth.'

Bill nodded, clearly identifying with the experience, but then asked, 'Why the Fleet Air Arm?'

'I was in my first term at Dartmouth, and we were on the parade ground, when a flight of Blackburn Ripons flew low overhead. I still remember the roar of their engines and the happy faces of their observers as they flew over us. For me, it was love at first sight. I can't say it was the same for the Chief Gunnery Instructor who was trying to drill us at the time, because it disrupted the whole class, but from that day, all I wanted to do was fly with the Fleet Air Arm.'

Bill nodded companionably and said, 'I joined out of contrariness.'

Clive looked at him oddly. 'Tell me about it,' he said, 'if only to compensate for "Admirals All".'

Nobly ignoring the jibe, Bill obliged. 'There was a particularly unpleasant instructor at Dartmouth in my time, a Lieutenant Commander Birchfield.'

'I remember him,' said Clive, 'a most unpleasant man. He was a gunnery specialist, as I recall.'

'He was, and it was for my failure to excel in that discipline that he gave me six strokes with his sword scabbard. I remember it vividly. He told me I'd never make a gunnery officer as long as I lived, and some latent spark of defiance led me to say, "I don't care, sir. I'm going to join the Fleet Air Arm!" I hadn't thought of it until then. It just came out after the sixth stroke.'

'What was his reaction?'

'He was incandescent. He shouted, "Only a half-wit like you would join the Fleet Air Arm!" He was so adamant that I made up my mind on the spot to join the Fleet Air Arm as soon as I could.'

'I'm glad you did, old man,' said Clive, laughing, 'if only for the sake of that story.' He beckoned the steward. 'Two more pink gins, please, Newbolt.'

The steward had just left them when there was a burst of static on the Tannoy. 'D'ye hear there! D'ye hear there! This is the Captain speaking. Firstly, let me welcome the Air Group, who, in case some of you missed it, joined the ship within the last hour. Secondly, I can now satisfy your curiosity about our deployment. We shall sail in five days' time for Gibraltar, thence the Mediterranean, where I expect we shall be kept quite busy. I shall tell you more when I receive further orders. That is all. Thank you.'

'The Med,' said Bill, 'the lovely, sunny Med.'

It could have been much worse, but Clive was conscious that it might be a long time before he saw Penny again. In the meantime, though, he had a job to do, and he had to concentrate on that.

25

LESSONS IN MANNERS AND MATHEMATICS

W ave after wave of Nazi aircraft crossed the Channel, and the ships of Coastal Forces might have presented easy targets, but the enemy's objective was clearly the RAF fighter stations, which they were pulverising almost into oblivion. 'Almost' was the word, because somehow, fighters were still intercepting and, according to the press and the BBC, taking a heavy toll of the attackers.

'They're trying to soften up the air defences,' said Petty Officer Rankin. 'They'll need to do that before they can invade. It stands to reason.'

'Why's that, Cox'n?' It seemed to Wilf that when someone said, 'It stands to reason,' the reason was seldom obvious.

'Their navy got a bloody good hiding in the Norway Campaign, as you know, so an invasion by sea would be impossible, to begin with, anyway. No, I reckon they'd start by sending in their army by parachute. That's why they want to deal with the RAF first.'

It made some sense to Wilf, but an important question remained. 'If that's the case, Cox'n,' he said, 'why have they lined up all them invasion barges we've been hearing about?'

'That's for when their army's taken over the main installations and starved the Andrew of fuel oil and ammunition.' The petty officer shook his head, smiling. 'Don't worry, Greg, it won't happen, 'cause for my money, that Hitler hasn't a clue. He's an ex-pongo, so what does he know about crossin' the oggin? His lot have only ever had to walk up to a frontier post and say, '*Hände hoch*!'

'What's that mean, Cox'n?'

' "Hands up". My dad was taken prisoner in the last war, and he told me that.' Reflecting on that isolated phrase, he said, 'Bloody silly language, isn't it? Bloody silly people, really. I mean, why else would they follow a clown with a daft haircut and an even dafter moustache? If he can't find a decent barber in Germany, how does he expect to find his way around in a foreign country? That's what I'd like to know.'

Such homespun wisdom was of some comfort, and so far, the enemy were across the Channel or, at worst, flying overhead, but Wilf had a closer look at them later that day, when MLs 97 and 98 were ordered to search for the crew of a Junkers JU88, which had been reported as heading for the coast and trailing thick, black smoke from a damaged engine. The humanitarian consideration in carrying out such a rescue came second to the possibility of procuring intelligence from any survivors, and the latter purpose made the operation both necessary and important.

Happily, the Royal Observer Corps had been able to provide the time of sighting as well as the aircraft's course, and the lookouts on board 97 sighted the dinghy twelve miles north of the French coast. The captain sent the signal, 'My bird, I think,' to ML98 and reduced speed to make his approach. Under Wilf's supervision, a party of ratings lowered a scrambling net and stood by to help the survivors out of their boat. One airman seemed to be in distress. His arm was hastily-bound in a blood-soaked bandage, and he was clearly in pain, so two ratings supported him, guiding his feet up the net until he was on board and could be given further help. He thanked his rescuers in an emotional torrent of German, which only Ordinary Seaman Brewer understood. The latter made what was presumably a soothing reply, and the airman was taken below.

The other three survivors followed, two of them thanking their rescuers, one in English, the other in German, but Wilf took the line that good manners were welcome in any language. Unfortunately, the fourth member of the German crew, an officer, failed to agree. Speaking to Wilf with visible hostility, he said, 'Enjoy this moment, English sailor. Soon your navy will be in the hands of the Third Reich.' That alone would have been enough to antagonise Wilf, but then the officer compounded the insult by spitting forcefully in his face. Wilf was about to hit him, but then he hesitated. Striking an unarmed prisoner was a serious offence, in addition to the fact that he had an example to set to the deck party. Instead, he placed his hand on the officer's chest and pushed him backwards. Realising his plight, the German panicked, flailing wildly with his arms in a forlorn attempt to right himself, but gravity was not to be denied, and he tumbled backwards over the side, where the guard rail had been removed to enable the rescue. He hit the water and submerged, breaking surface a few seconds later and screaming, 'Help me! Please! I cannot swim!'

Wilf seized a lifebelt and dropped it as close to the struggling German as he could get without braining him with it, shouting, 'Take hold of that, you Boche bastard!' 'Boche' was a word his father had picked up in the previous war, and it seemed right for that moment, sounding as it did, rather like a splash. In an aside to Brewer, he said, 'You'd think all the Master Race would know how to swim, wouldn't you, Brewer?'

Brewer was unable to reply, being helpless with laughter.

The terrified German was gripping the lifebelt desperately, so Wilf towed him via the attached line as far as the scrambling net. 'Right, get yourself up here,' he said, 'and no more playing silly buggers. Right?' He waited until the miscreant was almost on deck, and heaved him unceremoniously on board. 'Right, lads,' he told the deck party, 'you'd better put the guard rail back where it belongs before somebody else falls overboard.' There was a chorus of laughter, and Wilf straightened up to see the first lieutenant with a revolver in his hand. He waved it at the German in an unspoken but unmistakeable order to descend the ladder, and then said to Wilf, 'You're to report to the captain on the bridge, Gregory.'

'Aye, aye, sir.' Wilf took the bridge ladder, reconciled to receiving, at the very least, a reprimand for his action. He might also lose his hard-won leading rate. He stood on the bridge and saluted.

'Leading Seaman Gregory,' said the captain, returning his salute, 'your rescue was well executed.' His shoulders began to shake and, unable to control himself any longer, he gave way to laughter. 'Both rescues, in fact.' Making a fresh effort to control himself, he said, 'I saw what happened down there.' His shoulders shook again. 'It was only to be expected that a landlubber would have difficulty keeping his feet in this swell, but it was unfortunate for him that he should trip and fall overboard. Well done, Gregory. Carry on.'

'Aye, aye, sir. Thank you, sir.' Wilf took the ladder to the wheelhouse, thinking as he went that, for reasons of security, there was usually so little he could tell Esme and his family, but now he had a good story, and one they would all enjoy.

* * *

The captain had promised the crew of HMS *Illustrious* that they would be kept busy in the Mediterranean, and that turned out to be the case. In company with the battleship HMS *Valiant*, they were escorted into the Mediterranean, where they were soon in action against the Italian air force, the *Regia Aeronautica*. The Fulmar fighters shot down several Italian bombers, and it seemed that they were collaring all the action. That was until the Swordfish were flown off to attack the Italian seaplane base at Rhodes, their bombs leaving the installations wrecked and unable to operate. More was to follow, because, with the news that the Italians had invaded Egypt, they took to the skies again and carried out an attack on the port of Benghazi, sinking a destroyer and two supply ships. Another destroyer was sunk, subsequently, when it hit a mine laid by one of the Swordfish.

It was during this time that Clive received his second letter from Penny, the first having reached him in Gibraltar.

Dearest Clive,

I hope things are going well for you, wherever you are. I must say they'd be pretty boring for us if it weren't for the test match taking place here. Everyone's sky-high about it, and we're doing so well. Only this morning, I saw that yesterday's score stood at forty-four for seven, England still batting!

Clive read that and scratched his head. Because of the war, no cricket matches were being played. Then it dawned. Penny was referring to the battle going on in the air, hence her 'sky-high' remark. It was the biggest wonder she'd got away with it, but he was glad she had. It was good to know that the RAF were holding their own.

I receive regular bulletins from Grandpop, of course. He's been plagued with toothache, apparently, and when he could stand it no longer, he went to see your dad. Why are men such softies when it comes to dental treatment? He should have gone much sooner. Anyway, the tooth had to come out. He was surprised that the experience was quite painless, but I could have told him that. He said, also, that he had quite a chat with both your mum and your dad. He was particularly taken with your mum. You wouldn't think he'd still be susceptible to that kind of thing at his age, would you? Oh well, we live and learn about these things.

My ring is still greatly admired, and rightly so. Do you remember the jeweller saying it was a good time to buy it? I saw my boring brother-in-law before I left for work, and quite predictably, he said the same thing, and for the same reason. Honestly, if it hasn't a pound sign in front of it, it's meaningless as far as he's concerned, just as my sister is only interested, nowadays, in baby clothes and nappy rash. I'm expecting it to be born with a permanently serious expression, a book of knitting patterns and an accountancy qualification. If you and I decide to have a family, I hope we'll be more human than that and not bore everyone with it.

Before I set to work again, there's something I must ask you. What does XX^n mean? You write it on all your letters, and I think that I, of all people, should know. Don't you? Do let me know. Meanwhile, take the greatest of care. I miss you madly.

All my love,
Penny XXXXX

Clive decided there was no time like the present, so he took out his notepaper and made a start.

Dearest Penny,

I'm surprised at you. When you were striving manfully at your school, did you learn nothing about indices? Something with a tiny number two next to it is 'squared' and therefore multiplied by itself once. With a tiny three, it is 'cubed', which means it's multiplied by itself twice, and when it has a tiny 'n', it means 'multiplied by itself forever and ever. Therefore, kisses to the power 'n' means… well, you can work it out for yourself.

He broke off when the Tannoy crackled its usual warning.

'D' ye hear there, d' ye hear there. Swordfish pilots and observers are to report to Commander (F) at seven bells of the afternoon watch. That is all.'

He put the letter away until he was able to concentrate on it.

* * *

Penny was in the wardroom at Chatham with Third Officer Marigold Dawlish from Message Handling. Marigold had been telling her about Dennis, her fiancé, who was currently serving in a destroyer.

'I have to prompt him all the time,' she said.

'What do you mean?'

'Well, whatever we do has to be my idea. I had to prompt him into popping the question, and then into buying… you know.'

Penny looked at her with genuine puzzlement. 'No, I'm afraid I've no idea.'

Marigold looked around her to make sure they weren't being overheard, and said, 'When he was being… you know, persuasive, I had to remind him to buy the necessary.'

Penny gave that some consideration and decided that she had a rough idea of what her friend was talking about. 'I see what you mean,' she said, although she was still a little hazy.

'What about yours? Is he quite insistent?'

'No, I can't say that he is.' She was uncomfortably conscious that she was in uncharted waters, and she was relieved when Marigold said, 'Give him time. He will be, but anyway, I've said enough about Dennis. Yours is a pilot, isn't he?'

'Yes, he's serving in HMS *Illustrious*, and from what I've been able to gather from Coding, he's in the Med.'

'Lovely, warm, sunbathing weather,' said Marigold.

'Yes, except that there's a war going on there, as well.' She signalled the steward to come over. 'Same again?'

'Yes, please, and you're right. I'm awfully sorry, Penny. That was clumsy of me.'

'Two gins and orange, please,' Penny asked the steward. Neither of them had been able to acquire the taste of gin with bitters.

'Two gins and orange, ma'am.'

'Don't worry,' said Penny when the steward was gone. 'Everywhere we go, we're treading on eggshells, so clumsiness is unavoidable. I do worry, though. I'd be inhuman if I didn't.'

'Me too,' said Marigold. 'I've now got Dennis located in Western Approaches, and that's none too peaceful.'

To steer the conversation away from the war as much as for any other reason, Penny said, 'Before Clive went away, we were talking about our both being in Cinderella branches of the service, as far as the old curmudgeons at the Admiralty are concerned, and he said that there would come a time when flag officers would admit that the Navy would grind to a halt without the Wrens.'

'True enough.'

'Well, of course, C in C Nore said just that when he visited us.'

Marigold frowned. 'I missed that,' she said.

Penny broke off to sign her mess chit and take the two drinks. 'Thank you.'

'It's a pleasure, ma'am.'

'Yes,' she said, returning to their conversation, 'he told us the Navy couldn't cope without us.'

'What a lovely man.'

'That's what I said.' The subject of war was difficult to avoid, and Penny had another anecdote she wanted to share. 'Another thing that Clive told me,' she said, 'was that there would come a time when the Navy would need to engage an important target a long way beyond the range of the guns of the fleet, and that was when the Fleet Air Arm would be properly appreciated.' Being strictly honest, she said, 'He was actually talking about the Swordfish at the time, because that's his particular love.'

'Really?'

'Yes, on our first evening together, he told me that until an hour or so earlier, the Swordfish was the most exquisite thing he'd ever seen. When I asked him what had caused him to change his mind, he said it was seeing me when I opened the door to greet him.'

'Ooh.' Marigold went into a mock swoon. 'Does he give lessons? If he does, Dennis might benefit from a few.'

'He does it quite naturally. Actually, I told you that because he really believes what he said about the Fleet Air Arm. The only thing is, I'm almost hoping it won't happen. It's silly of me, considering what he does for a living, but I can't bear to think of him being caught up in something so awful.'

26

KINDNESS AND SUSPENSE

HMS *Illustrious* continued to be at the centre of hostilities, escorting a convoy to Malta, her fighters shooting down a number of attacking aircraft, but next it was the turn of the Swordfish.

On the thirteenth of October, a force from *Illustrious* and *Eagle* carried out a strike on the Italian airfield on Leros.

It seemed strange to Clive that an aircraft designed for torpedo bombing, spotting and reconnaissance should have spent the war so far operating largely as a dive-bomber. The exception was the strike on Benghazi, when his flight had attacked the shipping there with torpedoes, but even then, half of the Swordfish force had been used to lay mines. The Swordfish really was living up to its nickname 'Stringbag', the aircraft capable of carrying any type of weapon. Secretly, however, he was simply proud that the Swordfish had acquitted itself so well, and that was the thought uppermost in his mind as he flew through the night towards Leros.

In the glow of the full moon, the sea was like a vast sheet of planished metal. The tideless Mediterranean was as still as the cloudless sky above it, and the shimmering path of light was a reminder of the time he'd spent with Penny, when they'd stood on the seafront and observed almost the same picture. The song, 'They Can't Black-Out the Moon' sprang to mind, and he remembered dancing to it, and Penny had mentioned it as well. He decided, then, that it was better not to think about Penny when he was flying. Quiet though the night was, he needed all his concentration.

214

The two squadrons roared on, keeping rigid formation, a constant reminder that no aircraft or crew was alone. Unchallenged, they approached Leros.

When they were still a few miles distant, searchlights began probing the darkness, and Clive could imagine gun crews nervously elevating and training their barrels. A few impetuous souls opened up while the Swordfish were as yet out of range, but most held their fire until the force was less than three miles away.

Two minutes later, the leading aircraft dived on its target, releasing its bombs at a thousand feet. The rest followed, destroying gun emplacements as well as hangars, workshops and parked aircraft. The anti-aircraft gunnery was thick and fierce, but not, so far as Clive was aware, noticeably accurate. He knew it wasn't true of Italian defences generally; the strike on Benghazi had attracted skilful, accurate fire, so it seemed that on this occasion they were lucky.

In a remarkably short time, the strike was complete, and the force made its way back to *Illustrious* and *Eagle*. It had been a straightforward and successful operation, but Clive wondered how many would be as easy.

* * *

Much of the task of escorting convoys through the Channel fell to ML97's flotilla, and even though the Luftwaffe had switched targets, at least for the time being, the merchant ships, mainly colliers, were still threatened. The chief danger came from the fast, heavily-armed E-boats, which now had the benefit of the French Channel ports. Wilf, the cox'n and the captain knew that they outgunned the motor torpedo boats and motor gunboats so far available, and that it was only by wily deployment that British coastal forces were able to combat them. They also knew that, if the MTBs and MGBs were outclassed, the outlook for an ML, with its inferior speed and basic armament, was less than inviting. Even so, they were charged with the protection of convoys sailing the stretch of water now known familiarly as 'E-Boat Alley'.

* * *

From time to time, when she was going about her duties, Esme would hear gunfire in the Channel. The noise carried easily on the prevailing wind, and it was difficult not to hear it. Some of the women at the British Restaurant would comment on it from time to time, but such remarks were made in passing and with little thought. For Esme, it was different. She'd lost Len at sea, and while relations between them had been less than idyllic, she'd felt the loss and all its attendant emotions. She hadn't been fooled, either, by Wilf's airy talk of only 'sometimes' going to sea. When she thought about it sensibly, she realised that anyone based on the Channel coast must be in the thick of the fighting. The sounds of gunfire told their own story, and to lose Wilf would be even worse than her previous experience. In the brief time she'd known him since their reunion, she'd learned that, unlike Len, he was kind, loving, gentle and caring, and she knew that if he asked her to marry him, she would agree without hesitation. The prospect of losing him was too terrible to imagine. Because of that, she applied herself to her work in the steam-filled kitchen, trying all the time to dismiss her worries for the man who now meant everything to her.

* * *

The two, lean, grey shapes on the horizon could only be E-boats, and with their prodigious speed they would be on to the convoy within minutes. Like protecting sheepdogs, MLs 97, 98 and 95 placed themselves between the E-boats and the colliers.

The order, 'Depth charge crews, set to "Apple" ' meant that the captain was preparing to get in close. The depth charge was an anti-submarine weapon, but it was equally devastating when it was laid at its shallowest setting beneath an E-boat, and in the absence of a gun armament to challenge that of the enemy, it was worth trying. Wilf checked the settings and gave them his approval. Elsewhere, gun crews trained their weapons on the approaching raiders and waited for the order to open fire. Wilf was pleased with his Hostilities Only ratings.

The enemy vessels, now clearly identifiable as E-boats, separated to make their final approach. As they did so, they opened fire on the escorts.

'All guns,' ordered the captain, 'open fire!'

Wilf saw the tracer from one of the E-boats as it plunged beneath the bridge. Less than a quarter of a minute later, the captain ordered, 'Leading Seaman Gregory to the wheelhouse, at the rush!'

Leaving the ratings on the depth charges, Wilf followed the first lieutenant on to the wheelhouse ladder. With no trained sick berth attendant on board, the officer carried a first-aid haversack.

Wilf entered the wheelhouse and saw what he'd feared. The first lieutenant was kneeling beside the Cox'n, who was bleeding copiously from a head wound. Naturally concerned for his superior, but conscious of a more immediate need, he seized the wheel and called into the voice pipe, 'Wheelhouse – bridge!'

'Bridge.'

'Leading Seaman Gregory taking over the wheel, sir. The Cox'n is receiving attention.'

'Thank you, Gregory. Steer two-seven-five.'

'Steer two-seven-five, sir.' Wilf spun the wheel and caught it, bringing the ship's head round to starboard. 'The course is south eight five west, sir.'

The first lieutenant, who had been applying a field dressing to Rankin's temple, looked up and said, 'The Cox'n is dead, Gregory.'

Wilf glanced down at the pool of blood on the deck, grimaced at the loss of the man he'd come to think of as a friend, and called, 'Wheelhouse – bridge.'

'Bridge.'

'The Cox'n is dead, sir.'

'Thank you, Gregory.' The captain's tone betrayed his regret. 'Ask the first lieutenant to join me on the bridge.'

'Aye, aye, sir.' Turning to the green-faced sub-lieutenant, he asked, 'Did you hear that, sir?'

The officer appeared to be in a daze. 'What, Gregory?'

'You're requested to return to the bridge, sir.'

'Oh, right.' Still dazed, he left the lifeless body of the cox'n and mounted the ladder.

'Bridge – wheelhouse.'

'Wheelhouse, sir.'

'Hard a-port.'

'Hard a-port, sir.' He spun the wheel. 'Wheel's hard a-port sir.'

217

'Midships.'

'Midships, sir. Wheel's a-midships, sir.'

'Starboard ten.'

'Starboard ten, sir. Ten of starboard wheel on, sir.'

'Midships.'

Wilf repeated the order and heard the captain order, 'Let go depth charges! Full ahead together!'

Wilf answered the order and rang down full ahead on all three engines. Almost immediately, he felt the surge of power. A few seconds later, he was conscious of a different sensation. It was as if the ship were being thrown from the port side. It happened again, and he knew that the depth charges had exploded. He heard the captain's voice again. 'That's right, you bastard! Bugger off home!' Then, in a more sedate manner, he said, 'Wheelhouse, half ahead together, steer two-seven-five.'

Wilf rang down 'half-ahead together' and altered course accordingly, reporting back as he did so.

'Just to keep you informed, Gregory,' said the captain, 'the enemy is one wicket down and one retired, hurt. Steady as she goes.'

'Steady on two-seven-five, sir. Thank you for that.' So, one E-boat had been sunk, and it sounded as if the other had resisted the invitation to join battle with three slow and poorly-armed MLs. Meanwhile, beside him lay the lifeless body of Petty Officer Rankin, an excellent cox'n and a thoroughly likeable man.

Much later, ML97 returned to Dover, where Rankin's body was taken away pending his funeral and burial or cremation.

'It's a tragedy, Gregory, I know,' said the captain, but you acquitted yourself well as Acting Cox'n. I was pleased, as well, with your HO ratings on the guns and depth charges.'

'They're good lads, sir,' agreed Wilf.

'And well-trained. Clearly, you have special ability in that field.'

'Not really, sir.' Recalling Rankin's surprise that he'd spared the recruits the Whale Island treatment, he said, 'It's all done by kindness.'

* * *

There had been a sense of nervous anticipation in the wardroom of HMS *Illustrious* since the announcement that a strike was to be carried out against the Italian battle fleet in Taranto harbour, a fleet that outnumbered the British Mediterranean Fleet and which continued to threaten the Malta convoys. The operation was planned for the 21st of October, the anniversary of the Battle of Trafalgar. A more practical consideration for choosing that date, however, was the three-quarter moon, which would be most favourable. Infinitely less favourable, though, was the fact that, as the main fleet anchorage for the *Regia Marina*, Taranto was known to be the most heavily-defended harbour in Italy, and if its experience at Benghazi were any guide, the strike force was likely to meet the fiercest opposition.

Discussion and conjecture continued almost until the night of the operation, when pilots and observers were assembled to be told that Operation *'Judgement'* had been postponed until the 11th of November. A hangar fire in *Illustrious* had destroyed several aircraft, and contaminated fuel tanks on board HMS *Eagle* had led to her being taken out of the strike, but she nevertheless transferred five Swordfish to *Illustrious* for the forthcoming operation.

27

A FAMILY EFFORT

D amage and mechanical breakdowns meant that only twenty-one aircraft were available by the eleventh for 'Operation *Judgement*', and it was decided that they would form two waves. Only six aircraft in each wave would carry torpedoes, the rest carrying bombs and flares. Clive's aircraft was to be part of the torpedo attack.

Taking part in the first wave, Clive and Bill took off at 2045. As much of the space in the after cockpit of each aircraft was taken up by the long-range fuel tank made necessary by the 340-mile round trip, air-gunners were excluded from the operation.

The Italian fleet comprised rich prizes; no fewer than six modern battleships, seven heavy cruisers and seven light cruisers occupied the anchorage, with thirteen destroyers offering a secondary target. That was if the Swordfish could penetrate the harbour's defences. More than a hundred heavy anti-aircraft guns, almost two hundred machine guns and twenty-seven barrage balloons were set to deter any such attempt.

When the first wave of Swordfish arrived at 2230, it seemed to Clive that flares were scarcely needed; the muzzle flashes of the harbour defences combined with gunfire from the fleet itself illuminated the harbour more than adequately.

Each pilot and observer had memorised the layout of the anchorage, and Clive took his turn, entering the southern part of the harbour while shells burst and tracer-bullets marked out their deadly path around the vulnerable aircraft. At one stage, he felt and heard a flying wire part company with one wing, but he held on, because ahead of him was the gigantic, majestic battleship *Littorio*. Her name was displayed on her beam, and he could see the faces of the ship's gun crews as they struggled to depress their guns sufficiently to train them on the oncoming aircraft. Flying beneath the arcs created by the small-calibre weapons and between the wire cables of the barrage balloons, he chose his moment and, dry-mouthed, released his torpedo, checking quickly that it was running, before making his escape from the vivid, ever-shifting trap of anti-aircraft fire. He was too busy to notice whether or not anyone else had fallen victim to the defences; all his effort went into avoiding both the gunfire and the cables of the barrage balloons, and heading for the comparative safety of open sea.

Once they were clear of the harbour, he relaxed a little and followed the reciprocal course to the one that had brought them to Taranto. After a few seconds, Bill spoke to him via the Gosport tube, confirming the course.

Beneath his clothing, perspiration ran, and where it couldn't, it simply soaked the first garment it touched. Climate had nothing to do with it; it was the product of tension, of which there had been a great deal.

Bill's voice came again through the tube. 'I've counted seven aircraft, including ours,' he said.

'Well done, Bill.' Seven meant the possible loss of just one aircraft. He crossed his fingers for its crew, but marvelled at the same time. From its very inception, the strike on Taranto had sounded like a one-way trip, and the relief was incalculable.

They met the second wave on its way to the target and silently wished its crews luck. Should they need to carry out a second attack, they too would need all the luck they could find. The enemy would be ready and thirsting for revenge. Clive flew on, the cool night air making his perspiration more unpleasant than ever.

In less than two hours, they sighted *Illustrious*, waiting for them like a mother hen, and they made their landing to report what they knew, which was very little. They'd made their attack, but had seen little result. It seemed that a second strike would have to be made, after all.

* * *

221

With considerable damage to her superstructure and the loss of one key senior rating, ML97 was once again confined temporarily to Dover harbour. Exceptionally, 48 hours' leave was granted, and Wilf called at the British Restaurant to tell Esme.

When he arrived at the door, a doughty matron in a no-nonsense pinafore and turban said, 'What do you want, Jack? You servicemen get your rations where you're based.'

'I haven't come for a meal,' he explained. 'I just need a quick word with Esme. I won't keep her more than a minute.'

Her face softened. 'So you're the sailor she's told us about. All right then, but you really will have to be quick.' She seemed about to leave, and then she said, 'Before I go, Jack, come here a minute.'

Knowing what was to follow, he stepped inside and waited.

'I can't let you go without touching your collar, can I?' She touched the blue jean fabric and said, 'I can't resist this, either. I'm sure Esme won't mind.' Mischievously, she kissed his cheek before hurrying off to the kitchen.

When Esme saw him, she looked around her anxiously. 'What have you come here for?' she asked.

'Don't you start, Esme. I had to let the other one kiss me before she'd let me see you.'

She laughed. 'I don't believe you.'

'Listen, I've got forty-eight hours. I have to be back late tomorrow, but I've got tonight free.'

'Lovely.'

'I'll come round and collect you at eighteen-fif— six-fifteen.' Thinking again, he asked, 'What time do you get away from here?'

She looked up at the clock. 'Four o' clock. Another hour yet.'

'Okay, I'll call for you and we can go home together.'

'Right.' She looked around her again nervously. 'Can I have a kiss, too, before you go?'

'Of course you can. For all we know, it might be the next thing to be rationed.'

* * *

The second wave returned to *Illustrious* with a similar story. They'd hit their targets, but no one could report any appreciable damage. In the circumstances, it would have been impossible to see, anyway, but the crews were pessimistic about the result. Remarkably, however, only two of the twenty-one aircraft had been shot down, although their loss was felt by the survivors, who could now look forward to another strike in less than twenty-four hours.

*   *   *

Wilf and Esme travelled home on the train holding hands beneath Wilf's Burberry. To have leave again after so short a time was an unexpected bonus, and they intended to make the most of it.

'I was going to tell you in a letter about something that happened,' said Wilf, 'but I thought I'd save it and tell you about it properly.'

Esme looked uncertain. 'Are you sure you can?' she asked.

'This is one story I can tell you,' he confirmed.

'Go on, then.'

He told her about picking up the German airmen, and described the incident with the arrogant officer.

'The dirty horror,' she said, 'spitting's horrible, anyway, but spitting in your face was foul.'

'That's why I chucked him overboard.'

'You didn't.'

'Oh, yes I did.' He described the Nazi's impassioned screams as he begged for help. 'I don't know any German, so it's just as well he said it in English, or he might have drowned.'

'What did you do?'

'I helped him back on board, an' then the Jimmy – that's the first lieutenant – arrived with a revolver an' told him to get down below with the others.'

An airman said to the girl beside him, 'Honestly, the tall stories sailors tell, and they expect people to believe them.'

'Be thankful you weren't there, making your clever remarks,' said Wilf. 'I might have chucked you in an' all.' The laughter of the other passengers in the compartment silenced the embarrassed airman.

They left the train at Sandbrook and walked to Esme's house, where they kissed before parting.

'Six-fifteen, then,' said Wilf.

'Six-fifteen.'

Wilf walked home to be greeted by his mother. Naturally, he kept quiet about the action in which ML97 had incurred the damage, but in a quiet moment, he told his father about Rankin and about taking over the wheel in action.

'It's one of the saddest things in wartime, lad,' said his father, 'losing oppos, and it sounds as if your cox'n was a bit special.'

'He was, Dad.'

'Hush,' said his father, 'your mum's coming.'

Later, after they'd eaten, he told them about the German aircrew and the incident with the officer, which amused them, so he followed it by telling them about the airman on the train from Dover.

Soon, the time came to pick up Esme. In the absence of any alternative entertainment, they were going to the cinema again.

'Do you know what's on,' asked Esme, 'or aren't you bothered?' She'd sized him up quickly.

'I do,' he said. 'I had a quick look on my way home, and it's *All At Sea*, starring Sandy Powell. Any relation to any navy on this planet or any other is sheer fluke.'

'That sounded clever.'

'I learned it from one of the new lads. He was a newspaper reporter in civilian life, so he really is clever, but he's okay with it, if you see what I mean.'

'I think I do.'

Wilf bought two tickets for the balcony and they went upstairs. The usherette guided them to their seats and whispered, 'You're the one I've been waiting for, Jack.'

'What do you mean?'

'I've been waiting for somebody to come in here and *not* say, "Put that light out!" ' Shaking her head, she said, 'They all think it's screamingly funny.'

Wilf shook his head. 'There's some witty characters about.'

'Shush!' said someone behind them.

'See what I mean?' he said.

They watched the usual, fatuous nonsense on the newsreel and were relieved when the film began. *All At Sea* was a silly, knockabout comedy about an idiot who accidentally joined the Navy and foiled a spy plot. It was almost too daft to be funny, but it helped Wilf cope, for a while, with the death of PO Rankin, which had seldom been far from his thoughts.

Afterwards, as if by habit, they walked along the permitted ribbon of seafront and, against the unromantic backdrop of barbed wire and warning signs about mines, they declared their feelings for each other for the second time.

'It's maybe a bit soon to ask,' said Wilf as they emerged from a long kiss, 'but do you feel sometimes that you'd like us to make things more permanent?'

'No,' said Esme confidently, 'not sometimes. No, I can honestly say I feel it all the time.'

Encouraged, Wilf said, 'You see, I'm not earning very much as a leading hand, but when I get made up to petty officer, it'll be easier.'

'When will that be?' Her question sounded like natural curiosity rather than impatience.

'It would normally be another three years, but with a war on, maybe they'll do it sooner. I had to take over a petty officer's duties yesterday, so they know I can do it.'

'Why did you have to do that?'

'He got ki…. He got taken poorly.'

'Oh.' Oddly, she sounded disappointed. 'You don't think about that happening in wartime, do you?'

'It happens.'

'I suppose so. Anyway,' she said, 'it's something to look forward to, isn't it? Standing at the altar, I mean, with you beside me in your petty officer's uniform.'

'So it's on, then?'

'It's on,' she confirmed.

Now that they were formally committed to each other, they kissed on the strength of it.

* * *

Foul weather in the Mediterranean ruled out an immediate strike on Taranto or anywhere else, and it wasn't until two mornings later that a photo reconnaissance by the RAF elicited the surprising news that three battleships now rested on the bottom of Taranto harbour. The *Conte di Cavour* was out of the war for good, and the battleships *Duilio* and *Littorio* were seriously damaged and therefore unlikely to take any part in it for a long time to come. In one strike, the Swordfish had restored the balance of power in the Mediterranean, which meant that Operation '*Judgement*' had been a complete success.

* * *

Arthur Clement sat in his office, listening to the one o' clock news.

'Two nights ago, Swordfish aircraft from His Majesty's Ships *Illustrious* and *Eagle* carried out a strike on the Italian naval base at Taranto. The operation was carried out with great skill and courage in the teeth of fierce anti-aircraft fire, and it resulted in three enemy battleships and two cruisers being crippled as well as serious damage being inflicted on various shore installations. Only two aircraft were lost in the operation. Next of kin have been informed....'

Mrs Enright entered the office with a letter for his signature, and was about to leave, when Arthur said, 'Wait, Mrs Enright. Did you hear that?'

'Yes, sir. Isn't it good news? We needed some.'

'It's more than likely that Lieutenant Newing, Penny's fiancé, was involved in it.'

'Really, sir? Miss Dowling will be terribly proud.'

'I'm sure she is. They say that next of kin have been informed, so I think we can safely say, two days later, that he survived the operation.'

'I'm very glad to hear it, sir.'

Arthur signed the letter, and Mrs Enright took it to put with the rest of the post.

Less than half an hour later, he heard the telephone ring in Mrs Enright's office. A few seconds later, the extension on Arthur's desk rang.

'Hello.'

'It's Miss Dorling for you, sir.'

'Oh, good. Put her through, will you?'

There was a click, and Penny came on the line. 'Grandpop? I haven't much time. Did you hear the news? It's what Clive said all along. He said there'd come a time when.... Oh, but I told you, didn't I? Isn't it marvellous?'

'It was a special treat, hearing the news today, Penny.'

'I've spoken to Mrs Newing, so I know Clive's all right. How are things with you?'

'Oh, I'm doing my bit.' Remembering, he said, 'By the way, Chief Gregory's son, the lad who received the DSM after Norway and Dunkirk, was home on leave last night, and he popped the question to his lady love, a pretty local widow of twenty-five, Gregory tells me, so it's celebrations all round.'

'I'm delighted for them both. He did ever so well, didn't he? I think our little corner of England, and Sandbrook particularly, can hold its head up high.'

'Yes,' said Arthur, almost to himself, because it was actually the first time he'd thought of it. 'Our family.'

'What did you say, Grandpop? The line keeps breaking up.'

'I said, "Our family", because that's what we are. You've heard me say that the Navy is a small world and a big family, but Clive, Gregory and his son, you and I are a family within it, and we're pulling our weight.'

'That's right, Grandpop. It's a family effort.'

The End